Where Phantoms Tread

A Detective Lyle Odell Novel

Paul John Hausleben

Cover design by Paul John Hausleben
Cover Concept by Paul John Hausleben
The Detective Lyle Odell Logo, GBTKP LLC's logos and the designs are by Paul John Hausleben
All photographs by Paul John Hausleben

Published by God Bless the Keg Publishing LLC
Henrico, Virginia, U.S.A.

ISBN: 978-1-7330927-2-2

This is a work of fiction. Names, characters, businesses, places, events and incidents are either the product of the author's eccentric, strange and unusual imagination or used in a fictitious manner. Any resemblance to actual persons, living or dead or actual events is purely coincidental and it was not the intention of the author.

Dedication

To grilled cheese sandwiches at the local pub

Where Phantoms Tread

Paul John Hausleben

Contents

Acknowledgements

Many thanks and love to my family and friends. A tip of my Manhattan glass to Ms. Alejandra Lopez of GBTKP LLC for the beta reads, editing assistance, plot hole detection and most of all, for the encouragement and support. Ya super cool and a very brilliant chick!

"Reach for the sky and never stop reaching."

Paul John Hausleben

01 July 2021

Prologue

"Do you want a brandy? Something to steady your nerves?" Attorney Rexford Covington asked as he intently stared at Senator Monger with his hand poised on the top of the decanter.

The senator slowly nodded his head as he sunk into the chair. Once he settled into the chair, Senator Monger gripped the arms of the chair tightly, as if his life depended on him not falling out of the chair. As if the chair was a life raft afloat in the middle of the ocean.

"Yes . . . please a brandy . . . to steady my nerves. I need to steady my nerves. I am afraid that any steadiness from the use of brandy will only be temporary."

Rexford said while he twisted the top of the decanter, "Might be, senator. Might be."

He poured two glasses, three fingers deep with brandy, and then replaced the top on the decanter and settled the decanter back within a nest of other liquor bottles. Rexford picked up the glasses, walked over to where the senator sat, and handed him one glass while settling into the chair next to where the senator sat. Senator Monger took a sip of the brandy and then held the glass in his hands while resting it upon his lap. He nervously spun the glass around and around, and his eyes stared down into the carpet of the luxurious office inside of his sprawling home. The sun was setting, and the sunlight cast peculiar shadows on the walls and floor of the room. One of the sunlight beams broke into a prism of light, and the colors reflected on the carpet in front for the senator.

"Rex, she did not suffer, did she?"

Rex tilted his glass, took a sip of his brandy, and then placed the glass on a coaster on an oak wood end table that stood stoically next to the chair. End tables have no ears. But Rex looked around the office as if they did, or perhaps the other furniture did, or some ghosts were in the room listening.

"Don't ask me that question, Austin. This is all a very dirty business. Let's just put it all away forever. Relax. It had to be done now. For many reasons. The timing was crucial. Our inside man covered everything and the slimy doctor, covered the shift as planned. It had to happen now."

"I understand, but I need to know, Rex. If she suffered. I really do. At one time, I loved her dearly."

"Love is for chumps, Austin. You have higher aspirations than being a love-struck fool over some pretty chick. Look at you! Mr. Everything. You have good looks, power, one of the most powerful politicians in America and the most popular too. You have mountains of money . . . everything. You can have your pick of women. I can arrange any discreet affair that you feel that you need. Remember that the White House is still a realistic address for you to live in within five years or so. Remember, you love your wife, your family and your country. That is all that you love. Maybe your dog. Maybe you love your dog too."

Rex picked up his brandy, took another sip, and then set the glass back down. He stared intently at the senator and followed his eyes to the colors dancing on the carpet in front of them, and he realized that the senator had tears in his eyes.

"I don't own a dog. She was as beautiful as those colors are there on the carpet. She was a rainbow. A glorious rainbow."

The senator took a long sip of the brandy, paused, then downed the rest of the brandy and waved the glass in the air in an indication that he required a refill.

"She had to go. She was a fuse to a time bomb. A lit fuse sizzling towards detonation," Rex said as he pushed off on the arms of the chair that he sat in, stood up, walked over and grabbed the glass out of Senator's Monger's hands. The senator nodded, wiped away the tears and leaned back deeply into the deep folds of the chair. He was trying to bury his body in the chair to escape the pain of his existence.

In a low whisper laced with pain, Senator Monger spoke, "Tell me that it is going to be all right, Rex. Tell me again that no one will ever know other than us, and the hired hands that I have paid off handsomely. I have paid you handsomely, too. You are my attorney, but I feel that after all these years that you are my friend, too. Please reassure me that our secrets are safe. Only God can judge me now. And, I am afraid that he will someday. I think of how I began this journey, so innocent, so trustworthy, and so bent on doing good work for this country and its people. Now, the power and the glory and the lust of success feel like they are stones in my mouth."

Senator Monger ran his hand through his thick black hair and sighed. Right now, he did not look like the handsome, dashing, young successful senator from New York who was a front-runner in his political party. A darling of the media and a darling amongst his followers. A shoo-in candidate to run for the Office of the President of the United States of America. Right now, he looked like a beaten man.

Senator Monger spoke again with a voice laced with a heavy sob, "Tell me that no one will ever know, Rex. Tell me that law enforcement will not find anything to suspect, that this is anything but an unfortunate accident of a hidden lifestyle and terrible addiction. I need to hear it again. From you."

Rex held the glass in his hands and took a deep breath. With his free hand, he loosened his necktie and spoke with a powerful voice. A voice laced with some disgust at rehashing the details of what was certainly a sordid mess.

"No one will know. As far as any police investigation goes, the local law enforcement will rule her death as just another drug overdose in a city that suffers from a line of daily dead bodies, druggies keeling over right and left. Who knew that the precious, little, innocent Delilah had a hidden life of drugs and casual sex and dark days in Mohawk City? She is just another statistic. A casualty of an epidemic. I must admit that it is very convenient that she was originally from the lovely Mohawk City, New York. A den of sin and a pimple on the ass of upstate New York. Besides, the only homicide detective in, as they call it, Sin City is a drunken bum."

After speaking, Rex turned his back on the senator and set the glass on the table at the bar. He picked the brandy decanter out of the maze of bottles and lifted it, twisted off the cap, and poured another drink.

He spoke again, while keeping his back turned and said, "Detective Odell is an alcoholic, has-been. A worn out, mess of a man. He solved many cases in the past, but now, he is a chain-smoking, alcoholic wreck of a detective. My inside sources say that he could not solve a murder case if he committed the murder himself. He could not find a clue in his own pocket. This entire mess is so complex and has so many layers of madness to it, I am very sure that Sherlock Holmes could not figure it out. Certainly, not this drunken buffoon. I assure you, Austin, in a few days, he will be pushed out of jurisdiction by the hired gun federal officers, who we paid off for them to make a little side cash, anyway. Until they arrive, this loser, Detective Lyle Odell, will not find a single clue. He will feel as if her death was an accidental drug overdose and life will go on. And, you, my friend, will be the President of the United States of America someday."

Rex replaced the brandy decanter and picked up the glass, smiled, and walked over to Senator Monger. "Here. Sip, but do not chug it. You know how you drink like a fish when you are upset and we do not want the makeup crew having to paint the dark circles out from under your eyes before you have to act how surprised you are to hear of the death of your faithful assistant. You need to whip up some tears tomorrow, not tonight. I assure you . . . everything will be all right."

Senator Austin Monger took the brandy glass from Rex and leaned into the drink.

After a long sip, he lifted his eyes toward his attorney and said in a low whisper, "Rexford, I hope that you are correct. Not only is this our careers on the line, but now, our lives depend upon it."

Chapter One

Early Thursday Morning

The cellphone rang loudly. A cellphone that sat perched somewhat precariously upon an upturned plastic milk crate that was sitting on the floor next to Lyle Odell's reclining chair. The ringer on the phone was on the loudest setting. On purpose. Detective Lyle Odell opened one eye to look at the number on the screen. He groaned and moved in the reclining chair and strained his neck to read the number on the screen. He pushed in on the leg rest of the chair and reached for the phone, and when he did so; he knocked over the Irish whiskey bottle that sat on the floor next to the chair.

It did not matter because the whiskey bottle was empty.

It was difficult to grab the cellphone since it hung on the end of a charger. The battery was always dead, and his captain kept promising him a new one.

"When he received budget approval," the captain always told the good detective. Funny thing was that the captain always had the latest model cellphone.

The caller was persistent. Odell did not pick up the call, and it went to voicemail. However, they called right back. Odell's head pounded. His eyes could not focus, and the Devil danced on his brain but also poked his stomach with his pitchfork. It was a difficult night. Difficult, to say the least. Now, Odell focused his eyes enough to read the number on the screen and the time. Odell recognized the number for the overnight desk sergeant's phone at the front desk at Mohawk City Police Headquarters. This only meant trouble. It was just past two in the morning, and the last time that Odell recalled was around nine or thereabouts. The empty whiskey bottle explained the headache, the sick stomach, and the time of the call spelled out trouble.

Finally, through shipwrecked eyes, Odell circled in on the phone, pulled the charger out of the jack, hit the green button and growled, "Odell here," out of the corner of his mouth with a painful reverberation, practically causing his pounding head to lift off his shoulders.

"Sergeant Hawkins here. Ah, sorry to wake you up, Detective Odell, but there has been another. . .."

"Not too sure that I was actually asleep, sergeant. More as if I was borderline comatose. Sorry. I digressed. What's up?"

"A dead body in a room in the Langley Hotel. A young woman. Looks like another drug overdose. There are no outward or obvious signs of foul play. At least, that is what the responding patrolman reported. Paramedics are there and reported there were no revival chances. The crime scene boys are already on the way. You told me to call you on every drug overdose, and always dispatch the crime scene boys."

"Yes. Perfect. Good work sergeant. Those were my requests, indeed. Oh, geez. More drugs, huh? Okay, yes, I will get my act together and get out there. The Langley Inn, huh? The only fancy joint in the entire city."

"Yes, the dead woman was originally from Mohawk City, but now . . . she works, well, she did work in the government. Federal government."

Odell paused as he kicked a pizza box on the floor and at his feet, out of his way, and slowly stood up from his chair. He flipped on the light on the end table and squinted from the feeble light rays as they pierced his brain with pain. He debated picking up the empty whiskey bottle, but quickly crossed that off the list because he knew that his head would split if he bent over and he might lose the contents of his stomach.

"Federal government. How so?"

"She was the personal aide and assistant to Senator Austin Monger."

Odell processed the information in his pounding head. "Monger, huh? Everyone's darlin'. Damn . . . that means the dead woman is going to be Ms. Delilah Murdock. From the wealthy and powerful Murdock family. Oh boy. Nothing is easy. Okay, well, I am getting dressed now. Ah, Sergeant Hawkins, ah, can you send a patrol car to pick me up? Sorry, but I am not really in any condition to drive. Safely and lawfully, that is. These Friday nights are a bitch, Sarge."

"It is early Thursday morning, Detective Odell. Thursday."

"Oh yes, so it is. Thanks for the calendar, check. Anyway, honestly, taking forward steps and standing upright is enough of a challenge right now. I do not need to be driving. Therefore, a patrol car would be nice."

"Sure, Detective Odell. I understand. Gotcha covered."

Odell hung up with the desk sergeant. His eyes searched the room, and he stepped on the pizza box and then found the pack of cigarettes that were next to the empty whiskey bottle.

As he groaned in discomfort to bend over and pick them up, Odell mumbled, "Now, I need to find the damn lighter."

A stocky man with an oval face walked into the hotel room. He turned and looked at the emergency medical personnel, then to the police officer taking notes, and held his hand out to the officer. The officer scanned the man, who was offering him a handshake, and the officer remained aloof. His suit was sloppy in its fit and wrinkled, his necktie was too short and it hung askew, and his hair stuck out in many directions and in unkempt waves, and his face had a five o'clock shadow. Maybe, because of the events of the last few days, his face had a seven o'clock shadow. His eyes looked like they had witnessed an explosion of sorts. There was a distinct odor of stale booze emitting from his breath, as well as every pore of the man's body.

"I am sorry, sir. This room is off-limits. You have no business here. Did you not see the barrier tape across the door and in the hallway? Perhaps, you wandered into the wrong room. Let me assist you in finding the correct room," the police officer said as he dropped his notepad and pen on the bed and went to assist what he felt was obviously an intoxicated hotel guest who had partied too much in the hotel bar.

One of the older paramedics, who knew the good detective from crossing paths with Lyle many times over the years, chuckled at the patrolman's reaction and words, stood up from his work, where he was scouring a desk in the room for evidence and said, "Forgive him. He is a rook, Lyle. Patrolman Dennis Baker, please, meet Mohawk City Police Detective Lyle Odell. Ah, ah, Lyle is a homicide detective. Mohawk City's finest and, in fact, only homicide detective."

Odell smiled as Officer Baker scrambled for covering his mistake and fumbled for words while shaking the outstretched hand of Detective Lyle Odell.

"Oh sorry, detective. I am a rookie. One month on the job. I have heard your name around headquarters, just never had the, ah, ah . . . pleasure to meet you, sir."

Detective Odell's eyes went up and down to the now very nervous young police officer's uniform, and then he studied his face. He buzzed his hair high and tight; everything was perfectly in place as far as his uniform went. He wore military-type side zip boots on his feet, and the boots had a spit shine on them that Odell thought he could see his own reflection in the polish of the boots. The young officer had it together.

"Nice to meet you, Officer Baker. Police officers should not lie. It is seldom, if ever, a pleasure to meet me. No one enjoys my company. Regardless, no harm, no foul, as far as thinking that I was some wayward drunk stumbling back to my hotel room. I most likely would have had the same reaction. Right now, I am sure that I am a train wreck of sorts. I am a drunk, just not a wayward drunk or a drunk looking for a place to crash. Unfortunately, Irish whiskey is part of my heritage. My liver is doomed. I am thinking of getting onto the liver transplant waiting list now, as a prelude to a transplant." Odell stopped speaking and pointed at the hotel room floor, where the young officer's uniform cap had tumbled off the bed and fell down onto the floor. "Better pick up your cap, Baker."

The officer looked down, nodded and scrambled to pick up his cap and he did so, and in one motion, grabbed his notepad and pen from the bed and hustled in an effort to pull his poise together. It seemed as if the unusual appearance and some of the words of Detective Lyle Odell had caused the young officer to lose some discipline. Detective Odell scanned the scene inside the hotel room with a careful study of his dark eyes. It seemed as if he purposely did not focus his eyes or any intent on the dead body of the young woman that sat in a chair in front of the desk in the room. He scanned the entire room, while paying particular attention to the carpet on the floor, but when he did so, the good detective did not move his feet much, if any. Up and down, his eyes went. And other than where the dead woman sat, Detective Odell seemed to take in the entire scene. Odell attempted to adjust his necktie and after looking down and noticing its length and the condition of it, he quickly abandoned that effort. He seemed to make another quick but careful note of everything inside the room, even walking over to the closet in the room, opening the door and scanning the interior of the closet. After closing the closet door, Odell then looked at his watch. He then looked over at the emergency medical personnel and then at Officer Baker. Odell then stood straight and as tall as he could stand with his hands outstretched and his palms facing toward the ceiling of the hotel room and he closed his eyes and stood for a brief period, maybe a minute or more, as if he was deep in thought, or praying, or even falling into a trance. He then opened his eyes wide and scanned the room once more. No one said a word; it seemed as if everyone in the room awaited words or some direction from the good detective before speaking.

Officer Baker felt the detectives refocus and spoke first, "Is this going to be a crime scene for a homicide investigation, Detective Odell? Why are you here? It appears as if she overdosed accidentally. I called for medical assistance because I was not sure of a pulse or not. I was pretty sure that she was already deceased for a few hours when I arrived, but I called for medical, anyway."

Odell removed his eyes from his study of the hotel room. He studied the young officer, and after a few minutes of study and a pause, Odell answered, "Assumptions, Officer Baker can lead you down the incorrect path. Stay on the path. I received the call because the desk sergeant on duty is following my orders. These drug overdoses are becoming epidemic. Scumbag drug dealers are lacing opioids with traces of death and I want to find out who, and what, and whatever. I want to nail some of 'em. Too many dead bodies without visible wounds keep popping up in Mohawk City. Not only in the seedy, back alleys, but also in the fancy places. Like this joint is. If I can nail some of them and slap them with murder or manslaughter charges for selling tainted shit, maybe, the word on the street will be to stop trying to outsell the other guys and it will put an end to this madness. Anyway, I dunno if it is a crime scene or a homicide . . . . yet. To me, after all of these years, everything I see these days feels like a homicide until I prove otherwise. I am very cynical. Tainted. Anyway, time will tell."

Officer Baker stood upright and answered, "Yes, sir."

"Is the medical examiner on the way?" Odell asked the older paramedic.

"Yes, detective. On the way. It seems routine to us. Accidental overdose, but you are the detective. Other than checking for vitals, we disturbed nothing. Say, Lyle, even with the, ah, ah, disruption, to your evening and morning, the doc on call is slow out of the shoot tonight. You beat him here."

The paramedic felt comfortable enough with Odell to tease him a bit.

Odell forced a smile and took the comment within good nature.

"Yeah, a disruption all right. Ok, thanks. Say, Officer Baker, you were in the Marine Corps. Is that not, correct?"

Officer Baker seemed slightly surprised by Detective Odell's observation, and he looked at Odell and answered, "Yes, sir. I was. How did you know?"

Odell pointed at Officer Baker's boots and explained, "First, all the repeated sir bullshit, then your posture, but primarily, your boots. You stand upright as if you have a stick up your ass and only stain wax from the Marine Corps can shine boots like that shine. Old habits die-hard. You Marines spend a lot of time on protocol. It stays with you. Did you light the wax on fire to melt it a little?"

Officer Baker smiled and said, "I did. Yes, sir. The best way."

Odell shrugged, opened his suit jacket and tapped for his pack of cigarettes, mumbled, "Shirt pocket," pulled one out and stuck it in his mouth. "Don't worry," Odell commented as everyone stared at his actions, "heaven forbid that we produce second hand smoke in this blessed world of living in a utopian bubble. I will not light it. Not yet, at least. I just need to taste it. Maybe I will smoke it later. Outside. Ah, yes, melted wax. I used a plain, white tee shirt to polish mine." Odell looked at the young officer, who now clearly did not know what to make of the disheveled, old gumshoe, and waited for the rest of the statement. The unlit cigarette bounced in the mouth of Detective Odell while he spoke. "In the Coast Guard. I was a Coastie. You guys think that basic in the Marine Corps is the toughest. Let me tell you, the Coast Guard is no joke. Liberty in Cape May was awesome, though. The Jersey Shore is beautiful and the bars in the area were top notch. Anyway, Officer Baker, you and Sergeant Grundy were the first responders on the scene."

"Yes, sir. Wait! How did you know that I had a partner and that it was Sergeant Grundy?"

Detective Odell removed the cigarette from his mouth and stuffed it in his jacket pocket, while mumbling, "Suit jacket right-side. Even in this era of understaffed Mohawk City police ranks and budget cuts, rookies do not ride alone. When I pulled up, I saw him sleeping in the passenger's seat of the patrol car on the side of the hotel. He is exhausted. He will order you to drive when you wrap this up. I now know that originally, Grundy was driving because he parked the patrol car in the fire lane. That is a no-no. You are a Marine. You follow rules and you would have parked the car in a proper spot. Besides, Marines never walk on grass. You would have had to walk on the grass island if you drove the patrol car because the grass island is on the driver's side. Asphalt is on the passenger's side. I walked up to the car and checked. Grundy was lost in a slow drool and a loud snore. Old Grundy did not move a muscle. Even with the constant cup of coffee that he always has in his hands in his lap, he could not stay awake. I spotted the reference manuals and textbooks on official police procedures and tutorials from the police academy on the dashboard. I knew right then and there that Grundy's partner was a rookie. Still reading up, even if you are now on the job. Good move, because old Sarge Grundy is not going to teach you too much of anything these days. Other than where to get the best coffee and grilled cheese sandwiches in the city. Grundy is overworked, as are all of us here are. These days, he is not in the training type of mood. I understand. It is very difficult. Great guy, though. Outstanding man and police officer. None better."

Detective Odell turned and pointed at the carpet near the doorway of the room. It was a plush carpet, with a deep pile, and although the carpet now had many imprints, there were a few imprints that differed from the others. There was also a small coffee stain on the carpet, just inside the doorway threshold.

"Look, there. Grundy took a few steps into the doorway of the room, saw the scene, determined it was just another drug overdose, gave you instructions on the procedure, turned and spilled a little of his coffee, and then he left. He is a little overweight and wears low quarters. His footprints in this fancy carpet are different from all the others. The imprints are going to be very important. Please try not to walk around more than you already have because the dead woman has bare feet. By the way, Grundy will spill his coffee when he wakes up because he did not snap the lid on the cup correctly, even after he realized that he spilled some of it. Please, radio his sleepy ass and ask him to come on in now."

Officer Baker tried rather unsuccessfully to hide his shock and awe at the amazing observations and testimony of Detective Odell. He skipped his usual, "yes sir" and substituted a slow nod, pulled his two-way radio off his belt and called down to Sergeant Grundy. It took two calls in order to inspire a response from the sleepy sergeant. After transmitting the radio call, Officer Baker tried to cover for his partner just a little with the detective.

"Sergeant Grundy said for me not to touch much of anything, to take careful notes of the hotel room and of my discussion with the hotel staff. He said that he badly needed to use the restroom and he would wait for and then direct the medical responders to the room from the hotel lobby. He also said that he was going to use the lobby restroom and then have a smoke."

Odell waved to the rest of the crew and said, "Sure. Whatever. Too much coffee and too many grilled cheese sandwiches. He had the runs. I get it. I am not here to bust on Grundy. I only outrank him on active investigations. I am just a detective. After all, I am sure that I am still drunk by the standard of blood alcohol limits, so what the hell would I care about a sleeping sergeant cruising to retirement. I am glad that he had the good sense to use the lobby restroom and not this one. Okay, while we wait for sleeping-not-so-beauty, let's take a break, guys. Time out for a minute or two. I need a recap of the details. Try to stand where you are and not walk around too much. Paramedics, please, if you have decent cameras on your cellphones, then snap pictures of the carpet for me while we stand and talk." The medical crew all nodded and took out their phones and snapped pictures of the carpet while they discussed the events up until this point.

"Go ahead, Baker. Give me what you have here. Only what you have on your notepad, please. No other opinions or observations. Yet."

Officer Baker nodded. He opened his notepad and began to thumb through it. Settling on a page, Officer Baker began to read his notes aloud, "We arrived on scene at one-fifty-two this morning local time. The deceased is Ms. Delilah Murdock. Twenty-nine years of age and her driver's license is from the State of Maryland. She has a

Bethesda, Maryland address and a federal identification card on file with the front desk. We have not touched her purse yet. She works in Washington, D.C. and the desk clerk reported that he is sure that she works for New York Senator Austin Monger as a personal assistant to the senator. Federal senator, that is. The desk clerk reported that she stays here quite often. He claimed to know her fairly well. She is, or was, an attractive woman and apparently was very friendly and outgoing. She stayed here every few months or thereabouts. He also said that she is originally from Mohawk City and visits family here. Perhaps, a sister or a cousin. Sometimes, she has a boyfriend or what the clerk assumed to be a boyfriend or a male acquaintance who would check her in, and the desk clerk seemed embarrassed by that fact. I think that is against the rules and policy and procedures, but they look the other way because she is a frequent guest, they have her credentials on file and she is thought to be a very important person. According to the records, she checked in around three this afternoon."

Officer Baker stopped speaking and looked up at Odell, who now had closed his eyes and was leaning on the wall of the room near the restroom entrance. When the words stopped, Detective Odell opened his eyes, ran his hand through his unkempt hair, and that only caused it to stick up in even more different directions.

Odell waved his hand in the air to indicate for Officer Baker to continue speaking and then, instead, Odell suddenly spoke, "Interesting. Very solid, note taking Officer Baker. Solid. Impressive. Did the desk clerk say that he saw the deceased upon check in?"

"Only from afar. She stood at the main entrance, waved, and let her friend or boyfriend arrange for a check in. That is not standard procedure."

"Understood. Once more, solid note taking. I suppose that you interviewed the desk clerk in the hotel room after coming to the room and while waiting for the medical team to arrive. Specifically, in the room? I mean that everyone stood in the room."

"Thank you, Detective Odell. I served as a military policeman in the Marine Corps, and once my tours were over in the Middle East, I worked for a private security contractor in the combat zones. I guess that I am only a rookie within certain parameters. Civilian world, that is. As far as where we stood, no, sir. I spoke with them in the hallway outside the room while we waited for the medical team to arrive. Both the desk clerk and the houseman were quote, upset and creeped out by the death and preferred to stay clear of viewing the body. The hotel desk clerk made the call to police headquarters when the houseman found the body. The houseman was responding to the room to inform the deceased that she left her car headlights on and another hotel guest reported it to the front desk clerk. He found the door to the room slightly ajar and unlocked. I made careful note of his testimony because he said it was only slightly ajar, but ajar enough for him to see the lights on the desk lit in the otherwise dark room. The houseman knocked and called numerous times and when there was no response, he pushed open the door, found her in the chair and he immediately radioed the front desk and here we are."

"Did the houseman specifically say that he walked into the room and checked on Ms. Murdock?"

Officer Baker glanced up at the good detective when he heard the question and narrowed his eyes. He was deep in thought.

The young police officer then looked at his notes and reported, "He said that he took a few steps to a spot in front of the bed. He could see the vomit running out of her mouth, the pill bottles on the desk, the wine bottle and the wine glass, and her head tilted back, much as you see her now."

Officer Baker pointed at the scene with the young woman still seated in the chair in front of the desk, a trickle of what appeared to be vomit ran out of the side of her mouth, an open bottle of red wine and a half-empty glass of wine sat on the desk in front of her. There were pill bottles with various loose pills scattered along the surface of the desk. It was the first time that Detective Odell had studied the desk scene, or he had even glanced in the direction of the dead woman. Even now, he only glanced very quickly, and then his eyes returned to Officer Baker's face.

Officer Baker continued, "Since she did not respond to any voice, or give any indication of a response, he fled out of the room because he was. . .."

"I know. Creeped out," Odell finished the statement.

"Yes, sir. Creeped out. In his defense, it is not too often that a hotel houseman working in the only fancy, high-end hotel in all of Mohawk City finds a dead body."

"I guess. Did you walk up to the body to examine the scene?"

No sooner did the question leave the mouth of Detective Odell and hang in the air when everyone turned to face a voice from the hallway.

"He did. I took two steps into the room and watched when he walked over. Felt her neck for a pulse, and shook his head. Another druggie dying from an unfortunate overdose. I've seen too many of them. This is routine nowadays. I gave Officer Baker specific orders, told him to call it in, and I would wait for the medical team in the lobby. I needed to hit the restroom and catch a smoke or two."

It was Sergeant Grundy. Grundy made his appearance on the scene known with his testimony.

Grundy fervently dabbed at a large coffee stain that pervaded his white uniform shirt while mumbling, "Damn, plastic lids. Don't fit right."

He was as tall as he was round. His gun belt hung around his huge waistline, like a life preserver clinging to a wave. His thick jowls shook when he spoke and his wavy, almost white hair was curled up along his neck, where he had rested his head on the seat of the patrol car while he napped. He had sad eyes and yellow-cigarette-stained teeth.

"Oh hey, there, Odell. Do not judge me too harshly. The kid is a rook, but he is not a rook, if you know what I mean. He was in police work in the military and he is pretty damn sharp. Besides, how are you standing upright? You smell like a whiskey distillery."

Odell reached out his hand to the old sergeant, and the sergeant shook hands with Detective Odell.

"Nice to see you, too. I do not judge anyone, Grundy. I will not judge you. You do not judge me. I only investigate. Nothing is routine and nothing is easy. Please keep that in mind."

After speaking, Detective Odell turned to the medical team and to Officer Baker, and waved, while saying, "Okay guys. Medical, you can leave. Thank you very much. I will wait for the M.E. I will sign off on all paperwork. Please, let's get out in the hallway. Try to walk on the carpet outside of the normal walk patterns. Please text me the pictures from your phones. Here is my business card. Right-side pocket suit jacket."

Odell dug around in his right-side suit jacket pocket, and at first, he pulled out the previously handled cigarette, which he tucked into the top of his ear and it balanced precariously on its perch, then he found some business cards and handed them to the medical responders. Most of the cards had peculiar liquid stains on them.

"Will do," the older paramedic said, as he took a card and walked by Odell and Grundy. "Take care, Lyle," the paramedic added.

Grundy nodded to the paramedic and then turned to

speak to Odell, "Oh please, Lyle, don't make this into anything other than what it is! A rich, spoiled gal, playing footsie with a high-rolling pretty boy senator that gets nothing but bullshit done in the senate, but everybody loves because he looks like a movie star. She was a hottie, she probably banged the senator and anyone else that she wanted to bang, got money thrown at her right and left and was so bored with her life that she was popping pills and getting drunk every damn day."

Grundy paused in forthright commentary when he realized that the reference to intoxication might have hit home with Detective Odell. He stumbled within the pause for a few seconds and then dismissed the thoughts and continued with his statement. Odell caught his pause for what it was, and Odell allowed a smirk to form on his face. Odell knew what everyone, including his peers and fellow officers, thought of him. He was an alcoholic stumblebum. A has-been. A washed-up loner, loser of a fool. Lost in police work, searching dark corners and alleyways for clues and digging into things that most police officers generally thought were a waste of time. Just another drug overdose. Close the case. Stamp it, accidental death by an overdose, and move onto the next case. Yet, his copious inducement of alcohol did not yet taint Odell's sharp eyes to the point where they missed the clues the others missed. His mind was numb, but not numb enough not to seek justice.

Grundy continued, "It was a terrible accident. She was drunk, sucking down wine while waiting to get a little piece of action with some local stud, and she screwed up and mixed up the pill doses with gulps of wine. Too bad. Another statistic. That's the end of the case. I have worked two doubles and it ain't gonna be a triple."

"Assumptions, Sergeant Grundy," Detective Odell once more tried hard to adjust his necktie and then gave up and patted the shoulder of Sergeant Grundy, "are the downfall of detectives and the dreams of criminals. Sometimes, we are just as far into the game as we are out of the game. That is what the bad guys count on. Keep that in mind."

The elevator floor bell dinged a loud alert, everyone could hear the elevator door open and then slam close and within seconds, a man with a stethoscope around his neck, and wearing a haphazardly buttoned white coat, rushed down the hallway in the direction of the room. Everyone assumed this was the medical doctor on call.

"I am so sorry for the delay. It has been quite the night so far," the doctor said as he rushed into the room. The doctor wore bedroom slippers on his feet. "Two deaths by accidental drug overdoses earlier tonight. I barely fell asleep when this call came in. Hello, I am Doctor Mikhail Barken from the Medical Examiner's office. I am filling in here tonight for a few days for the regular medical doctor, Doctor Kent. I am on call. I am up from Albany."

He displayed a badge and credentials, and Lyle leaned in and studied them, as did Officer Baker.

Odell stepped back. He lifted an eyebrow and carefully studied the doctor.

"Okay. Nice to meet you, doctor. Ya missed a few buttons," Odell said as he pointed to the white coat buttoned incorrectly. The doctor sheepishly looked at his coat, undid the buttons, and buttoned it correctly.

Odell growled out the words, "Ya did not need a white coat. A regular shirt and an overcoat would have worked. It is early April, but still cold out there. And you do not really need the stethoscope. I guess you need to make her death official and all. However, I assure you that this poor woman is stone cold dead. Anyway, filling in for Doctor Kent, huh? Okay. I am Detective Lyle Odell. This is Officer Baker, and this is Sergeant Grundy. I understand about the night so far, doc. I think. Anyway, there she is. Try to catch all the details, but try not to walk around the room too much. Stay off the beaten path, so to speak. The carpet tracks are important. Officer Baker will stay with you. We will be back after a smoke."

Odell nodded at Officer Baker, who nodded back, and the good detective tugged at Sergeant Grundy's uniform sleeve while he removed the cigarette from his ear.

"C'mon, Grundy. I am dying for a cigarette and dying while I smoke 'em."

"I will join you. Are you taking jurisdiction? Lyle. Do you see something?"

"Maybe, I see something, George. Maybe not, but yes, I will take jurisdiction."

Odell took a few steps, suddenly turned, and yelled out in the direction of Officer Baker, "Your MOS was 5811, but was your, B-billet Marine Security Force, Baker? I mean, an SDA? Cuz, ya awfully friggin' sharp, Baker."

Officer Baker, who was in the process of leading the doctor into the room, looked up and smiled.

He answered, "It was."

Odell nodded his head, waved his hands in the air, and said, "The expert attention to detail and the fantastic note taking gave it away. Thank you. Please, carry on."

The two policemen made their way to the elevator, and Odell tugged hopelessly at his tie once more. "Say, George, do you mind if I borrow the kid for a few days?"

"Sure, Lyle, if it will mean that I can catch some damn sleep. He is not a bad kid. Local guy returning home after the Marine Corps, as a sort of hero from combat that no one really notices or cares about . . . despite everyone saying that they care. He saw some shit over there in the Middle East. He is a little uptight. He is all yours. The schedule officers are milking the kid like a cow. Killing me. I ain't exactly twenty-five years old, anymore."

"Gotcha. I understand. By the way, where do I get a good grilled cheese sandwich in this city?"

The elevator bell dinged, and the doors opened. The two men stepped into the car.

"Gulliver's. Fifth and Main. Downtown. The damn thing always has bubbly melted cheese and burned and crispy edges on it. I swear, Lyle, it will be the death of me."

Odell leaned back a little into the wall of the elevator. He contemplated the testimony of Grundy and studied Grundy while the doors closed and the elevator began to move.

"Really? Gulliver's? My source told me that it was Hal's Diner out on Route Five."

Grundy turned and looked at Odell and shook his head while explaining, "Ya the detective Odell, but ya sources got it wrong. Look at the size of my belly." Grundy grabbed his rather large belly with both hands and shook it around as evidence. "C'mon, Odell, the evidence speaks for itself. I am a foodie and it is Gulliver's. Plus, I wash it all down with a few ice-cold beers."

"I would say the belly evidence put your testimony over the top. However, I usually don't drink beer, George," Odell offered as the elevator stopped and the doors slowly opened.

"Damn, your loss, Odell. Nuthin' like a few cold ones mixed with gooey grilled cheese and burned edges. Usually, ya get out of there with a tab under twelve bucks. Chuck a few bucks to the bartender for a tip, and bang! Ya fat, dumb, and bloated. As I usually am."

"Sounds rather . . . appealing, George. In a gluttonous sort of way."

"Fifteen bucks at the most. That is . . . if ya drink the tap specials and order a side of fries. Ya missin' out on one of the simple pleasures of life, Lyle."

As the two police officers exited the elevator and turned in the direction of the exit for the hotel and the smoking area, Grundy waved his hands in the air and commented, "Then wash it down with that Irish whiskey ya love. Your choice, Odell. Your choice."

Chapter Two

Left Hand-Right Hand

Dr. Barken ran his hand through his thick gray hair. He glanced up as Detective Odell and Sergeant Grundy both returned to the hotel room. His eyes quickly scanned Odell, and they studied him before the doctor spoke.

Clearing his throat, Dr. Barken said, "Make this the third drug overdose on this so far, very horrible night. I will initially determine her death accidental . . . she choked on her own vomit while in a drug and alcohol induced coma. Lethal combination of alcohol and those pills. I suspect they are opioids laced with whatever super-high-test wretchedness the street is lacing them with these days. The labs can give us the full report, but whatever high it gives these addicts, they sure come back for more . . . until they, well, just don't come back," Doctor Barken finished his statement. He glanced at the dead woman and shook his head. "What a shame. Such a beautiful woman, too. The world at her fingertips. Awful." Dr. Barken placed his medical examination tools in his bag and picked up a clipboard with standard forms printed upon them. "I would guess her to have passed about six hours ago or thereabouts," he said while beginning to complete the form, "we can rely on the autopsy results for what is ambiguous here. I think it is rather cut and dry. I confess that I am very curious as to what could be in that pill bottle."

While Officer Baker and Grundy watched the doctor

complete the paperwork, Detective Odell finally glided over to where the dead woman sat in the chair. It was the first time that Odell closely examined the scene. At first, his eyes glanced at the woman's face, and then he studied her hands rather carefully and surprised everyone by fumbling around in his jacket pocket and pulling out a small foldable magnifying lens. Detective Odell carefully unfolded the lens from its small leather case and he leaned in with the lens over his right eye and appeared to be studying the dead woman's hands, or more specially, her fingernails. After carefully studying her fingernails, and with a grunt and groan, Odell slowly made his way to the floor and ended up on his knees. He wobbled a little and Officer Baker, who was now right beside the detective, and obviously deeply interested in Odell's studies, placed his hand on Odell's shoulder to assist in steadying him.

"Easy now, Detective Odell," Office Baker said, "still a little woozy, huh?"

In return for the steadying hand, Odell only mumbled, "Something like that. Say, doc," Odell said while leaning in close and now fishing a small flashlight out of his jacket pocket to add to the examination arsenal. "Why are you saying that this is initially an accidental overdose, ruling?" Odell turned on the flashlight and leaned in to examine the dead woman's toenails with his lens, and he spoke in a barely audible voice just above a mumble, "You later said it was rather cut and dry."

Odell leaned in closer and he was carefully examining the woman's toenails while Officer Baker and Sergeant Grundy stood with puzzled looks planted upon their faces. Doctor Barken stopped writing his report and looked over at Odell on his knees. Now the doctor seemed puzzled too. The doctor placed the pen on the clipboard and tilted his head at a different angle in an effort to determine what it was that the detective was checking.

"I always put a disclaimer in there. Therefore, I stated

initially . . . pending autopsy results . . . but I have been doing this for a long time and my experience enters into my opinion. I was simply offering my opinion there when I said cut and dry. In my opinion, it is cut and dry. Accidental. If I might ask, what in the world are you checking?"

Odell switched off the flashlight, leaned back on his knees and rocked a little before answering, "Sure you can ask, doc. I am checking her nail polish techniques and specifically, her toenail polish applications. Say there, Officer Baker, give me a boost up, will ya?"

Sergeant Grundy chuckled a little at the scene and the doctor studied Odell while Officer Baker gripped the detective under his arm and helped pull him to his feet.

"Are you under the influence of alcohol, Detective Odell?" Doctor Barken asked.

"Ya don't need to be a doc to figure that out," Odell growled and pointed at the doctor's feet and said, "you are in bedroom slippers because you were climbing in bed when this call came in. I was climbing into a bottle of Irish whiskey. I had to climb out of the bottle in order to get here. Do not worry. I did not drive here. A patrol car picked me up. Baker, where are her shoes?"

"Sir, on the floor right there next to the side of the bed. Right there, Detective Odell."

Officer Baker pointed to the shoes, and Odell's eyes followed his finger.

Odell nodded, stuck his hands into the inside pockets of his jacket, and fumbled around a bit and shook his head. In a show of slight frustration, with a slight waver and wobble that hinted at the effects of his early evening activities, Odell removed his jacket and he dropped the jacket onto an empty chair next to him. He fumbled through the jacket pockets as the jacket sprawled on the chair, and he finally found the object of his probing and pulled out rubber gloves.

"Here they are. Could not reach them."

Grundy wiped at his eyebrows and then his forehead in a puzzled reaction to the detective's actions; the doctor shook his head, picked up his pen, and resumed completion of his report. Officer Baker studied Detective Odell and made a note of his wrinkled shirt, hanging untucked from his pants, his leather belt looped through the belt loops of his pants, but missing two loops while it made its way around the waist of the detective. All of this was in stark contrast to the immaculate appearance of Officer Baker, who looked as if he could be a poster model for a perfect image for a police officer. Most of all, Officer Baker's eyes noticed that Detective Odell's leather shoulder holster hung over his right shoulder, but there was no weapon tucked in the holster.

While Detective Odell pulled on the rubber examination gloves, Officer Baker stated, "You don't have a weapon in your holster, Detective Odell."

Now Grundy and the doctor both turned and studied the rumpled detective for his response.

"Nah . . . seldom carry one these days. Most of the time, when I conclude a case, the bad guys are not in a shooting mood. I usually have the bad guys cornered and dead to rights. No need to resort to shooting."

Odell leaned over the body, carefully picked her purse off the desk, gently opened the latch, and carefully examined the contents. He placed the purse back down in the original position, once more took out his lens and flashlight and carefully flashed the light over the dead woman's dress and studied it carefully while gently poking in and around the hip areas of the dress with his gloved hands. He then turned and walked over to the shoes, carefully examined them while they sat next to the bed, and waved to Officer Baker. "Please, Baker, take a few photos of these shoes before I touch them.

"Yes, sir."

Officer Baker pulled out his cellphone, walked over, and snapped off a few pictures. When he finished taking the pictures, Odell once more dropped to his knees, very carefully lifted the shoes, and closely examined the heels of the shoes without greatly disturbing their positions on the carpet. The shoes were a women's slip-on loafer. After a close examination, Detective Odell carefully left the shoes in the same position; he used the bed for leverage and wobbled to his feet. For a few moments while everyone remained silent, his eyes scanned the entire hotel room, and then he eyed the sliding exterior door hidden behind the drapes. Odell walked over to the curtains, he gently parted the curtains and then studied the lock and handle on the door, he cupped his hands over the glass and peered into his hands in an effort to shut out the ambient light and he peered into the darkness.

"Humph . . . first floor hotel room. Ground level. A walkway out there. Leading to the parking lot. I wonder if that is where they parked her car. Most likely out there in one of the spots close to the building. I don't see any headlights on out there. I guess the battery finally lost power and drained."

Now the use of the word "they," caught the ears of the doctor, Officer Baker and Sergeant Grundy. All three of them looked up and carefully studied the detective.

Grundy spoke first, "They, Lyle. Whose they?"

"That, Sergeant Grundy, is the question of the night. Do you see many overdoses in Albany, Doctor Barken? It is an epidemic here, and I agree in the fact that I want to see the lab analysis results of those pills."

"I saw a few, but I can't recall ever seeing three in one night, detective," the doctor mumbled in a slightly somber tone. It seemed as if the detective's unusual methods and careful examination had caused some pause and an element of wonder to the doctor. As if he did not anticipate the seemingly intoxicated detective to be able to function at a high level, or at any level at all.

"How long have you been working here in Mohawk City, doctor?"

"On and off for a few weeks or so. Coverage for vacations of the regulars and such. Can you sign my paperwork, detective? I imagine you will call for the coroner's office to remove the body to the morgue. I want to go get some sleep. Who knows what tomorrow will bring?"

Odell nodded. He gently pulled at the rubber gloves and removed them from his hands, crumbled them up and stuffed them in his pockets. The doctor handed the clipboard and the pen to Detective Odell, who took the pen, glanced at the check marks on the report and some of the notes, and signed the report.

"Thanks, Doctor Barken. Please leave copies with Officer Baker. Go and get some sleep. I will eventually make the call, but I am not calling the coroner's office to pick up the body just yet."

The doctor took back his clipboard and thumbed through the copies to pick out the reports to give to Officer Baker, when suddenly Detective Odell's statement hit home. All three of the men looked at Odell, and the doctor's face turned into puzzlement.

This time the doctor spoke, "You're not calling now? Why?"

Odell walked over to the chair, picked up his jacket, and slipped it back on while standing next to the woman still sitting dead in the chair at the desk.

"This woman was left-handed and left footed." Odell pointed at the desk and at the dead woman. "Her fingernails are painted unevenly on her left side. She was not accurate with her right hand. For such a perfect woman, her toenails and fingernails on the left side are painted wobbly. The right-side is perfect." Odell turned and pointed at the shoes on the floor next to the bed. "Her left shoe sole and heel are worn more than the right-side is. Her laterality was totally on the left side. Only about ten percent of the human population is totally left-handed, left footed and left sided. Animals . . . we don't know so much yet." Odell continued to explain to the astonished group as the body posture of all three of the men changed from dismissal of a drunken detective, burned out by years and years of investigating homicides in a seedy old worn-out city to astonishment at his adeptness. "Yet, lookie there, the wine glass is on the right-side of the desk. The pill bottle too and her purse is on the right-side of the desk, there. Yet, this woman was left-handed. And the carpet, well, we have been walking all around now, but initially, I could see marks here and here . . . drag marks. I want to receive those pictures from the medical crew and check them carefully. Use some software enhancement to see the marks."

Odell leaned over, pointed to the carpet, and blinked his eyes as he studied it carefully. "This is a looped pile carpet, easy to make it look fancy when you use a vacuum on it. Gives the room a plush and luxurious appearance." Odell ran his hand over the carpet. "Expert executive housekeepers pride themselves on making fancy vacuum marks on these commercial loop piles. Have to satisfy the guest, ya know." Odell stood up and flexed his back while tilting backwards.

"Under the lens, there are carpet fibers on the heels of those shoes. And dog hairs, too. Inside here. Must have been on her feet and-or stuck to her socks. Silver and black dog hairs. Cannot wait to get them to the lab. Oh yes," Odell pointed at the door, "the lock latch was not locked on the door. Beautiful young woman, ground floor of a hotel, dark walkway, not a good idea to leave it unlocked."

"Maybe she never realized that it was unlocked, Odell," Grundy offered.

"Maybe, but doubtful. I think that a big, strong person carried her dead body up the walkway from her car in the parking lot. This person dragged her through the sliding door while holding her under her arms, placed her in the chair, and staged the scene. Under her arms, because if you look there . . . under her arms, her dress is askew in and around her armpits. I bet her brassiere is askew too, but I will not examine that closely until help arrives. That is because he hooked her under her arms to drag her body along. This person had an accomplice, because someone unlocked the sliding door from the inside. There is only a spot or two of dirt on the carpet, a remnant of a wet leaf, here and there that tracked in from outside on the shoes or body of the strong person," Odell said while he pointed to the carpet in various locations. "This person did not realize that she was left-handed. Furthermore, Officer Baker and Sergeant Grundy, your testimony upon arrival was that the houseman came to notify the deceased that her car headlights were still on . . . correct? That is how they found her body."

"Yup, that is right on, Lyle," Grundy answered.

"Strange, no car keys anywhere in the room, or in her purse, or in the small pockets on the side of her dress. No car keys because she did not drive her car because she was already dead. They drove her here and staged this scene as a diversion. A rather poor one at that. Rather easily figured out. Someone else drove the car and the bad guys or gals screwed up by not leaving the car keys here. If we recall Officer Baker's impressive note taking of the testimony of the desk clerk on duty . . . something about another man, a boyfriend or friend, or someone else, checking her in, seeing her from afar, having her credentials permanently on file, a frequent guest who spends a lot of dough, something about breaking the rules but looking the other way. Huh? Okay. We do need to speak with the desk clerk because he just might be very helpful with those very important points. Anyway, my gut feeling is that she unknowingly drank wine spiked with whatever is in those pills, to make them super-drugs, and she died as you said, Doctor Barken, by choking on her own vomit. However, I think that this poor, beautiful woman only wanted to enjoy a few glasses of wine. However, the wine had evil intent mixed in. This . . . gentlemen . . . is a homicide."

Odell looked at all three men and then wiped at his brow. Some emotion at the conclusion that Odell just announced set in silently and heavily upon everyone in the room. Especially on Lyle Odell.

"That poor beautiful woman. Such a gorgeous woman, and so young. I wonder what would bring her to such an awful fate. What did she know that required silencing?" Odell turned and glanced at the young woman's body still slumped in the chair, and he wiped the touch of mist at the corners of his eyes.

"Such an evil world that keeps us employed. It weighs on me more and more. The evil. The disregard for human life. It becomes worse every day. The things that I see and have seen. Anyway, I promise that I will find out . . . mark my words . . . I will find out. This one will not be easy. I can already feel how complex and ominous it will be, but we will persevere. Yes, indeed." Odell looked at the doctor and said, "Sorry, Doctor Barken, this is anything but cut and dry. Office Baker, Sergeant Grundy, please make a call into headquarters and get me a crime scene investigation team." Odell tugged at his necktie to loosen it, even more than it already was. "Please, damn . . . I need a cup of coffee. I fear that I am sobering up now. The clues will be dull now. Oh well. I might have all that I need for now. Or at least until the crime scene crew arrives."

Odell ran his hand through his already tousled and messy hair and made it even messier that it was. If that was actually possible.

The three somewhat shocked witnesses to his investigation and his amazing abilities stood silently and stared at the oval faced detective. A detective with messy hair, a wrinkled suit jacket, a loose and askew necktie, unpolished shoes and now somewhat clearer eyes. He looked as if he worked in any occupation other than police detective work.

After a long pause, Odell gently asked, "Please, maybe in the hotel lobby . . . can we find some coffee?"

The cellphone of Attorney Rexford Covington signaled an incoming call, and even if the screen did not indicate a name, Rexford Covington knew who was calling. He was not pleased with the call coming in, nor was he happy to think of the person associated with the number. He was borderline furious. But in front of Senator Monger, Covington needed to conceal his emotions. Senator Austin Monger took his hand off his forehead, from where he sat in his chair opposite his attorney. The senator was now a little numb from the brandy and the weariness of the day and the awful events of the same wore heavily upon his soul.

"Trouble?" The senator asked as he looked first at the cellphone and then at the face of Rexford Covington.

Covington quickly whipped up a cover and with a wave of his hand in a ploy of dismissal; the attorney played the scene to the hilt. Covington was a legend in the courtroom, and it was easy to see why. Half-attorney and half-actor, but mostly a scoundrel.

"Please, no, just a call that I need to take. Another client. Please relax. Take another sip of your drink and lean back. I will be right back."

Covington scooped up the phone, stood up, and walked by the senator, who weakly nodded while reaching for the brandy glass on the end table next to this chair. The glass top of the elegant oak wood table reflected the colors of the brown liquid courage remaining in the glass, and the facets of the glass reflected and captured the light from the one table lamp on in the entire room.

"Client privileges with the usual attorney-client privacy. Sorry, please excuse me. Just a corporate client with a routine matter. Trying to leverage a rather messy buy-out of a wealthy but somewhat inept majority shareholder. You know how it goes with business," Covington said with a nod and wink, while he gently patted the shoulder of the senator. "I will pour us refills when I return. This will only take a minute or two."

Covington slipped out the door and caught the call before it went to voicemail.

He walked a few steps and lowered his voice, carefully checked the long hallway and the door to the senator's den and spoke angrily in the cellphone, "This had better be damn good for you to call this phone. I told you only emergencies, and emergencies are not what I need to deal with right now. Now, we have a phone record of us speaking and that is not good. Speak!"

The voice on the other side of the phone also reflected the weariness and treachery of the day, "Sorry. Yes, but it is an emergency. It is . . . Odell."

"Odell? Why is this about Odell? I don't need to hear any bullshit!"

"We . . . I might have underestimated his . . . abilities. He is declaring a crime scene."

Attorney Covington leaned back and sighed deeply while holding the phone at his side and staring at the ceiling. He wanted to scream at the sky, but he knew that he needed to remain quiet and return to the senator quickly.

Borrowing upon his legendary courtroom tactics and acting skills, Covington gathered his thoughts and spoke, "Underestimated, huh? Crime scene, huh? I thought this guy was a raging drunk who could not find a clue in his own pocket. Is that not what you told me?"

"I did. I mean, that was the word on the inside from our guy. The guy is a terrible drunk. Irish whiskey flows through his veins along with his Irish heritage and blood. He was half-in-the-bag when he showed up, looking as if he crawled out of the police drunk tank or a dark alley downtown and I swear, despite the alcohol . . . he is friggin' amazing. Like some, kind of modern-day, Sherlock Holmes. He even carries a magnifying lens. In fact, he might be better drunk than sober. At first, he did not say anything other than small talk and a few words, and then he put it all together."

"A modern-day, Sherlock Holmes. You are kidding me with this call. Correct? Kidding. Just a joke, right? What the hell do you mean?"

"No joke. I wish that I was kidding. I mean, he put the scene together. Exactly as it went down. Additionally, there was a little screw up with her car keys and we left the headlights on in her car by mistake."

"Car keys? Headlights? Mistakes? So, you are dumb-asses! Explain! Now!"

"Yes . . . her car is in the parking lot but the keys are not there, or in her purse or on her body or on her person. Odell discovered that . . . almost right away. One of us has them. Somewhere. I need to check my bag and check with the other guy. I mean, it was a hassle to drag her in there and set her in place. Dead, body and all. We left the headlights on and that is how the houseman found her dead body. I mean that is really no big deal. They would've found her, anyway. I am beside myself here. The guy does not miss a trick."

Now Covington's blood boiled. Yet, he suppressed his voice while getting his point across. "Wonderful. A *little* screw up, no that is a major screw up. A simple detail and you screw it up. Look, I paid you handsomely. Perhaps, we picked the wrong guy. Regardless, we are not going down. Not the senator. Not me. No one but you. Do you realize the implications of this? Senator Monger is the senior federal senator from New York. The media loves his bleeding-heart, save the world, liberal politics, his movie star good looks and his white-toothed smile. He is going to make a run at the White House for his next mailing address. That is why she had to go. I will ride his coattails, pocket a ton of dough, grab my thirty-six-year-old hot little Latino with a body that melts paint off the walls and I will disappear with her to an island somewhere and enjoy the fruits of her vines and of my efforts. You are a stupid son-of-a-bitch . . . take care of all of this. Now. Somehow. We are not going down. You are. Do whatever it takes, even if it takes killing off the stumblebum drunken detective and burying his drunken ass in a shallow grave somewhere. Take. Care. Of. This. Or, you can join the gorgeous chick in seeing who can push up daisies on their graves quicker. Understand."

"I do. I will handle this. I have a plan."

"Good. Never call this phone again. Ever."

Covington angrily hit the red button to end the call. He gently tucked the cellphone into his suit jacket pocket, and he took a deep breath and ran his hands over his hair to smooth the edges. He tightened his necktie, stood up a little straighter, and composed his emotions once more. With a few strides, Rexford Covington was back in the den and he put on his best smile. Upon hearing the attorney reentering the room, Senator Monger turned and anxiously glanced Covington's way and studied his face. The senator still held the brandy glass in his hand. A now empty brandy glass.

"Is everything okay, Rexford?" the senator asked with a furrowed brow and deep lines entering his handsome face.

"Everything is fine, Austin. Purely routine," the attorney lied as if he was a fine Persian rug.

"A refill?" Rexford Covington asked with a pretend smile and a singsong voice, and with an outstretched hand that did not tremble in the least.

That is because the tremors were on the inside.

Chapter Three

Mack

Police Officer Dennis Baker walked out of the men's restroom, down the hotel hallway, and met Detective Lyle Odell in the lobby. Odell sipped a cup of coffee in a waxed paper cup, and the detective's eyes carefully scanned Officer Baker's face and his body posture.

Officer Baker caught the study, and it unnerved him just a little.

"What, do I have toilet tissue on my shoe or something?" Baker asked.

"No, no toilet tissue, Baker," Odell answered over the rim of the cup. "You, okay? Did the sight of the beautiful woman sitting there dead and my determination of a homicide upset you? Or unnerve you? I would have thought that in the Marine Corps you might have needed to deal with a few dead bodies or some of the uglier sides of life. Grundy told me you were a combat vet. You look a little uneasy there," he added.

"I am fine. Sorry. Yes, I saw some nasty things while I was serving in country. I just had to go to the restroom. Kind of badly. You know. I did not want to leave while you were investigating in the room . . . I held it. Your methods were fascinating, sir."

"Understood. You had to go badly, huh? I guess so. You were in there for a long time. Yeah, it happens to all of us. Do you want a cup?" Odell asked as he pointed with a finger to the coffee station set up in the corner of the hotel lobby.

"No, it will make me run to the restroom again, sir," Baker said, and Odell chuckled at the comment.

"Damn, I really need a cigarette, but right now, I need this coffee more. Look, Officer Baker, please call me, Odell, or Detective Odell, or Lyle, but please, do not sir me to the hilt. I am fine without the military protocol. I don't warrant fancy."

Baker nodded and cut off his words when he began to answer Lyle, "Yes, sirrrr, ah, Detective Odell."

"You still look shook up, Baker. How old are you?"

"Thirty-one, Detective Odell."

"Did you know Ms. Delilah Murdock? Grundy told me that you are from Mohawk City. Did you grow up here in Mohawk City? I cannot think of any reason that you would return here after your service in the military unless you had family roots or a young woman here. She was only a few years younger than you are."

"No. I did not know, Ms. Delilah Murdock. Heard of her . . . everyone has heard of the rich and powerful Murdock family, but I did not know her. Yes, this is a return home for me. Family reasons. I supposed she went to fancy private schools. I was a poor kid who went to public schools. We would never have traveled in the same circles."

Odell studied the young police officer, nodded and blinked a few times and mumbled, "Welcome home, Baker."

Officer Dennis Baker then nervously went about checking his uniform to make sure that nothing was askew after his restroom trip. He seemed not to want to make eye contact with Odell and the detective noticed that fact yet chose not to comment on it.

"Say, I spoke with Sergeant Grundy about you when we went for a smoke. I think that you cramp his style and are in the way," Detective Odell spoke the words, then lifted the eyebrow of his left eye and focused in with the same eye while gauging the reaction of Officer Baker to his statement.

Officer Baker shifted his body weight and tilted his head a little while commenting, "I do seem to get on his nerves. Perhaps, I am in his way of his normal routine. I am not sure."

"I gotcha. Well, do not let it bother ya too much. Grundy is an old salt, and he is a little grumpy these days. Who knows? Anyway, I asked Grundy if I could use you for a little assistance in this case. Normally, I am a one-man-band and Grundy is not in the training mood, so it works out rather well. Your observation, reporting, and military experience will come in handy for me. Besides, you always carry a service weapon and that might come in handy too."

Now, Officer Baker gave Lyle his full attention, and he stopped worrying about his uniform and the exact positioning of his patrolmen's badge and smiled widely upon hearing of the new assignment and the prospect of a little in-depth police action.

Baker's eyes flashed while he spoke, "This is wonderful news, Detective Odell. Thank you for the opportunity. This is exciting and I will not let you down. Besides being in his way and cramping his style, I felt as if I was getting a little stale with riding with Sergeant Grundy. He is not really the most engaging guy to work with, and not my idea of an ideal example of a police officer. A little cynical and worn out, I suppose."

"And I imagine that I am not your ideal example of a homicide detective, either. Messy suit, longish hair that requires a comb and a high and tight. I need a shave. I seldom carry a service weapon, and here, I show up with watery eyes and smelling like a whiskey distillery and stale cigarettes. Not exactly ideal. Huh, Baker?"

The young officer did not comment. He took a deep breath and withheld his words. That told enough of his opinion.

"I get it. These evil bastards should know better than to commit murder and horrible crimes when I am home staring into Irish whiskey bottles. However, it does not work like that, Baker. Evil does not take any days off. In our meager defense, this job will do that to you, rook. This is my twenty-eighth-year on the job. Twenty-four as a homicide detective. Come see me in twenty years. If I am still around."

Baker toyed nervously with the position of his patrol officer's cap and decided that a simple answer would suffice rather than a long comment. It was obvious that there was much to learn about the complexities of Detective Lyle Odell. Police Officer Dennis Baker realized after witnessing his amazing investigative abilities that there were many reasons for him to stick close to Odell's side.

"I do understand, Detective Odell. By the way, where is Sergeant Grundy?" Officer Baker asked while glancing around the lobby.

"He was guarding the hotel room, but he locked it up and went for a quick smoke. He will go back to the room and then meet the crime scene crew when they arrive. I would have joined him for a good puff on a cancer stick or two or three, but you were in the head. Besides, I needed the coffee to push along my sobriety and to wait for you to tell you that you are on the team now."

"Oh, yes, thank you. Yes, a smoke. Both of you do that a lot. And the doctor?"

Lyle laughed and took a long sip of the coffee. It was cooler now.

"He could not wait to go home to bed. I think that I pissed him off by countering his determination and the results of his examination. Anyway, I want to speak with the desk clerk. He is on a break. He should be back any minute now. Get your notepad out, Baker. Take careful notes. As you did previously."

"Yes, detective. I have my pad right here. Pen too." Officer Baker tapped the top pocket of his uniform to confirm the presence of the writing equipment. Lyle Odell simply raised his eyebrows at the young police officer's zealousness.

"So, you married, Baker? I do not see a wedding ring."

"Oh no, Detective Odell. I don't have a steady gal. Yet. I do have my eye on a young woman, and we keep some company occasionally, but right now, during my probation period, I am too busy to pursue her much. How about you?"

Lyle shook his head and he forced back a smile.

"No, Baker, I am not married. Never been. Who wants to marry an old drunken detective that endlessly pokes around for clues in dark corners and sticks his mind, body, and soul into immoral situations and carries the burdens of cases upon his shoulders and the stink of evil on his person? Besides, I ain't exactly a movie star in the looks department. Not like you are. Ya, a sharp-looking kid."

Officer Baker initially did not comment. Instead, his eyes studied the old detective, and he absorbed the profound testimony into his soul. It appeared as the young police officer's eyes displayed a little sympathy at Odell's words and his situation. A lifetime of investigating homicides could make you more than worn out.

"I guess it is a difficult life and career, detective. I can see how after all these years that it weighs upon you. What do you do for fun, Detective Odell? I mean, do you have any hobbies? I am an occasional trout fisherman and I like to target shoot too."

Odell took a last sip of the coffee; he carried the empty paper cup over to a nearby trashcan and tossed the cup inside before answering the questions from Officer Baker.

"I guess that you expect me to say that I drink for fun. I do not drink for fun and I do not have any hobbies. My work is my life. Do not have much else going on over here. No family. Not too many friends, just a few guys on the force who can stand hanging out with me for a few hours here and there to catch a beer or a shot or two occasionally. I guess for fun, I poke around for clues where phantoms tread. That is what I do, Baker. Clues are as phantoms are . . . they are all around us. We just need to open our eyes in order to see them. When I find them, then that is when the drink comes in. It erases the pain of finding the phantoms. Lookie over there, Baker. Is that the desk clerk that you spoke with now returning from his break?"

Officer Baker tried hard not to dwell upon the words of Detective Lyle Odell, and he followed his finger pointing in the direction of the front desk of the hotel.

"Yes, that is him."

"Good. Pen and pad ready, Baker. Follow my lead. Let's get this case rolling and start here by seeing what it is that he knows. First reactions are important."

The front desk clerk busily shuffled through some papers and he typed away at the keyboard of a computer. When he looked up to see that it was Officer Baker and another man, the desk clerk held a quick frown for just a brief moment. Odell nodded to Officer Baker for him to take the lead and speak first.

"Hello there. Sorry to bother you again. I know this has been a difficult evening shift for you and that you have work to do, but this is Homicide Detective Lyle Odell from the Mohawk City detective bureau. I briefed the detective on the high points of our previous conversation and now, Detective Odell would like to ask you a few questions."

The young man was nervous. Very nervous. He nodded, and his eyes went from Baker over to Detective Odell. It was easy to see that he was the same as all the others who first encountered the rather unconventional looking police detective. The desk clerk was a tall, thin, Caucasian male who appeared to be in his mid-twenties or thereabouts. He had close-cropped black hair, wore two silver stud earrings in each of his ears, and wore a neatly trimmed beard. He was a good-looking young man, and Detective Odell made a careful study of his reactions while they looked each other over.

Odell spoke first and with a wave of his hand in the air, Odell broadcasted his usual recognition of his appearance and a person's reaction to a homicide detective, looking as he did.

"Yeah, I know that I look like hell torn apart and flamed over and out. However, if you were home sucking down gallons of Irish whiskey on a Wednesday evening, and now Thursday morning, when this call came in, well, you would look as I do too."

The young man almost laughed and instead, he nodded his head and answered, "An honest cop. Interesting."

"Best to put all the cards out on the table, ah, ah, Officer Baker, do we have the particulars on," Odell leaned in to read the desk clerk's nametag and continued, "Timothy?" Without waiting for Baker to thumb through his notepad for reference to his previous notes, Lyle leaned in closer and waved his hand in the air for the desk clerk to tell them his last name.

"Mackie. Ah, ah, ah, my name is Timothy Mackie. Everyone calls me Mack. No one calls me Timothy or Tim. Mack works."

"Okay, Mack, that works for us, too. Are you nervous? You seem fidgety."

"I have a ton of work to do. My partner, Ronnie . . . he is making rounds of the checkouts and slipping the paperwork under the doors. If I could . . . I would go to the office and collapse in the chair there. I am very, very upset. Not nervous. It has been a very rough night. To say the least."

Odell nodded. He then tapped his shirt pocket inside his jacket; he pulled a pack of cigarettes out of the pack, tilted it over and shook one of the cigarettes out of the pack.

While waving the cigarette in the air, Odell asked, "Say, you don't mind if I stick a cancer stick in my mouth here? I promise that I will not light it up. New York State laws and such for evil second-hand smoke. I just need to taste it. I am overdue for a puff or two."

"Honestly, it is against the rules, Detective Odell. You need to go outside. Even if it is not lit."

Odell nodded, stuck the cigarette in his mouth anyway, and while it dangled and bobbed along the edge of his mouth, Detective Lyle Odell sent the first wave of salvos across the bow of the young hotel desk clerk.

"I gotcha. Against the rules. Sort of like a hotel front desk clerk not making a careful and in-depth inspection of identification credentials of a hotel guest when you check them in, huh? Officer Baker takes very careful and comprehensive notes."

Detective Lyle Odell was very good at his job.

Very, very good.

Mack frowned, and this time, he made no effort to hide his reaction. He put his head down, toyed with the stack of papers on the desk, and then his eyes darted back and forth as he checked for any other hotel workers nearby or any other persons in the lobby. It was now close to four in the morning, and there was no one else around.

"Look, detective, yes, I broke the rules. Please, jobs are hard to come by here in this crummy old city. We barely make it now on this income. I live with my old man and he lost his job a long time ago and never found a decent job after that. My mom is dead." Mack twisted his head and spoke out of the side of his mouth, "Ah, ah, c'mon now, detective. You are not going to tell my general manager, are you?"

"Sorry about your mom and the tough times. Lookie here, Mack, the rules are the rules. No promises. Things eventually come out in the end. Often . . . it is out of my control. Let's worry about that ticky-tacky bullshit later. We have to wade through some turbulent waters first. Tell us more about Ms. Murdock."

"She was a frequent guest. I knew her quite well from her staying here, and we were rather friendly in a . . . well . . . ya know, in a casual sort of way. This has been simply awful. Very upsetting. It is not every shift that we find dead bodies in hotel rooms. Especially when it was Ms. Delilah Murdock. I really looo . . . liked her. She was very . . . nice." Mack finished speaking, and he looked down at the floor, back to his paperwork on the desk. He nervously shuffled the papers and wiped a hint of a few tears away from his eyes. Tears that he tried unsuccessfully to hide from Detective Odell and from Officer Baker.

Odell removed the cigarette from his lips and tucked it into the wrinkled pocket of his shirt. He was giving the young man a few moments of introspection and a chance to gather his emotions.

Odell was good at his job. Very, very good.

"Especially, Ms. Murdock, huh? Nice, huh? You liked her or something like that, huh? You had the hots for her, huh, Mack?"

Mack blinked his eyes rapidly and took a deep breath before answering, "Well, sure I did. I mean, sitting up there dead and all with vomit coming out of her mouth, you most likely could not tell—but she was drop-dead gorgeous. Beyond beautiful. I bent the rules, was extra nice to her, and someday, I hoped that she would give me more than a smile, a twenty buck tip and a wave or two."

"Gotcha. Yes, she was quite beautiful. Even in death. I was young once, too. I was never as handsome as you are. Nope, never were and never will be. Ya, a good-looking young man. I was always an ugly mug, but I understand about the attraction. Twenty buck tip, huh?"

"Yes. Well, most often she did not hand it to me. There was always some hotshot guy with her. He always checked her out, left the card keys to the room and dropped a twenty-spot for me and five bucks for the houseman and he was gone. He picked her up from the rear walkway. Drove her around when she was in town. You know, she was originally from Mohawk City. She has family here. I imagine that is the only reason a gorgeous, successful woman from Washington, D.C. would ever return to this dump of an old city. To visit family."

Odell, without hesitation, jumped in with more information.

It seemed as if he knew everything.

"Yes, she had family here. The Murdock family. A wealthy lot they are. Made a fortune on the backs of many Mohawk City workers. The factory still stands. Abandoned on the south end of the city. Weeds poking up through every crack in the parking lot. The bricks of the factory are crumbling. They sold their gloves, socks, hats, and garment manufacturing business before it all gave out here in Mohawk City. They sold the name and the brand to an investment company, which did as all these companies seem to do, and they stole the brand, and they stole the reputation and the name and they moved the manufacturing to Mexico. Lost jobs. Murdock. They have a mansion on the north end of the city. I guess they banked all the dough."

"That's them. Right on. You know your shit, Detective Odell. She worked for that clown, Senator Monger."

"Clown, huh?" Odell asked and then lifted his eyes toward Officer Baker to infer that he should take a break from his feverish note taking mission and jump into the questioning.

Baker took the hint, stopped writing, and held his pad and his pen at his side while asking, "Why is he a clown, Mack? Seems as if everyone loves the guy. Handsome, charismatic, compelling political arguments to help everyone who is suffering from the economic downturn here in upstate New York. He is originally from around these parts. He seems to understand our issues here."

"Might be, but I think he is a phony. My old man says it too. Smiling jackass. Gonna save the world. Tax the hell out of us to do it too. Doesn't do much more than smile and wave to the crowd."

"Taxes are the answer to every liberal politician's save the world plan, Mack. Then all the taxpayers complain and pull the lever the next time for the same dope. It is an endless cycle of pain and confusion. Come on now, you seem to have your fingers deep into the good senator's platform." Detective Odell paused, studied the young man very carefully, and then added, "You seem to be rather involved in politics, Mack. Are you?" Odell asked and persisted in his quest for an answer and for a deeper connection.

"Not really, just that guy grates my ass."

"Have you ever met him? Has he ever been here?" Odell pried a little more into the obvious animosity that Mack held toward the popular Senator Monger. A senator, whose faithful and gorgeous assistant just died. An assistant who stayed here frequently and whom Mack had a strong attraction to. . ..

"I never have seen the guy here. Only seen him at a rally in Mohawk City when he was running for reelection a year or so ago. Bernie Withers claims that he has seen him here one day. Or, so he says. With Delilah."

Officer Baker looked at Odell and then to Mack and asked a question, and at the same time, he answered Odell's looming question. Officer Baker was proving to be quite intuitive of his new boss, and his actions and his words.

"Bernie Withers? The houseman who found the body?" Officer Baker asked, while recalling his notes and the previous testimony of events.

"Yup, one and same and no offense to the detective here

but Bernie, likes to," Mack made an imitation of tipping a glass to his mouth in reference to drinking while his eyes darted between Baker and Odell.

"No offense taken, Mack. I admit my faults. Where is Mr. Bernie Withers now?"

"Went home. Too, upset at finding the body. It creeped us all out for sure, but Bernie took it as an excuse to run home and drink. I am still shaking, yet, I stayed on because I need this job and I cannot leave my partner, Ronnie, alone. Withers did not care. He took off and left us alone on the shift. Just Ronnie and me. By the way, Ronnie did not see anything. Look guys, I have to reconcile a night audit and as much as I would like to. . .."

The front doors to the hotel lobby opened and Sergeant Grundy appeared around the corner of the main hallway at the same time that the crime scene investigation team burst through the doors carrying their specialized equipment.

"CSI is here, Odell. Ya coming, or should I let 'em in?" Sergeant Grundy asked. Five CSI officers now stood in the lobby, and they each nodded in the direction of Detective Lyle Odell. Odell recognized the team leader, Sergeant David Pegg, as a veteran of numerous investigations.

"Hey there, Pegg. Sorry to drag ya assess out of bed. Do not miss anything, Pegg. This is going to go in circles for a few rounds."

"Apology accepted, Detective Odell. We never miss anything. You know that."

"Thank you, please, Grundy will get you in. I will be there in a few minutes." Pegg nodded and Grundy turned heels as the CSI team followed Sergeant Grundy to the room.

"Crime scene investigators? Holy shit! I mean, she overdosed . . . she liked to. . .."

Mack was shocked and then clamped his mouth shut in mid-sentence.

"Liked to what?" Odell asked.

"Nothing."

Odell eyed the desk clerk carefully and then waved his hand in his direction. "Can you get a hold of Ronnie on your two-way radio there, Mack? Can you call him to the front desk right now to cover for you? We need to speak in private and about something very serious." Odell pointed to the two-way radio sitting on the front desk and Mack nodded, picked up the radio, and made the call. A few minutes later, the lobby elevator sounded the floor alarm bell and a short, slightly overweight young man with a wrinkled and an untucked shirt and a necktie that the young man tied too short and left askew, walked into the lobby and headed to take up the post behind the front desk. Odell studied the young man, then tapped Officer Baker on the arm, nodded his head in the direction of Ronnie, and spoke just above a whisper, "I like how that kid, Ronnie, dresses. He might have a future as a homicide detective."

Officer Baker tried hard to hold his stoic pose, but a small smile slipped across his face.

"Everything, okay here, Mack?" Ronnie asked while trying to tuck his shirt into his pants.

Mack glanced at Odell and Baker and then to Ronnie and said with a grimace on his face, "Not sure. Thanks for covering. I will be right back. I hope."

Mack walked out from behind the front counter and pointed in the direction of the shuttered cocktail lounge on the opposite end of the lobby from the front desk.

"We can sit and speak privately in the lounge. Breakfast prep is still a few hours away." The three men walked in silence into the cocktail lounge, and Mack selected a chair at a high-top table. Odell and Baker joined him at the table. Concern washed over Mack's face, but he remained composed.

"Are you okay, Mack?" Officer Baker asked after a study of his face in the dim lights of the closed cocktail lounge.

"I am okay, Officer Baker. Am I being arrested for sumthin'? I can't afford an attorney. I can't afford much of anythin'."

Odell cleared his throat, ran his hand through his messy hair and achieved the unachievable, because his hair became messier.

With a dismissive wave of his hand in the air, Odell spoke honestly, "Once more, Mack, let's not dwell on ticky-tacky stuff right now. We are going to get to where we need to be, and you can help us. We will help you too. Lookie, Mack, this is a homicide. Some evil bastard or evil bastards killed the lovely Ms. Murdock."

"You think that I had something to do with this, Detective Odell? I mean come on now, I am just a hotel desk clerk. Who would murder Delilah Murdock? My god. She was so special!"

"That is my job to find out whom, what, and that sort of thing. So, you say, Mack, about being just a desk clerk. Not too sure that you do not have a few side gigs rolling, too. Jobs are scarce and you barely make it now. Your words – not mine, Mack. Look, we are going to help you, but you need to help us, too. Straight up now, how long have you been sellin' weed to Ms. Murdock?"

Mack was clearly stunned, his eyes opened wide, and he studied Detective Odell carefully as did Officer Baker, who seemed just as surprised at the question as Mack did. Before Mack could even answer, Odell fired another question at Mack, "And since we are being so open and honest in our efforts to assist each other, how long were you lovers?"

Mack took a deep breath and then exhaled, while not removing his eyes from Detective Odell. Upon exhaling, Mack offered up a statement, "Sure, let's be open and honest. No offense, but, Detective Odell, you look like you live in a box in a dark alley in the heart of the city. Yet, ya one of the smartest sons-of-bitches, I've ever met. How did ya know about sellin' the weed? We have been on and off lovers for a few years. At first, just casual sex, drinks, some smokin', some escape from the world. Her world was much different from mine. Ha! To say the least."

Mack once more shook his head, lowered his head, then looked away from the table and stared out at the cocktail lounge and then to the bar in the lounge. Tears rimmed his eyes. Odell reached out and patted the young man on the shoulder, and Odell squeezed his shoulder hard in a show of support.

Mack nodded, composed his emotions and continued, "We used to sit right over there at the end of the bar. After my shift or on my day off. I used to kid around with Delilah and say that we were like Lady and the Tramp in our relationship. I think that a few months ago, I fell in love with her, though. Not sure, she wasn't getting there too. It was special." Odell nodded, and Baker remained silent. Odell motioned for Baker to take notes, since the young officer seemed to forget his role due to the awe of Odell's compassion, and his perception abilities, as well as being aware of Mack's emotions. Baker quickly grabbed his pad and pen and began to take notes.

"Mack, this much I can figure out from here, Ms. Murdock came here to smoke weed, relax and not have to stay at the stuffy Murdock mansion and endure all the pain it brought to her life, but still, she needed to visit her family and such. I knew that she smoked weed in the room on her visits here because of the ozone machine in her hotel room. In the corner, near the edge of the bed. You put it there, Mack, to erase the weed smell. You always put it there for her when she called you to let you know she was making the trip home."

Odell looked at Officer Baker and asked, "Did you see it, Baker? I will have CSI inventory all the items in the room."

Baker simply shook his head to indicate that he had not seen the device, and Detective Odell did not pause long enough for Baker to comment before continuing with the explanation and details.

"The ozone machine kills the weed smell in the room." Odell waved his hands in the air and almost whispered, "High voltage burns the air."

The volume of his voice increased a little, "I deduced that you were the plug by your words about her, your body language, the little slip-up about how she spent her recreational time, and by how badly you needed money. Don't worry, right now, we have bigger and better things to worry about than a small-time dealing of weed by a poor city guy. Ms. Murdock did not get along with her family and was not really fond of her father and her sister."

Odell waved back and forth in the air and continued, "Maybe, I am not too sure as of yet, but maybe, the sister is like the father is. Kind of, mean, nasty, conceited, and greedy. Time and investigation will determine her demeanor and role in all of this mess. Delilah is close to her mother, if I had to guess. You initially struck up a friendship after her many visits and by making small talk, because you told her how your dad lost a solid job at the Murdock's manufacturing factory and when you found whom she was and whom she worked for, you two bonded. Ms. Murdock sympathized with your plight because she realized that her father sold Mohawk City, and some very loyal workers up the river to sell the business to overseas pimps and pocket even more of a fortune than the Murdock family already have. And smiling, Senator Monger did shit to help everyone. I know that Delilah and you feel differently, but the truth is that the senator could not do shit to help. Money talks and bullshit walks."

Mack nodded his head and mumbled, "As I said, Detective Odell, ya a damn genius. Ya right on about everything. Delilah did not get along at all with her dad. That is why she started staying here. She wanted to visit her mother and avoid her dad. You would never know that she was wealthy and affluent. Delilah was very down to earth, and I know she did what she could to help this old city by pressuring Senator Monger to help us. Delilah could not do too much . . . she was only an assistant to him in his office. She only mentioned that she had a sister once. I actually forgot about her having a sister until you mentioned it. Are you Sherlock Holmes in real friggin' life or what?"

Odell ignored the question.

"Lookie, Mack, this is evil bullshit. The bad guys are going to play you for the fall guy. They know you were occasional lovers, and the really, really bad guy or bad guys, know that she was falling for you and you for her too. It caused a rift because of something that will require some awfully hard digging and intense detective work, and I know this might cause you some pain, but I suspect that Delilah spread her love around a little." Odell checked Mack's face for a reaction to his statement with a quick glance, and then continued, "Sorry. No man enjoys hearing about sharing a lover. Anyway, the bad guys are coming for you, Mack. Officer Baker here will arrange for twenty-four-seven protective custody for you and your father too, an attorney and all the things that you will need to stay safe. To stay alive."

Mack was clearly stunned now, and his face turned ashen at the warnings and words of Detective Odell.

"What the hell do you mean, safe and alive? I sold her weed, we hung out, smoked and drank, talked for hours, and we made love and had fun together. I meant her no harm and did not hurt anyone. I would never hurt her. I loved Delilah."

"Exactly, Mack. Exactly. You are the fall guy for this evil bullshit. The second victim of this horrid mess. The evil dudes are aware of everything about the relationship between the two of you. It plays perfectly in their plan. They will seek you out, kill you, make it look as if you committed suicide because you are so distraught over sellin' your beautiful lover some bad shit for a special sort of high before Delilah and Timothy Mackie had a wild sexual tryst. Some of the bad shit that is killin' addicts all over this city. Your old man lost his job to the Murdock's, greed, you have animosity toward Senator Smiles, and you are a poor kid from the city . . . yakity-smackity. These are very evil persons. Some might be professionals at evil, others might not be, Mack. Regardless, I assure you that they are very evil persons and you are the perfect fall guy now. Sorry, Mack, I am factual. Overly so."

Odell once more held onto the shoulder of Mack and comforted him as best he could.

"Officer Baker will stay with you and take care of everything."

Officer Baker nodded at the words and continued to jot notes in his notepad, while Odell continued to explain, "I realize you have your job duties to attend to and I need to meet the CSI team, so a few more questions. Are you okay, Mack?"

Mack nodded but put his head in his hands for a few seconds and wiped his eyes and face with his hands before uncovering his face.

"Remember, Mack, we are here to help you. By the way, that inquiry into your status was not one of the questions. Now, to the questions. One, you told Officer Baker that Ms. Murdock waved to you from afar when she checked in. Baker . . . that is the word that Mack used. Correct? Afar?"

"Roger. Afar," Officer Baker said while expertly flipping his notepad to the correct page and tapping the words with his pen. "Afar."

Odell said, "Thank you. Mack, was she wearing a hat? As in a wide-brimmed sort of hat?"

Mack's eyes widened at the suggestion, and he seemed slightly aghast at the question.

"Yes, as a matter of fact . . . she was. Delilah liked to

wear hats, but I never saw her in that particular hat before. I figured that it was new. How did you even know to suggest that? Was her hat in the room?"

"Nope, no hat in the room. That is why I suggested it. I may look like a drunken fool and a bum, but *I am* a detective. A homicide detective. Specifically. Mack, please, I need you to think very carefully. Did Ms. Murdock wave to you with her left hand or her right hand?"

Mack screwed his face up and shook his head a little. He closed his eyes and thought as Baker and Odell carefully studied him and waited for his answer.

"Right hand. She waved with her right hand."

"Are you sure?"

"I am. Positive."

"Okay. Great. Very astute. You have hit on a key point in this case and confirmed it in my mind! Wonderful! Thank you. Now, please, Mack, exactly where is, afar? You specifically stated from afar. Show us."

Mack nodded; he stood up and waved for Odell and Baker to follow them while Mack explained, "I need to walk over to the front desk to get a heading on it."

"Great, Mack. We are following. This is very important. Please take your time," Odell said, while tugging at his suit jacket in a futile effort to cover his wrinkles and his shirt, which was now hanging out of his belt not only at his hips but also toward the front of his pants too.

Mack stopped at the front counter, opposite the position that he was working in when he checked Ms. Murdock in, and studied the scene in order to reenact it in his mind and to be accurate. Ronnie stood behind the counter carefully studying the situation and Odell put his fingers to his lips and looked in the direction of Ronnie in an indication for him to remain silent. Ronnie nodded and made himself busy behind the counter and averted his eyes from the situation.

It was very obvious that Mack was trying very hard to

help. After a careful study, Mack pointed in the direction of the front doors of the lobby for the hotel.

"She was outside there. Standing beside the large planter with the small evergreen tree in it. Right next to it. She smiled and waved to me from there."

Odell glanced at the spot, nodded and pointed to Officer Baker and instructed Baker, "Thank you, Mack. Baker. Please, let's have CSI measure that distance and record it. Here-to-there. Be triple sure that there is no hat in the room. I did not see one, not in the closet or around the room. Triple-check for me. I was a little wobbly a few hours ago."

"Roger, Detective Odell," Baker noted, and jotted down the instructions in his seemingly never-ending notepad.

Odell now turned to Mack and said, "A few more questions. This mysterious man who always checked Ms. Murdock in. Security, bodyguard, limo driver? Maybe a lover or boyfriend? Could you describe him? Any name?"

"Yes, to all except the name and a boyfriend or lover. Nope, not a lover. I am sure of that. And Delilah never mentioned his name or his role. I am sure that he was protection for Delilah. A big guy, dark. Always, dressed in an all-black suit and he drove her here in a fancy black limousine. Muscle-bound dude. Big. Never says too much. I suppose he works at all of those jobs that you just named. She was a big shot assistant to a high-powered senator in Washington. She had a great body, was stunningly beautiful, captivating, and commanded grand attention. Of course, when she visited her family, she would bring a driver, bodyguard, dude."

"Yup, and this was the same man who checked her in today?"

"It was."

"Yet, Delilah's car was left here today."

"Yes. I did not see another driver or her car pull into the lot. I guess that I was busy and missed it. There are no cameras where Delilah usually parks her car, and I know that she told me that she wanted her car here. Bernie spotted the headlights on when he emptied the trash out there at one of the exit doors and another hotel guest also reported the car's headlights were on."

Baker wrote feverishly in his notepad, and out of the corner of his eyes, Odell caught his partner's actions and he suppressed a smile.

In so many ways, Odell knew that he picked the correct man for the job.

"Is that because you wanted to have her car around so you could drive it later on after you met her in her room after your work shift? If you wanted to go out after having some romance together."

Mack blinked his eyes, but other than that, he did not react to the words of Detective Odell. Mack was becoming used to Odell's genius powers now.

"It is, yes, it is, Detective Odell. My car is a pile of junk."

"Thank you, Mack. I know this has been a difficult situation for you in so many ways, but you have been a trooper. A tough guy who was put in a bad spot because of love. It kinda sucks. I know that we have been major pains in your ass, but please, heed my warning and help us to help you. Okay? Don't wander. Baker will be right here. Looks as if Ronnie needs help now," Odell added with a smile and an outstretched hand.

Mack and Odell shook hands, Mack solemnly nodded, and as Odell and Baker began to walk away, Mack went back to working on his night audit.

Odell grabbed Officer Baker by the arm and explained, "I need to catch a smoke or my head is going to burst. I will head up to join Grundy and the team in a minute. You stick around with Mack. Begin to make the calls for our plans for protection for Mack."

"Will do, Detective Odell."

Odell nodded his head in the direction of the front desk

and mumbled while tapping his jacket for the cigarette pack, and then recalling the loose cigarette that he previously stuffed in his packet, Odell grabbed at and then he plucked that same cigarette out of its temporary confinement.

The cigarette radically bent at the end.

It pointed straight downward.

Odell did not even notice.

Odell looked around the lobby and checked the front desk for the presence of Mack, but Mack had gone off to the office to perform his night audit. They were alone in the lobby.

"This case is still in its infancy, but when we dig deeper, we will find out that this case is layered into complex evil. It is a very complex case. I can feel it. Mack's old man worked at the Murdock factory. He, along with hundreds of others, lost their jobs. Hence the animosity towards Senator Extremely White Teeth. Mack and his dad think that the senator could have done more to help with the situation. Ms. Murdock was sympathetic to the entire situation. That commenced their love and connection. All of those facts and more make Mack the perfect fall guy. Anyway, it is a shame about Mack. The poor kid does not have a chance unless we protect him. Please find out when his shift ends and call in a patrolman to guard the kid. We are going to need to protect him twenty-four-seven until we can uncover a little more of the facts. Without protection, Mack will be dead within a week. I do feel, as though Ms. Murdock actually loved the young man. Poor desk clerk or not. He is a very handsome young man. A dirt-poor guy, but they were deeply in love. They had a deep connection. I can feel certain things. Delilah Murdock. A beautiful, compassionate, and very wealthy woman involved with a federal senator. Mack's analogy about the lovey-dovey dog story is right on target. Mack and Ms. Murdock's love might have helped trigger much evil. I dunno yet, just a gut feeling that romance had much to do with all of this. Anyway, this is a classic, Baker. A classic case. Very complex."

Officer Baker cleared his throat and stared at Detective Odell. "If I might be a little curious, Detective Odell. I have one question, Lyle. I have been following along with you to a certain extent. Honestly, much of this seems to be merely your theories at this point. Yes, some of your investigation methods are amazing and impressive, but I am lost, and it is not that I totally disagree with your findings, but in light of what Mack said, some of your theories do not seem to hold water. I have to say that damn . . . my head is spinning. I am not sure how you arrived at where we are and it will take me some time to run it all around in my brain, but one thing sticks out to me. How do you still think that Ms. Murdock was murdered in another location, her body brought her to the hotel room, and the scene staged? I mean, in light of what Mack told you about waving to her and she waves to him. I assume you still think this to be the case. Perhaps Mack is not the fall guy. Maybe they decided to graduate from weed and try some stronger drugs and he did lace her drinks with high-test and killed her because she, as you said, shared her love around. Maybe, Mack found out about that and we are protecting the murderer, not the fall guy. I am confused unless you changed your ideas and think that Mack is fudging the entire waving scene. I understand that I am simply a patrolman, but I do have investigative sense . . . and honestly, I am not following this, sirrrr . . . I mean, Lyle."

Officer Baker caught his mistake and corrected it, and then shook his head and studied the detective for a reply. The young police officer was befuddled.

"I understand your confusion, Baker, and appreciate the bouncing of theories and questions back to me. I respect that and encourage it too. It will be of great assistance to me in solving this case. Uncovering *all the* bad guys. No changes in my theory. The bad guys killed Ms. Murdock in another location and brought her dead body here. I am anxious for the autopsy results and to see what the CSI team uncovers. No lies. Mack is telling the truth as he saw it happen. He skirted the check in rules, met with the usual muscle-bound dude, and he waved to Ms. Murdock. Ms. Murdock waved back. He was the plug for her weed habit. They were close. They were lovers. They fell in love."

"I don't get it, Lyle. If he is not lying . . . how is that even possible?"

"Because Delilah Murdock has an identical twin sister. Ms. Ireland Murdock. Just as beautiful, just as shapely, just as wealthy and just as connected. However, in light of the murder of her sister, and Ireland's potential role in all of this mess, I need to dig a little deeper into Ireland Murdock. I know quite a bit about her and the family because I study many things and people in this old city. Our circles overlap because of their immense wealth. And potentially, great wealth can lead to criminal intentions. Perhaps a trace of something evil might run through Ireland's veins. I should not prejudge her, though. Ireland has all identical features to Delilah except that Ireland always dyes her hair red. Hence, the hat. I would have thought that it would be easier to forego the dye and wear her hair in her natural color, but these gals are quite vain, nowadays. Ms. Murdock waved to Mack. Ms. Ireland Murdock. Not, Ms. Delilah Murdock."

Baker's eyes narrowed and his mouth fell open but before he could even pose a question, Detective Lyle Odell, stuffed the cigarette in his mouth, pulled his suit jacket around his body, turned and went to walk out the front door of the hotel. He stopped in his tracks; the cigarette dangled precariously from the edge of his lips as if it was a tightrope walker on the high wire.

He turned and pointed at Officer Baker and commented

as the cigarette danced on his lips with the rhythm of his words, "Weird name for a gal. Ireland. I guess they are Irish. Over half of the city is. Anyway, weird first name. Don't ya think? These wealthy folks sure are eccentric. Oh, yes, by the way, Ireland is right-handed. Technically, that is the only difference between the two sisters. Please make a note of that, Baker. Please take very careful notes. They were so identical that even Delilah's lover could tell the difference between the two sisters. A man who knew every inch of her naked body could not tell the difference. Amazing. Even if it was from afar. Please arrange the protection for Mack, but don't give him the inside scoop that we know so much. Okay? Thank you."

Odell then turned and quickly walked out the front door of the hotel.

When he did so, Officer Dennis Baker shook his head and quickly walked to the front desk to explain to Timothy Mackie what was happening in his life right now.

To follow orders.

He figured that it was best for him not to get too deeply into the complex and amazing mind of Detective Lyle Odell.

After all, he might get lost and never return.

Chapter Four

Always, Bring Coffee

It seemed as if the pounding on the front door of his house was taking place from some far-off, distant land. Perhaps from Morocco in Africa, or in Uzbekistan. . .. On the other hand, perhaps the noise came from even farther away. Detective Lyle Odell opened one eye, tilted an ear, and realized that he was incorrect. The pounding, or specifically the frantic knocking, was at his front door. The front door to his house. He opened another eye and peered around the inside of the living room of his house. He was still wearing his suit. If you could call it a suit. He was sitting in his easy chair and he looked all around the floor for signs of empty Irish whiskey bottles or a whiskey glass. He was in the clear. Head not pounding. Check. Eyes not feeling as if they would pop out of his skull. Check. No whiskey bottles. Check. Knocking at the door and a voice calling his name that sounded as if it was from Officer Dennis Baker. Check. Listen once more. Okay, double check. It is Baker.

Odell pushed in the footrest on the easy chair, pushed off on the arms and the chair folded up and in on itself. The action propelled Lyle Odell up and out of the chair and with some effort; he stood up and slowly made his way across the floor and to the door.

"Detective Odell! Lyle! It is, Baker! Are you okay in there?"

'Bang! Bang! Bang!'

Odell spun the doorknob and swung open the door just

as Baker had gone to pound on the door with his fist for another round. Odell looked up and caught the fist in mid-air, and Baker jumped back. Startled. Odell was a mess, but he was a lot stronger than Baker could ever imagine.

"Oh, geez . . . sorry, Detective Odell. I was banging on the door . . . here . . . and worried about you. You were not answering, so I had to bang. Hard."

"Ah yeah, I heard you, Baker," Odell said while dropping his grasp on the fist of Office Baker. "I was sleeping in my chair. Come on in. Close the door behind you. Please. Why are you banging on my front door as if the entire damn world is on fire? It is only," Odell glanced at his wristwatch and then sighed a little while, saying, "oh shit. Eleven in the morning."

Baker stepped into the house and slowly closed the door behind him as his eyes glanced around the living room. Lyle Odell was not the world's greatest housekeeper. Empty pizza boxes and some spent Irish whiskey bottles remained piled high on top of a small wastebasket near the easy chair in the corner of the room. Right next to a plastic milk crate that seemed as if it served as a makeshift end table.

Odell caught the young officer's eyes staring at the waste can and explained, "Yeah, well, hell, at least, I sort of put them in the waste can. Piling stuff on top counts for throwing them away. I did not drink when we left the investigation. I typed my report and sent it along with a few emails and then I just crashed in the chair."

Baker slowly nodded as he studied Odell and said, "Well, I have been calling your cellphone endlessly. You did not pick up your phone, so I rode over. We have some interesting developments."

Odell ran his hand through his messy hair, and it became even messier.

"Battery is deadsville on my phone. The phone needs a new battery and I don't keep up on the charging routine because it is a pain in my ass. Mack is under protection, and okay?"

"Yes, he is fine. I checked in with the team a few minutes ago. All is quiet there. Mack has a day off today. It is just that Captain Tucker wants you down at the station. . .." Odell cut off the words of Baker and interjected with his usual uncanny and otherworldly predictions of situations that were not predictions because they were the truth.

"Yeah, yeah, yeah. I know. The captain has federal agents in his office. Up from Washington, D.C. and they are all hot and bothered because I declared the death a homicide. They want suppression from the media to protect the fancy senator and are claiming jurisdiction in the case." Once more, Odell astounded Officer Baker with his amazing detective abilities.

"Yes. Exactly correct, Lyle."

"And when I did not answer my phone, Captain Tucker, and you, to a certain extent, both figured that I tied one on and you came to rescue me. You both did not check your inbox of your email for the report and another message that I typed up a few hours earlier and sent to both of you for review instead of drinking myself silly. I dabbled in a touch of the Irish whiskey but did not go to the far side. Hung on the edge but did not go overboard. Only went to sleep a few hours ago and was deep in a sleep drool until some young police officer came pounding and knocking on my front door thinking the worst of me. Actually, I do not blame you. I would have thought that I was half-in-the bag too. I would think that the autopsy reports should be in our inboxes too. Doctor Kent returned to work early this morning, and he is a very efficient and timely sort of fellow. I told Grundy to make sure to tell the coroner's office to include you in all emails and reports and such, Anyway, I need coffee." Odell waved in the air in direction of Officer Baker and asked, "You did not bring a coffee by chance, did you, Baker?"

"No, sir. Sorry. Sorry that I did not read the reports yet. Captain Tucker was pretty adamant of me alerting you and bringing you into headquarters."

"I understand. Tucker gets that way. Especially now, because he is a short-timer. Only six months before he hangs it up. No sir stuff, Baker. Please. We have been down the sir road already. Moreover, you did not bring any coffee. Unreal. No coffee. Still calling me, sir. Two strikes. Always, if you need to bang on my door like some wild man, you must bring me coffee, Baker. Please. No coffee equals no banging. I will make us some instant coffee. I would offer you a chair, but there are not any chairs. Only my easy chair and you might not want to sit in it. You will smell like cigarettes and stale whiskey and a fancy pants, tight-ass Marine as you are would fret over your uniform all day. I will smoke too. Sorry, Baker. Job-related hazards. Oh, by the way, to keep your perfect police uniform in order . . . ya might want to remove that dog hair all over your right leg of your uniform pants. There is a lint roller in the closet there. I do occasionally wear my dress uniform. I lint roller my dress uniform so at least, occasionally, I look better than a hum-drum rag-a-muffin looks."

Baker immediately looked down at his pants leg and, in a frenzied rush of wiping, swiped at the hairs on the lower portion of the leg of his pants. He looked up at Odell as he did so, Odell held his hands out at his sides in a casual gesture.

"Ya know . . . I wear it for official funerals and parades and such. I did not know that you have a dog for a pet. Seems as if dog hair would drive ya nuts."

Baker continued to wipe and answered, "Ah, ah . . . I don't detective. Must have been the dog outside the diner where I stopped this morning for breakfast. His owner was . . . ah, ah, walking the dog and I bent down to pet him and say hello. Friendly sort of dog. A mutt . . . I think."

"Always nice to be friendly to the taxpayers. It is nice to

promote that picture-perfect-postcard image of a police officer that ya are there, Baker. We need taxpayers on our side. Lint roller. Top shelf. There." Odell pointed at the closet and said, while turning to leave the room, "Be right back."

Odell disappeared into the kitchen, leaving Officer Baker standing in the middle of the living room. On worn hard floors. Very worn. Baker walked over to the closet, opened the door, and peered inside. It was musty and dark and sure enough, there were two or three uniforms under dry cleaning wraps hanging on hooks in the closet. One dress blue uniform and two standard police officer's uniforms. Surprisingly, the uniforms were spotless, creased, and pressed. Baker spotted the lint roller on the top shelf, plucked it off the shelf, peeled a fresh sticky layer, and rolled the hair off his uniform. The roller captured quite a bit of dog hair, and Baker shook his head and swore a little under his breath at the accumulation.

"Damn dog," Baker mumbled. He carefully checked his uniform for any more lint and hair and satisfied with the results; Baker closed the closet door and after glancing at the waste can piled high, Baker shook his head and set the lint roller down on the only end table in the room. While the faint odor of a burning cigarette emitted from the kitchen, Baker lifted his patrolmen's cap, rubbed his high and tight haircut and sighed while looking around the interior of the home. Odell's easy chair sat in the corner of the room, an ashtray overflowing with spent cigarette butts sat on the end table. The hairy lint roller stood on end next to an ancient table radio. The table radio looked as if it was a museum piece. It had a brown wooden cabinet and a light brown speaker grille stained with nicotine smoke. The table and its contents sat rather wobbly next to the chair. Baker's eyes caught the empty whiskey bottles and the pizza boxes piled high on top of the waste can, and a few scattered newspapers tossed carelessly around the base of the chair. Every wall had an off-white paint on it, off-white from nicotine, or perhaps the paint was simply very old. On the other hand, perhaps it was a combination thereof. Cigarette odor hung in the room as if it were vines of tobacco drying in a shed. The living room only had one other chair in the entire room. A steel folding chair that appeared to have seen much better days. No sofa, no love seat, just the easy chair and the rather sad, steel folding chair. And the plastic milk crate.

The dining room was empty.

To say that the house was sparse in furnishings was an understatement. In fact, it was barren. No ornaments, no pictures on the walls; no decorations of any sort. In the opposite corner from the easy chair was an antique television on a rolling cart, with rabbit ear antennas sticking precariously up in the air. Odell still used rabbit ears for reception. . ..

It was obvious that television viewing was not high on Detective Lyle Odell's priority list. Officer Baker heard a teakettle whistling away in the kitchen. A few minutes later, after some banging around in the kitchen, Odell appeared, carrying two coffee mugs.

"Here," Odell handed one mug to Officer Baker, "the mug is clean. I promise. You can keep it too. It can be your reminder never to show up again without coffee. I hope you drink your coffee black because I am a little sparse on supplies such as milk and sugar and a few other things."

Baker took the mug and nodded his head while pointing a finger around the house.

"I noticed. Sparse seems to be in the décor department, too. Oh, thanks for the lint roller. I did not want to set it back on the shelf in the closet with it being full of hair and your waste can, well, it is kind of full for me to peel a layer off the lint roller and dispose of it."

"Yeah, well, it is not exactly a luxurious life that I lead. I am going to do better in the future with the housekeeping around here. Gonna keep everything spotless. Cleaning will give me something to do with my downtime. Anyway, I have not much use for extra stuff, Baker," Odell said while taking a sip of the coffee and smacking his lips as the caffeine provided the first trickle of an energy boost. "Let's roll and save Captain Tucker from the wrath of Washington, D.C. at its best. I suspect that these federal boys are just phonies. Some losers on the take trying to make some side hustle dough from the bad guys. We will find out soon enough. The deep dark caverns of politics have many layers of corruption, Baker. Many layers."

Officer Baker glanced at Detective Odell. His eyes traveled up and down while studying the wrinkled shirt, the messy hair, the unshaven face and the fact that Odell wore the same clothes and suit jacket from yesterday and earlier this morning.

Lyle read his mind, "Don't worry about how I look, Baker. You are handsome enough for both of us. Captain Tucker has been my commanding officer for twenty years. Damn well, don't want to shock him into an even earlier retirement with me showing up all squared away. I need the clout of Captain Tucker on my side with this case. It is going to cause some major ripples in some big ponds, Baker. Lots and lots of ripples."

"Nice of you to show up today, Detective Odell," Captain Lawrence Tucker growled as Odell and Baker entered Tucker's office. "And to look so eager and . . . detective-like too." The captain added as he waved his hand in the direction of Odell in reference to his appearance.

"Well, yeah, sure. Captain Tucker. My pleasure. In my defense, yesterday was my day off, ya know. I had full disclosure with Sarge Hawkins when he called me in. Sarge made the call, and I did what I had to do. And I stayed up even later to type up my report too. Kind of running on empty now and Baker showed his true rook colors and screwed up and stopped for breakfast but did not bring me any coffee."

Captain Tucker stood up and forced back a smile while waving in the direction of two men dressed in black suits sitting in the guest chairs in front of the captain's desk. Black suits with federal agent identification badges hanging on the lapels. Captain Tucker was around sixty-two years of age; he was tall, and very handsome with a square jaw, chiseled features, close-cropped white hair and a perfect build. He looked as if he was the picture-perfect example of what a veteran police captain should look like. He also was a close ally of Detective Lyle Odell. Tucker had seen Odell's magic and had been a witness to his genius, many, many times before and despite Odell's haphazard appearance, his penchant for Irish whiskey, his chain-smoking, and his eccentric ways and helter-skelter type of approach to investigations, Captain Tucker knew that Odell was above reproach in honesty, integrity, and he was good at his job. As in, very, very good. As in exceptional.

"Agents Whitehouse and Stickney from the Federal Bureau in Washington, D.C., please meet Detective Lyle Odell and Officer Dennis Baker. Homicide Detective Lyle Odell," Captain Tucker introduced Odell and Baker to the two federal agents, who both stood up and the group exchanged handshakes and greetings. The agents gave the once over to Odell's appearance, but neither of the agents commented on such. Not unless their stares, study and frowns qualified as a comment. Both agents looked as if they were advertisements for the cover of the "Federal Agent Manual for Perfect Agent Appearance" instruction manual. Stoic, black, dark sunglasses, perfect suits, bulges for their weapons under the suit jackets in and around the shoulder areas, polished shoes, and piercing eyes.

Agent Whitehouse spoke first in a monotone voice, void of any discernible accent, "Nice to meet you Detective Odell and you too, Baker. We, ah, ah, can see that it was a rough stretch of a few days for you, Detective Odell. Anyway, we both read your report. Your chain of command was very cooperative to provide us both with copies, and we would like to inform you. . .."

Odell cleared his throat and began to speak.

"Please, let me cut ya off and jump in here and say. . ." Odell said while tapping his suit jacket pockets for his cigarette pack. After not finding any, the detective reached in the pocket of his pants and after still coming up empty and upon the pointing suggestion of Officer Baker, Odell found the cigarettes in his shirt pocket, pulled out the pack, tapped one cigarette out and plunked it into his mouth, "Thanks, Baker. I will not smoke it. I just need a taste of it. Let me fill in the blanks for you two federal types. You disagree with my declaration of a homicide, ya want to cite the toxicology report of the autopsy results as obvious evidence of the cause of death of Ms. Murdock and ya want to take over the case and use your jurisdiction to close it all up tidy and nice as an accidental drug overdose. Because, Senator White Teeth has an image to protect and we cannot have messiness putting any stains on his teeth. Now, can we?"

Now, Agent Stickney spoke and Agent Whitehouse smiled as he did, "I am the senior agent in charge of this investigation, Odell, Agent Bruce Stickney." Same monotone voice. Same lack of an accent, but the same piercing dark eyes. "I see you are perceptive and anticipate some of the reasons. . .."

Detective Odell interrupted again, "Let me guess. Ms. Murdock had a copious amount of alcohol in her blood, due to sucking down glasses of wine, along with oxycodone and clonazepam. A fatal drug interaction. Top it off with a cherry and some whipped cream of traces of

THC because she enjoyed relaxing with some cannabis."

"Oh, so I see that you are not perceptive at all. You read the autopsy report already?" Agent Stickney asked.

The cigarette dangled from the edge of Lyle Odell's lower lip as if it was stuck there with a dab of glue. Bobbing up and down as he spoke, as if it was a lever to his mouth.

"Have not read any reports. I was sound asleep in my chair until Baker here came pounding and screaming on my front door because you two agents of bullshit came waltzing up here from Washington, D.C. to take charge. Take charge of what? Are you two bananas gettin' sum side dough for this gig? By the way, unless my captain here says so, you are not in charge of anything around here. Ms. Murdock was an intern, then an aide, and now, an administrative assistant to Senator Smiley. She is not a senator. Some evil person or persons killed her here in my horrible, rundown mess of a city. Not down by you boys in some federal building. Ya have no jurisdiction here. She was a gorgeous young woman with a knockout body, from a powerful, wealthy, and influential long-time Mohawk City family and a young woman, who most likely was sharing her body and love with lots of those high rollers in D.C. and maybe, even Senator White Choppers liked to dabble in a little after-hours love too. I will find out. I always do."

Odell removed the cigarette from his mouth and turned to Officer Baker and asked, "Didn't you grab us coffee from the coffeemaker outside the door, Baker?"

Officer Baker did not say a word; instead, he picked up the paper cup filled with coffee from the credenza of Captain Tucker and handed the cup to Odell.

"Thank you very much. You are gaining rook. By the way, Ms. Murdock took the clonazepam to minimize panic attacks. She had a history of them. Once, when she had to speak as Valedictorian for her class at the graduation from the fancy, upper crust, overpriced university she attended and once or twice when working as an aide to Senator Monger and she panicked on the floor of the Senate. That is why she moved from working as an aide to working in the office. Cannot have your gorgeous, young, aide flipping out while running paperwork to the senator during sessions and before important votes. Ms. Murdock was no dummy. She was a brilliant young woman, very cultured, very educated and intuitive. She was a skilled pianist, and violinist but she could never play in front of large audiences because of her anxiety and ensuing panic attacks."

Both of the federal agents tried their best to burn holes in the mind and body of Detective Lyle Odell with their intense stare from those piercing eyes. Agent Stickney nodded to his partner, and it was a signal for the agent of lesser rank to take over the less than professional portion of the conversation. The part where the agents needed to attack the character of Detective Odell, since it seemed as they, as many others before them, underestimated the skills and intelligence of Detective Lyle Odell.

"Ah, detective, we can see that you did a little homework here on this case, but we feel it is cut and dry . . . you were not, how shall we say here . . . at your best earlier today when you arrived on the scene. Drunk on duty now. Tsk, tsk, your captain here might not enjoy reading the emails and a report filed by the medical examiner on the scene about how you smelled like a whiskey still. Your reputation for loving too much Irish whiskey precedes you. Anyway, your entire investigation is flawed. The desk clerk obviously gave Ms. Murdock some opioids, in hopes of an extra happy love session after his shift ended, she took the clonazepam, and drank too much wine and unfortunately, the cocktail from Hell did not . . . agree with her. An accidental overdose. Case closed. Your captain here, will, read the autopsy report and your report, overrule you, even if the case goes along any farther, then the prosecutor and attorney general will do the same, laugh at your flawed report and silly investigative antics, and agree that it is ludicrous. The case is over and done with. Ooooo-ver."

Agent Whitehouse was the tough guy in the duo.

Agent Whitehouse tapped the printed copy of the report with his hands.

He then added, "Instead of arresting the local plug for peddling weed and pills, this, Timothy Mackie, who might have even fed her high-test drugs because they are killing addicts all over Mohawk City, and he could be a punk who leads you to more important drug sources, you put the young criminal in protective custody." Agent Whitehouse leaned in towards Odell and Baker while Captain Tucker took his seat behind his desk and sat without saying a word. "Maybe, you need to lay off the bottle, Odell. Take a few days off and relax. Check into rehab. Dry up. Save your career. If you actually have one. Because you are hinging your case on some hearsay, some type of Sherlock Holmes-like-bullshit-tidbits of amazing investigative clues with carpet pictures and left hand versus right-hand bullshit and twin sisters posing for each other and drag marks and dirt and weeds on shoe heels. All through your magnifying lens and bloodshot eyes. Do you smoke a pipe too, or just those bent up ciggy butts? Do you wear a deerskin cap?"

The agent thumbed a single thumb in the direction of Officer Baker and smugly commented, "I suppose Baker here is Watson."

"Only smoke cigarettes. I never had much luck with a pipe. No deerskin caps. I think they would make my head itch and my hair is messy enough. As far as Baker goes, well, time will tell. Anyway, I guess this is the point in your intimidation diatribe where you pull the ace out of the deck and tell me that my investigation is really over and done because I blew it with the car keys." Odell tilted the cup of coffee over and sucked the last drop out of the cup. He looked around for a trashcan. Captain Tucker pulled his chair away from behind his desk and pointed at the trashcan hidden underneath the desk.

Odell dropped the cup into the can under the captain's desk and mumbled, "Thanks, Cap." Odell's voice grew stronger, more forceful and powerful while continuing, "Ya know, where you tell me that Odell, Baker, Sarge Grundy, and the CSI team all missed the car keys that were actually on Ms. Murdock. Maybe in a pocket of her dress that we missed or something like that." While the agents remained silent and staring, Odell turned to Captain Tucker and asked, "Cap, please, can you open the email that I sent to you around six this morning. The one email that you did not open yet because I did not receive a read receipt on it yet. At least, as of the time that I last checked. The same aforementioned prosecutor and attorney general are copied on the same message as is young Watson here."

While everyone waited, Captain Tucker nodded, turned to his computer and reached into his uniform to find his eyeglasses. Captain Tucker placed the eyeglasses on and with a few taps on the keyboard of the computer and a few clicks of the mouse—Captain Tucker studied the screen. The movement of his eyes were telltale signs that he was reading the email that Lyle Odell mentioned.

Upon clearing his throat, Tucker read the message contents aloud, "Regarding the case of Ms. Delilah Murdock and my unpopular ruling of the case as a homicide, I thought it would be prudent to send this email message to everyone with a time and date stamp hours earlier than the release of the autopsy report results. Due to evidence, circumstances, and to a certain amount of gut feelings for lack of any other description, I am convinced that upon undressing of the body and a careful examination and notation of all the contents of the deceased, the doctor and medical assistant or assistants performing the autopsy will find the deceased car keys somewhere on the dead person's body. Most likely in a dress pocket. This is contradictory to my report that even after careful investigation, the detective, responding officers and crime scene investigation team found no car keys on the dead body while in the hotel room. This, of course, is a key element to my theory that Ms. Murdock died elsewhere and her dead body was brought to the hotel room to simulate an accidental overdose as a prelude to partying with the desk clerk and her casual lover, Timothy Mackie. This is a very complex and disturbing case, and unfortunately, we have inside persons or an inside person infiltrating our investigation and police department and very powerful persons influencing and manipulating the case from outside of the department and from within Mohawk City. These same persons or person recognized their grave error with the car keys and decided the best action was a poorly chosen reaction. I am afraid that the logbook at the morgue and official records and reports will contain many names of persons both serving in official and unofficial capacities who had access to the body both during transport to the morgue and in the morgue itself and this will make the case even more complex to solve. Additionally, the video system monitoring the body storage area will have malfunctioned and video not be available, until the attending doctor and assistants notice and correct the malfunction in order to record the autopsy. I will solve this case. You have my promise, and Ms. Murdock will not have been a victim who simply passed away in vain. I intend to protect Mr. Mackie at all costs. I will try to keep him alive because his testimony holds the keys to open many doors of questions and unfortunately, upon sending of this email, he becomes an even stronger target for elimination. Very Respectfully, Mohawk City Police Department, Homicide Detective, Lyle Odell."

Captain Tucker looked up at Officer Baker and Odell and then turned his eyes to the two agents who sat silently with faces void of any expression.

He then read aloud once more, "Time of this message is six-ten this morning. That is, as in—it was sent today. The autopsy results release time is nine o'clock this morning."

Captain Tucker cracked a slight smile and took a breath before asking, "Agents, do you have anything to add? Are we done here?"

Captain Tucker removed his eyeglasses and held them in one hand while studying the faces of the two federal agents. Agent Stickney stood up and his partner took that as a lead for him to do the same.

"No, Captain Tucker. Thank you. Nothing to add at this time. We are good. Please, might we keep this report?"

Tucker nodded and the two men extended their hands and Captain Tucker shook each of their hands, as did Officer Baker.

"Please, as a professional courtesy, keep us posted on the progress of the case. Please, Captain Tucker?"

"As much as I am able to do so. Perhaps, I will. Perhaps, I won't. Perhaps, I will dig around, drop a dime on your chain of command, and find out if this little trip here received proper authorizations. Perhaps, if you go away quietly, I won't."

The two agents turned to Detective Odell, both of the agents extended their hands, and Odell shook their hands one-by-one.

Agent Whitehouse spoke, "Sorry about the nasty comments, Odell. You know the drill. Sometimes, you need to play hardball. No hard feelings?"

Odell now had the same cigarette once more dangling from his mouth as it once more bobbed up and down, and all around.

The good detective answered, "Nah, no hard feelings. I just need to go outside and light this cancer rod up before my head explodes. Thanks for stopping by. Have a safe trip back to Washington. Stop by in Albany on your way back home and say hello to that clown of a medical examiner for me, will ya please? Ya know, the one who dropped a dime on ya squawking 'bout me being half-in-the-bag. What was his name? Ah yes, Dr. Mikhail Barken. Crazy guy. Filling in from Albany for a few days. Here and there, he says. Sounds like an amazing coincidence. The usual doc off on a vacation or an unexpected holiday? Who knows these days? We will dig deep into that fact. For sure. You know what else? He was wearing bedroom slippers. How about that one, huh? Bedroom slippers because we supposedly woke him up, and he did not have time to change because he was rushing to the crime scene. And, he wore a doctor's white coat too. Weird. A white coat, as if he was in an examination room. No overcoat. It was twenty-seven degrees last night. The guy was a mess. Supposedly, because we woke him up."

Odell removed the cigarette from his mouth and stared intently at the two agents out of the corner of his eyes.

"Bedroom slippers. Crazy-ass thing. Was it because he rushed and was sound asleep, all cozy in his bed, or was it because he did not want to wear shoes? Maybe shoes that would have matched the imprints in that fancy-ass plush hotel room carpet. Ya know, the imprints that I have so many pictures of and I have a good friend who happens to be a genius in computer enhancements of photographs, checking out for me right now. What was it you said, agent? Part of those pesky Sherlock Holmes-like-bullshit-tidbits?"

Stickney and Whitehouse did not say a word. Both of the agent's eyes burned hard and deep.

"Yup, give the good doc my best regards. I have a feeling that Watson and I will take a ride down to Albany and pay him a visit. Maybe, even, buy him a new pair of bedroom slippers and an overcoat."

Chapter Five

Messy Business

"Can you please either replace the battery in my cellphone or just get me a new phone, Larry?" Captain Lawrence Tucker leaned back in his chair behind his desk and studied Detective Odell sitting in the guest chair in front of his desk as Lyle fiddled with the buttons on the cellphone.

"Why? You will forget to turn the phone on, anyway. Or forget to charge it. Hell, you seldom carry your service weapon on duty or off duty, nor do you bother with a two-way radio, or a detective's car. Do you even have your badge on today?"

Lyle looked up, and a puzzled look appeared on his face. Then he wiggled a little in the chair and studied his belt line.

"Yup, the badge is clipped to my belt. Right here."

"Amazing. A part of the uniform intact on Detective Lyle Odell. Say, where is the rook?"

"I sent him to a desk to surf the electronic world and to dig up every item that he could on the Murdock family. I asked him to focus upon the demise of the factory here in Mohawk City and what it is that they do now to accumulate even more wealth than they did when they ran the factory."

Captain Tucker stared long and hard at Odell. He even narrowed his eyes in thought. But after a pause, the captain did not mention the Murdock family or the angle that Odell was working. Instead, Tucker moved to some praise of his homicide detective.

"Needless to say, but I will say it anyway, nice work on the investigation, the report and setting those two agents on their asses and then packing back to Washington. Your magic never ends, Odell. You never cease to amaze me. Honestly, I could have done without the doctor's report on your condition, but it *was* your day off, and Hawkins vouched for your honesty and for his own decision. I will handle that rather easily."

"I appreciate that, Captain. It was a rough week."

"I understand. I think. Lyle, I am, of course, particularly disturbed by your thoughts that there is a traitor in our ranks. Your thoughts and statement that someone inside is involved in this evil mess. Do you have any information on who, what, where? Or is this a trick to unearth some hidden behavior or clue or action? Or are you not going to clue in your commanding officer and keep this shrouded in typical Odell mystery?"

Lyle Odell seemed to be pondering his commanding officer's statement. He looked up, then ran his hand through his hair, and made his hair even messier than it was.

"Your hair is sticking up. As in, straight up," Captain Tucker said while pointing at Odell's hair.

"It is always sticking up, Cap," Odell said as he shrugged his shoulders. "Lookie here, Captain Tucker, I am sorry, but your last option is closest to the way this is rolling right now. My apologies, Cap, but right for now, I rather keep my suspicions in my head. I am spewing a ton of bullshit publicly while I create some smokescreens on my actual intentions. Yes, the typical Odell mystery stuff. I only have some vague clues and gut instincts at this point. I will keep it under wraps . . . unless you order me to spill my guts."

"I will let you roll for as long as I can. Eventually, the chief and the attorney general and some prosecutors as well as internal affairs will come sniffing at my door. I will hold them off as long as I can. Of course, I know your methods, as unusual as they usually are, and you have my support."

"Thank you. Much appreciated. I only need a few days. I plan to spend Saturday morning deep in research and then some interviews in the afternoon. If certain events occur as I suspect they will, then everything should come together by the end of the weekend. Then we have the funeral on Monday. I will be there in the shadows. Watching and waiting. Funerals for homicide victims are always ripe for picking out the phony mourners. They stand out like Southern Baptists in a cocktail lounge."

Captain Tucker withheld a smile and a chuckle at Odell's analogy, and at the same time, he admired his confidence at seeming to know everything that was going to happen before it even happened because that was part of the magic of Detective Lyle Odell. Above all, Captain Tucker knew that Detective Lyle Odell was very good at his job.

As in, very, very good.

"Captain, I will need your authorization to pull some human resource files for viewing and research on some officers and maybe some civilian employees here in the department," Detective Odell said while lifting one eye to his commanding officer to gauge a reaction.

Captain Tucker remained stoic and said, "I will authorize that. Please submit the list of names to me on the forms and I will sign off."

"Thank you, Cap. Going to go through them all on Saturday morning."

Captain Tucker moved some papers around on his desk and after doing so, he looked directly at Lyle Odell and his eyes demanded honesty. Even if it was going to be painful to accept.

"How messy is this case going to get, Lyle?" Captain

Tucker asked as he turned his attention from Odell's disorganization and his eccentricities to his genius.

"Messy, Cap," Lyle said while still pushing the buttons on his cellphone.

"How messy is messy?"

Lyle looked up from the cellphone and his eyes narrowed. He ran his hand through his hair and once more, he managed to make his appearance even messier.

"I dunno, Cap. I mean on the messy scale, with one being not so bad, to ten being a cluster-you-know-what, well, it is going to be an eleven."

Odell put his head down, went back to pushing buttons on his cellphone, and with his head down, the detective mumbled, "Maybe, even a twelve."

Captain Tucker sighed and leaned back in his chair and shook his head. "Damn. Just what I needed. I was so hoping to cruise to retirement without much bullshit. Lyle, please give me that damn phone. I will get you a new one. Geez."

Odell smiled and handed Captain Tucker the phone while explaining, "Okay. Thank you for a new phone. As far as the case goes, well, sorry Cap. I am still putting the parts and pieces together in my mind and creating a framework for the pecking order of evil. It is going to take me some time and maybe, a few bottles of Irish to sort out. I hate to tell you, but we have a turncoat or a number of turncoats working on the inside here in the department. We have the wealthy and powerful Murdock family and old man Murdock is not exactly having high tea and crumpets with the Queen of England. He was a mean, nasty son-of-a-bitch years ago and he ain't mellowed with age. All his dough just makes him meaner, greedier and nastier. By the way, Delilah and the old man were oil and water. That is why she always stayed at the fancy-ass hotel when she visited her mother. She and Mr. Murdock did not see eye-to-eye. That is why she sided with the desk clerk, because Mack showed her how his family suffered when Murdock pulled the plug on the factory and shipped the jobs overseas. Delilah was a sweetheart. Now, Ireland, well, I am researching her very intently. At his point, she is in limbo-land on my case radar. I need to weed through it all. Need to start with Dr. Barken, though. His appearance is an early key to unlock more clues in the case. Any ideas on why he was filling in for Doctor Kent?"

"First, that I heard of it was when you mentioned it. I can dig a little for you if you want me to do so."

"No. Thank you. I will dig. Don't want to sound any more alarms by having Detective Lyle Odell's top brass ask questions."

"Okay. I understand and of course, you have my support. This should all hit the newspapers and on-line sources very soon. Mohawk City media is going to have a field day with this. Everything is going to light up like a Hollywood marquee. It is not as if the Murdock family and their assorted casts of characters are popular around the city, but to lose a daughter as a murder victim . . . no one wishes that on them. It might be a blip on the national news only because Senator Monger is the media's darling. I will run the no statement interference for you, Lyle. I know you will avoid the media at all costs, but a homicide is going to bring out the howling wolves. I might get a few phone calls from the prosecutor and the attorney general. However, I know that once I give them the facts, out of respect for you, they will play nice and wait for the details and clues to unfold."

"Thank you, Larry. I appreciate that. Yes, I need a few days. No comment is the plan. I am keeping my head down. For sure."

"One more question, Odell, and I will let you on your way. I know that you want to go study the facts and chant and burn incense and do all the things that you do to unlock clues. Notice that I did not mention the Irish whiskey. Why the rook? Baker seems to be a sharp kid and all, nice military career, some private security work with one of those government contractors after his tours ended, his family has had some ups and downs over the years, I think that is why the kid joined the Marine Corps, but all in all, he has it all together. It is a feel-good story. The local good-guy returned home to serve as a police officer. I get all of that. But why did you recruit him to work with you? Other than the fact that Sarge Grundy would only teach him to drink coffee and eat grilled cheese sandwiches. The rook seems as if he would get on your nerves with all that Marine Corps square up stuff. Baker is an anti-Odell. The rook is a picture-perfect-postcard of a police officer. Hell, his socks have creases in them. Oh, yes, by the way, it would have been nice for you to check in with your immediate chain-of-command for permission before grabbing Baker. Grundy is all too willing to dump the rook, but it is part of his job to train them now that he does not do much of anything else."

Detective Odell waved his hand in the direction of his commanding officer and nodded.

"Yes, sorry, Larry. My fault on that one. No doubt that I should have checked in with you. It was a spur of the moment. Heat of the battle type of thing. I need, Baker at my side. For many reasons right now. His actions and interest in the case are most helpful to me in order to work toward conclusions quicker. Besides, I can fix my messy hair in the mirror polish of his shoes."

Captain Tucker smiled, and now it was his turn to wave with a hint of dismissal in the air and in the vague direction of Detective Lyle Odell. With the hint of a laugh, or at least a chuckle, on his lips, Captain Tucker proclaimed some truths. Truths from his side combined with his many years of experience of working with Lyle Odell. Close to twenty years of truths and experience.

"Woooaahh what a load of bullshit you just spit out to

me. Your captain! Detective Lyle Odell. A one-man-band for how many years? Over twenty? Maybe twenty-five? The ultimate loner? Lives alone, works alone, and stays alone. Generally, drinks alone too. The deep and eccentric thinker. Only friends on the force are Sergeant O'Malley, Sarge Grundy, and Captain Tucker and you only come over for dinner when Margie and I beg you to do so and meet for beers with me, Grundy, and maybe, Sarge O'Malley when we beg you. Now, you need some rook. Okay, I can smell it and I will not dig too deep. You need him. Good enough for me."

"Thanks, Captain Tucker. I appreciate you and your support. Do you know how to play the violin?" Odell's question caused a laugh, and then a puzzled look on the face of Captain Tucker.

"Me? The violin? No, Lyle. Why would you ask?"

"Because for now, with the media that is . . . it will be stonewalling and no comment, and then I will need you to play them as if they were fine violins. They could play a key role for us. That handsome mug of yours and all those ribbons always impress. I am such an ugly mug and never photograph too well. Besides, the violin might be a nice relaxing venture for you to take up when you retire, Larry. Very restful. Melodious. I love the cascades of violins in my favorite classical music. Anyway, once I have more, then you will know. Now, I need to dig a bit. After a smoke."

Odell spoke, then he rose from the chair with a push off on the arms of the chair with both arms, and he groaned a little as he rose to his feet.

"Okay, I will consider the violin in retirement, or maybe the guitar. Yes, I almost forgot that you are a classical music fan. Carry on, Detective Odell. Smoke if you have them, and Lyle," Odell turned to face the captain, "if this is going to be as messy as you predict . . . it might not hurt to carry that service weapon."

Odell nodded and added, "I will consider it. As I said, I

need Officer Baker. Aside from some other things, something tells me that the kid can handle a weapon."

"I've seen you shoot, Lyle. You are a crack shot, my friend. I am quite sure that you are the best shot in the entire police department. And, just for the record, you have more ribbons than I do. In fact, more than any active officer in the department and for the record, in the entire history of the department."

Odell shrugged his shoulders and turned heel for the door of the office. As he did so, you could hear him mumble.

"I keep 'em in a dusty drawer. No good place to pin 'em. Ya need a chest to display medals upon, and mine is sunken. See ya."

"A homicide! A homicide, Rexford. Unreal! You said this would be cut and dry and easy and unfortunate, but essential! Now, we have it on the news that my administrative assistant is the victim of a homicide! Back in her home city . . . a horrible city that just so happens to be within my state!" Senator Austin Monger loudly proclaimed a sorrowful rant while sitting behind his desk and while alternating between burying his head in his hands and lifting his head to wail. His attorney and the mastermind of all the latest parts and pieces of this wretched adventure, Attorney Rexford Covington paced the floor of the senator's office in Washington, D.C. while a television tuned to the national news reported the news of the murder of Ms. Delilah Murdock in Mohawk City, New York.

"Look, Austin, I know it looks bad right now, and your nerves are on edge, but let's stay calm and regroup. I assure you that no one can tie us to anything. Our inside person just underestimated this detective guy. This

Detective Lyle Odell. It was a slight miscalculation. Apparently, the detective is sharp. As in a modern-day Sherlock Holmes, type of sharp. Extremely sharp." Covington cleared his throat, swallowed, and added, "Genius sharp." After speaking, Covington stopped pacing and looked over at the senator for a reaction to his statement.

Senator Monger's face was flush with anger now, his usual good looks askew with pain etched on his face. "Sure, Rex and you assured me that the detective that would eventually show up to investigate the case was useless. A spent wreck of a man. The detective was too much of a drunk lush to think straight. Who could not find a clue in his own pocket? A raging drunkard? Now, suddenly, he is Sherlock Holmes! Great, just great! Look bad . . . ah yes, it looks really bad. As in dire straits!" Austin Monger, in an uncharacteristic action, banged his fist in anger on his desk and screamed, "This is our lives, Rex! Our friggin' lives that you messed with and concocted this evil scheme! Not just my political life and your law career, but our lives!"

Now, Covington also grew angry, he walked over, and placed his hands on the elegant and massive oak desk that Senator Austin Monger sat behind, the attorney leaned in, over the front of the desk, stared directly at the senator, and growled, "Scheme? A concocted scheme? Who came to whom for help here, senator? Who was desperate for help because you could not find a way out of the mess that you put yourself in? Who cannot keep his ding-a-ling stuck only in his wife, but needs to lure beautiful young women into every bed that he can find? Ms. Murdock was the one who you decided to have drunken after sex pillow talk with, and your loose lips and endless lust got your own handsome ass in a sling! Sooner or later, it was going to nail you, Senator Monger, and damn . . . did you pick the wrong chick to fall into bed with and pine over. I told you before, I could have arranged for many beautiful women, it would be discreet, and it would have been anonymous. However, no, you have to mess around with Murdock's daughter, put her in a high position within your office and then bang her every night. Nice move, dummy! Oh Rex, save me! Please, save me. You are nothing but a pussy."

"I am going to burn in Hell for this, Rex," Monger whimpered and leaned back into his chair as reality exhaled into his words.

"News, pal. News flash! Hold the presses! You were burning in Hell before this event. Drugs, multiple and endless lovers, money laundering, an evil scheme of using your influence and official federal senate role on the arms committee to weasel an illegal weapons deal to terrorists overseas and funnel dough into hidden overseas accounts. Illegal weapon sales to the enemies of our nation, who use the arms to attack our own troops and military. Funneling weapons, contracts and business to Murdock. Oh yeah, you were an angel floating on heavenly clouds before the scheme arrived to silence Delilah Murdock, Austin. A friggin' angel. Power, greed, the love of your own self, you are an evil asshole and came to me for help. So, let's get that out there and off the table right now." Monger buried his head in his hands once more and it seemed as if he fought back tears. Rexford Covington studied him carefully, shook his head, and walked over to the bar cart in the corner of the office.

"You need a few drinks. Your emotions are running over you."

Senator Monger lifted his head and gazed at the clock, and mumbled, "It is only ten in the morning. I have meetings at lunch. I don't want to smell like a whiskey distillery."

"Chew peppermint gum, Austin," Covington answered, while he uncorked a bottle of whiskey and poured two drinks into whiskey glasses from the decanter. "Here. Pull it together, Austin."

Rexford handed the glass off to Monger, who nodded, stared at the glass for a pensive moment or two, and took a long sip. Covington settled into the guest chair opposite Senator Monger and he, too, took a long sip of the whiskey and then set the glass upon a wooden coaster near the edge of the desk. While leaning back into the chair and trying hard to relax, Attorney Rexford Covington provided some details of where they were in the "situation." More details than he had previously released; perhaps, it was time to be more open with Senator Monger because if Austin Monger was not thinking with his male body parts, the senator was actually a brilliant man.

"Look, Murdock does not fully realize what happened. His lead-headed muscle man does not even understand it all. Murdock needs us and we need Murdock and I doubt he is grieving the loss of Delilah, anyway."

Monger looked at Rexford over the edge of the whiskey glass, and his eyes opened wide and then narrowed as he took a sip.

"She was his daughter, Rex. I am sure he still loved her."

"Delilah Murdock was a pain-in-his-ass. A pain in his wealthy ass. She did not toe the Murdock line and drink the sweet Murdock drinks. The old man thinks she had a terrible drug habit, dabbled a little too much, and she was cavorting with some lowly hotel desk clerk whose family wanted revenge on the Murdock family. The desk clerk is the key and right now, therein is the problem."

"How so, Rex?"

"The detective ruled a homicide and put the desk clerk, this Mackie guy, into protective custody. Otherwise, we could have eliminated him last night. Made it look as if he committed suicide. The distraught lover type of angle. Right after, he spoke with the detective. It would fit in place perfectly. We made a slight miss-step with the car keys, but that was . . . easily corrected. Our inside man could have easily made the staged suicide happen and we would be sitting pretty. Instead, we have two loose ends and one end with potentially loose lips. One we need . . . for now, the other one . . . we do not need any longer. One will take care of the other."

Senator Monger's telephone on his desk rang. He glanced at it, waved at it, and pushed the ignore button to send the call to voicemail. He took another sip of the whiskey and then titled the glass and finished it in one gulp.

Handing the empty glass to Covington, Senator Monger almost smiled and said, "I guess I better chew that gum, Rex. Refill. Please." Attorney Covington took the glass, stood up and walked over to the bar cart to prepare a refill. "What about the DOJ boys we sent to strong-arm the detective and his commanding officer into taking over the case? Did they make any headway, Rexford? You said you worked a deal with them too."

"No luck, Austin. The detective stonewalled them. Anticipated all the moves ahead of time and his captain is as honest as the day is long and supports the detective." Senator Monger studied his attorney while he returned to the desk, and when he received the whiskey, he took another long sip. The whiskey quickly worked some magic. His nerves calmed, and his emotions steadied out some.

"How much did that little dead-end stunt cost us?"

"Does it matter, Austin? You just said this is our lives. A little dough to some corrupt DOJ guys trying to go around their pensions and earn a few extra bucks. It does not mean a hill of beans. I did not tell them anything. Just to try to get the case removed to the federal level and squish it. They think it is just to qualm any poor reflection upon your political career. Those two fools mean nothing now."

"I understand, Rexford, and I trust you and know that you are doing all that you can do to help me. How about the little journal diary that Delilah used to write in all the time? Have you found it?"

"Austin, it does not exist. I already told you a hundred times that we swept her place here in D.C. and her car, and the hotel room and everywhere in between. It is nowhere."

Austin Monger displayed his despair. He slumped in his chair and mumbled, "It does exist. It never left her side. She wrote in it all the time. She told me that it was for her music and general notes of life. It does exist. We need to find it. It could have notes in there of our love life, of what I said to her, of everything. Please find it."

Rexford Covington stood in front of the desk of Senator Monger and put his hands on his hips and in a voice of frustration the attorney said, "Well, we cannot find it. I assure you that we have done everything to find it and if it existed and was not a figment of your drunken and lust-full imagination . . . it has disappeared. You best hope that it is gone forever and our supposed drunken fool of a detective does not find out where your little fling-a-ding-do hid it. Or we are all in a world of hurt."

"Then, I hope it is gone forever. Yes. This detective is a smart one. Genius sharp, you say."

Rexford Covington nodded and sipped his drink.

"Genius."

"Can we buy him off? Can we send him cases of whiskey for life, or some hot young women to fulfill his life? Can our inside connection corrupt him when he is in a drunken stupor? Ya know, it is Mohawk City and they do not call it Sin City for nothing. It is a dump."

"Tsk, tsk, Senator Monger. Speaking such ill of an area that you are so desperately trying to assist and pull out of their misery. My goodness, have some heart, Senator Monger. These are the people that you represent!" Covington shook his head in mock concern and finished his drink in one last gulp. "Can't buy out the detective. The guy is an eccentric hermit. Women mean nothing, money, means even less to him. The man is a minimalist. Just bottles of Irish whiskey and his work. Lives alone, drinks alone, and unfortunately, he is brilliant and above all . . . honest."

"Then how about?" Senator Monger made a slashing motion across his throat, and his eyes studied Attorney Rexford Covington. The attorney stood up, picked his empty glass off the coaster and slowly made his way over to the bar cart to prepare a refill of his drink.

With his back turned to Senator Austin Monger, "Eventually. Yes, it will come to that. It will be very tricky because of the detective's brilliance and the fact that his commanding officer is on his side. I am afraid there might not be another way. If this progresses a few more days . . . the detective might uncover so much more . . . unless we act quickly. We will take some steps today. First, we need to eliminate one of the ties to us . . . then . . . we can deal with Homicide Detective Lyle Odell."

Covington pulled the lid off the whiskey decanter and poured the glass half-full of whiskey. He turned and faced Austin Monger and lifted his glass in the air before taking a sip.

With a low whisper of a voice, the attorney growled, "Eventually."

"Thanks, for the reports, Doctor Kent. Very thorough and accurate," Detective Lyle Odell said, while thumbing through a report in the coroner's office of Mohawk City's Chief Medical Examiner, Doctor Patrick Kent. Doctor Kent was about forty-years of age, but he looked a few years older than his actual age. His once black hair was now salt and pepper, and his eyes were sad, and the skin underneath them hung as if they were dreary clouds before a rainstorm.

"As you usually are."

"Thank you, Lyle. Are you feeling, okay? You look rather, well worn out. Ah, no offense, detective, but more worn out than you usually look."

Odell looked up from glancing at the report, smiled, and said, "No offense taken. I am beyond being offended. Worn out, huh? As in a drinker's look, Patrick? Yeah, I am okay. Swimming in a sea of Irish whiskey. Do you have an extra liver in your laboratory of dissection down the hallway there?" Odell thumbed his right thumb in the air, in the direction of the autopsy room.

Doctor Kent did not comment.

"Patrick, you and I are in the same business. Staring at dead bodies and hanging out where phantoms tread forces you into some dark places and you seek escape with some even darker methods. Oh well, what the hell, ya going to do? Someone has to do it."

The doctor nodded and leaned back in his chair and his eyes traveled over to Officer Baker, who stood silently off in a corner of the small office.

"Oh yes, sorry." Odell caught the doctor's look, and Lyle introduced Officer Baker. "Officer Dennis Baker. Meet Doctor Kent. Baker-Kent."

Office Baker reached over and shook the doctor's hand while saying, "Nice to meet you, sir."

"Likewise, Officer Baker. Are you new?"

Odell, for some reason, did not allow Baker to answer, "He is a rook, Doc. He is helping me and driving me crazier than I already am with that constant sir stuff." Odell quickly shifted gears in the conversation; he tapped at the clipboard with the reports and added, "I read this autopsy report yesterday, but I need to go over some items with you. I hope that you don't mind, Doctor Kent. Ms. Murdock only had some cookies and crackers in her stomach, and maybe some orange juice. Did she not eat all day, except for maybe some breakfast on the airplane trip? That is interesting."

Doctor Kent nodded and said, "Yes. Might have contributed to the drugs working such evil with her bloodstream."

"Any sexual activity that day or recently. Or, more importantly, are there any signs of sexual abuse of assault?"

"No signs of any sexual abuse or assault. Any sexual intercourse was consensual and pleasurable for Ms. Murdock. No sexual activities within the last day or so. Although, she certainly was no virgin."

"Gotcha. Sort of like throwing a penny down a mine shaft, huh?"

Doctor Kent leaned even farther back into his chair, and his face went into an emotionless stare. The words came out slowly and deliberately.

"A rather unique and somewhat crude analogy, Detective Odell. From a battle-hardened detective's point-of-view, I guess that works. In fact, it works, even for a doctor."

"I mean no offense. I need the facts, Doctor Kent. Her sexual activity and sexual partners are of keen interest in this case. It is pivotal. I do not judge. I am sure that Ms. Murdock was a kind and lovely woman who slipped into some difficult circumstances. I am very sure of it, and it is a tragedy that she realized her true love too late. Anyway, my apologies for the perceived crudeness, but I have no medical training. Per se. No pregnancy?"

Doctor Kent shook his head and added, "I-U-D. In place and in good condition. Ms. Murdock had no underlying medical issues that I could detect. It is a terrible shame. Such a beautiful woman."

"It is a shame, and I will get to the bottom of this. Soon. Within a few days."

Odell looked first at Doctor Kent for a reaction to his prediction, and the doctor remained emotionless. The doctor knew very well the reputation of Detective Lyle

Odell. Odell then glanced over to Officer Baker, who at first moved his arms and hands from his side, to placing them behind his back in a clasp while he nodded.

"At ease, Baker. Relax. You don't need to be so damn uptight. We have this. Besides, you are screwing up. You are supposed to be taking careful notes." Officer Baker realized his error. He unlatched the button on his uniform shirt pocket and pulled out his notepad and pen and began to write.

"C'mon, Baker. Wake up. What are you doing? Did you have a late night chasing that one gal that you have your eye on?"

"No . . . siiiirrr, Detective Odell. No chasing. I am on it."

Odell then turned his attention back to the paperwork and continued to speak aloud, "The rest of the autopsy was what I expected. With the lethal cocktail of drugs. And the weed. Thanks for the additional photos of her toenails and fingernails. I have a few of those from the crime scene crew and some of my own, but needed some more."

Odell closed the cover to the autopsy report with a snap and returned it to Doctor Kent's outstretched hand.

"And, can I see the transport logbooks and sign-in sheets for the morgue visitation and body viewing? Please, Doctor Kent."

"You are welcome. I have the logbook and sheets right here, Lyle." Doctor Kent stood up, walked over to a credenza on the side of his office, and plucked some paperwork out of a wire tray sitting on top of the furniture. "Here you go."

Lyle nodded and took the sheets and mumbled, "Thanks" while he glanced through the logbook and then the sign-in sheets.

"Shame about the camera and video system going on the blink. So untimely," Detective Odell commented while flipping through the paperwork. He gently lifted his eyes to study the reaction of Doctor Kent and added, "Good thing that the techs repaired the system in time for the autopsy procedure."

Doctor Kent sat in his office chair, folded his hands, and answered, "Yes. Something about a power supply wire. Yes, we have the autopsy video in detail. When we realized the main system was down, we dug around for a back-up plan. We have the body prep recorded on a back-up camera. We covered everything except for the viewing, body identification, and the transport into the autopsy room. I did have a police officer standing by the entire time, as well as myself and my medical technician and assistant, Harry O'Shea. You do know, Harry. He has been with me for many years, Detective Odell."

"Yes, of course. Good man," Odell said and then added, "So, the transport team signed off, the CSI team too. All were involved in body transport, as well as Sarge Grundy and Officer Baker here. They were all in the hotel room and in the hotel together . . . that all is correct, and it all makes sense."

Out of the corner of his eyes, Odell caught Officer Baker shifting his feet and then changing his weight to a different foot.

Odell lifted his head, pointed at the other guest chair in the office, and said, "Sit down, Baker. If you need to do so. You don't have to stand and be stiff all the time. This is not guard duty in the Marine Corps. Feel free to become loose and sloppy as I am. Well, on second thought, please don't go overboard, Baker. Strive to find a happy medium. Perhaps, a little slouch will work."

Officer Baker smiled and waved in dismissal and mouthed that he was fine.

"Suit yourself. The official body identification was by Mr. Murdock, and let's see, we have Mrs. Murdock, Ireland Murdock, who is the identical twin sister, and we have this person."

Odell tapped at the name on the sign-in sheet and held it

up for Doctor Kent and Officer Baker to read. "Who is this, guy? This, Mr. Cortland McNealy?"

"He was, ah, a very large man. Lots of muscles. He was huge. . .."

Officer Baker jumped into the conversation and he pointed at Lyle and rather excitedly answered Lyle's question, "The bodyguard! The man with no name. Until now." Odell smiled at Baker's enthusiasm and nodded, as did Doctor Kent.

"Very good, Baker. The bodyguard."

"That makes sense, Lyle," Doctor Kent said, "Mrs. Murdock was a grieving mess, as was the twin sister. Mr. McNealy supported them both during the viewing. It was a very tragic and difficult scene."

"I can imagine. No with, Mr. Murdock?"

"Pardon, Lyle. What do you mean?"

"I mean that old man, Murdock, did not require support from Mr. Muscles? Either emotionally or physically?"

Doctor Kent shook his head and said, "None. He was quite solid. He only spoke with his official identification of the body. Never said hello or goodbye."

"How about Mr. Muscles? Did he shed a tear?"

"None. No tears, but Mr. McNealy was working hard to do his best to remain stoic and powerfully emotionless. His face told the story. He was very upset when viewing the body, but he held it together rather well. Perhaps, for the sake of the family. Perhaps, for his own sake and soul. Regardless, he was very impressive."

"Gotcha. Wonderful observations, Doctor Kent. Thank you. Very helpful, indeed. One last name on the sign-in sheet. This one is most intriguing."

Once more, Odell held the paper up for Doctor Kent to read the name. This time, Odell even tapped his finger on the exact signature and the printed name beside the scrawled signature. Doctor Kent leaned in and read the name, as did Officer Baker.

"Oh yes, Doctor Barken. He checked in with me to share observations from his initial examination on the night of the death and his on-call response." Doctor Kent leaned back in his chair, folded his hands upon his desk and announced rather proudly and forcibly, "He covered for me for a few days this week and that past weekend. My first vacation in a long time."

"Yes, that is what Doctor Barken mentioned to us when he rushed into the hotel room. He is a rather . . . nervous type of guy," Odell observed, and then lifted his eyebrows to study Doctor Kent's response.

Doctor Kent tilted his head and almost spoke out of the side of his mouth in a show of surprise at Detective Odell's observation.

"Nervous, really? I have known Mikhail since medical school. We attend Albany Medical College together. He is a forensic pathologist too. As I am. He is usually a Steady Eddie sort of guy. Perhaps, covering in Mohawk City had him frazzled. I noticed in reviewing the records of the past few days that I was away that we did have that one drug overdose this week in addition to this unfortunate case with Ms. Murdock. It is upsetting, to say the least. These opioids are laced with some poisons."

"No doubt. I am working on that mess too. In my spare time. Doctor Barken did not respond to that other overdose case. The poor kid made it to the emergency room and died there. Well, perhaps, Doctor Barken did not like my, let's say, condition. He observed that I was rather on an Irish whiskey bender, or recovering from it. It was a rough night."

"I see. Well, he is a doctor and trained to observe a medical condition. Ah, Lyle, were you, ah, intoxicated or sobering up?"

"I was. Both. Leaning toward sobering. My day off is Wednesday. I don't take vacations, Doctor Kent, and I asked to be on call no matter what came in. My choice. I don't hold a grudge. The doc was right on in his observation. Are you two friends? You and Doctor Barken?"

Odell waved his hand in the air and flip-flopped his pointy finger as he asked the question.

"No, not really. We are just acquaintances. We are distant connections, sort of because of the business and going to school together. Medical examiner, coroner, it is all the same and overlaps. I occasionally cover for him and he covers for me." Doctor Kent leaned in on his desk and paused as he pondered his last statement. Odell and Baker both studied the doctor's face and actions, but did not interrupt him in his thoughts. "Actually, it has been many years since he covered for me. Not that I often take vacations. The wife was screaming at me for this one. It was our wedding anniversary. My manager said that Doctor Barken was the only doctor he could find to cover me. It is usually Doctor Lynne Jeffries. You do know her, correct?"

"I do know, Lynne. Yes. Interesting. Congrats on the wedding anniversary, Patrick. Do you report to the City Manager?"

"I do. Yes."

"When did you put in your vacation request?"

"About a month or so ago. I think."

"Perfect. Thank you, Patrick. You have been very helpful. Honestly, I am dying for a smoke and will die because of my dying to have one . . . so . . . please, a few more questions and I will smoke and let you go about your work. Maybe five questions more. Where did you find the car keys on the body?"

"I didn't. Harry did. He said they were in an inside pocket of her dress. It was easy to miss them, Lyle. And the crime scene team missed them too. It happens, Lyle. Even with someone as good as you are and the CSI team too. Harry undressed the body and did the prep work."

Odell tapped the pointy finger from his right hand to his forehead a number of times, then ran his hands through his hair and sat back in the chair. It seemed as if the doctor's answer sent him deep into thought. Very deep.

"Can you call Harry in? Is he here?"

Doctor Kent nodded and answered while dialing his desk telephone, "Of course. He should be at his desk completing reports."

"By the way. That was not one of the five questions that I have, Patrick. That was spontaneous."

A few minutes later, after a gentle knock on the door, a tall, thin, pale-faced man of about sixty-years of age entered the room. He looked about the same as what Doctor Kent and Odell did. Too many dead bodies.

Harry O'Shea's eyes lit up and widened when he spotted Detective Odell and he warmly greeted the detective while Odell stood up and shook Harry's hand.

"Nice to see you again, Lyle. You are looking, ah, Odellish," Harry said as his eyes traveled up and down Odell's disheveled suit and appearance. Odell looked down at his suit and tie and attempted to straighten his necktie and center his belt buckle and tuck his shirt in, but it was all rather futile.

"I tied my necktie too short today. Harry, nice to see you too. It has been a long time, and this is. . .."

Odell went to introduce Officer Baker to Harry O'Shea, when to Odell's surprise, Harry warmly shook Officer Baker's hand and said, "Nice to see you again, Officer Baker. How is the training going? I thought you were stuck with Grundy. How did you end up in homicide with Detective Odell?"

Baker answered while glancing over at Odell, "It was, rather, what was the word, Detective Odell . . . spontaneous."

"Yeah, spontaneous things happen. Ah, how do you know each other?"

"Sergeant Grundy brought me by on one of my first shifts last week and gave me a tour. Harry and I met, then."

Odell studied Officer Baker's face and then Harry's face as he nodded in affirmation. "Part of your training, huh?"

"Yes, Detective Odell. That is what Sergeant Grundy told me."

Odell nodded and quickly turned to speak to Harry, "Harry, sorry to disturb you. I know that you are busy. Doc Kent tells me that when you did the body prep, you found the car keys to Ms. Murdock's car in an inside pocket of her dress."

Harry nodded and reported, "Correct, Detective Odell." Harry made a demonstrative move in the air with his hands to mimic the events. "Sort of one of those small pockets within the other one. At the top of the dress pocket. Right-side of the dress."

Odell's face broke into a wide smile as Harry testified to the discovery of the keys and the exact location.

"I only found them because I heard something kind of make a clink-type of noise when I set the dress down on the steel table. It caught my attention."

"Great testimony, Harry. Fantastic. So helpful. Thank you," Odell stated while running his right hand through his hair, and then tried in vain to smooth it out. He lowered his head and stared at the floor for a few moments and then lifted his head and spoke once again, "Harry, please think carefully and do your best to recall all the exact events. Was anyone with you when you did the body prep?"

Harry shook his head and closed his eyes and thought for a moment or two, "No, the techs were here working on the cameras and video but they are not allowed near any bodies for privacy and security reasons, so I waited until they checked the camera and left before I began the actual body prep. None of them guys want to see dead bodies, anyway. The tech said the trouble was not with the camera but in the video room equipment. . .."

"So, the cameras still were not working at this point?"

"Correct. The main camera system, that is. I dug around and found a spare video camera and a tripod and did the best that I could to record the body prep. Not ideal, but it worked to some extent. The techs fixed the main camera system in time for the autopsy."

"Excellent. The techs are not on the sign-in sheet, though. Is that because the body or bodies are all in the refrigeration?"

"Correct, Detective Odell. They signed in under the police officer's log sheets. Non-body viewing and non-access. The locks are on all the refrigeration vaults. They signed in as maintenance and repair workers and the officer escorted them and I, too, was in here, prepping for the prep, I followed all the procedures. Exactly. Been doing this a long time. I stay by the rules."

"I see that. Great work, Harry. Were they city maintenance or private contractors?"

"City I.T. Department. I know one of the guys."

"Perfect. Please, go on, Harry. Anyone else?" Harry nodded and thought once more, "The police officer was back outside the door controlling entry." Harry looked up and looked at Odell and then to Doctor Kent before continuing to relay the past events from his memory, "Doctor Kent was scrubbing and Doctor Barken left just before the techs came in . . . so no. That is, it." Odell nodded and closed his eyes when he did so.

"Barken was in the autopsy room? Before, you arrived."

"Ah yes, Lyle, he had just spoken with Doc Kent about the death and his results of the examination of Ms. Murdock's body in the hotel room. He wanted to share some details. You can see the sign in time that he signed in and compare it to my logging of the time when I actually began the body prep. He was covering when the call came in, so he said that he wanted to. . .."

"Harry!" Odell cut off Harry before he could continue and Odell shouted and extended his hand to shake the somewhat startled Harry O'Shea's hand, "He wanted to double-check the body for vomit in the mouth or marks on the body that show abuse or other such nonsense because that drunken bum, Detective Odell claims that her death was a homicide. You can tell me, Harry. I am a big boy. You won't hurt my feelings."

Harry nodded his head, and he resisted a smile.

"Yes. Close enough, Lyle. He referenced some reasons for viewing the body and you too, in sort of, that same manner. I think that he disagreed with your ruling that the death was a homicide."

"Thank you, Harry. You have an amazing memory and you have been of such great assistance. Thank you and please, it is nice to see you, but please, unless Doctor Kent needs you, let us allow you to return to your work." Doctor Kent thanked Harry; he said goodbye to Officer Baker and Detective Odell and left the office.

Odell nodded to Officer Baker, and Baker took that action to mean they were finished here. The young officer was becoming quite intuitive of the old detective's actions.

"Thanks, Doctor Kent," Odell said as he gripped both arms of the chair and rose to his feet. "Thank you so much. I will be in touch. Nice to see you again and one last question, do you pathologist-medical-examiner-coroner-types ever wear white coats when you respond to death scenes? I know you suit up when performing autopsies and such. I am thinking of emergency calls. Ya know, white coats . . . sort of like the doctor does when he examines me for my five-year physical and tells me my liver enzymes are off the charts?"

Doctor Kent tilted his head and said, "Five years, Lyle. Oh my. Yes, I do occasionally wear a white coat. If I want to remain sterile and not transmit something from my suit or clothes to a patient's body or a person or a dead body. I have a dog at home and she sheds terribly. I do my best to lint roller my clothes, but dog hair is a bitch. On the other hand, if I anticipate, yucky stuff such as vomit or other bodily fluids to have the potential to rub off on my suit, then I will wear a white coat. Suits are expensive, Lyle. Dry cleaning is hit or miss these days. Difficult to find a good dry cleaner around here."

Doctor Kent's eyes went up and down Lyle Odell's ramshackle suit. The suit jacket filled with coffee stains on the lapels, his dress shirt full of wrinkles, his belt buckle to the side and his necktie tied too short and hanging askew.

Doctor Kent smiled and added, "Well, most suits are."

Odell laughed and waved, and Officer Baker put away his notepad and pen into his shirt pocket. He reached and shook Doctor Kent's hand as they left the office. Odell leaned back and said, "Yucky stuff and dog hair, huh? Interesting. Gotta go smoke, doc. No use in allowing my lungs to escape any havoc. See ya."

"Good luck, Lyle. My autopsy simply showed a tragic overdose, but you are the homicide detective, not me. Good luck to you. I have no doubts that you will get to the bottom of this. Please, take good care of you."

"Thank you, Patrick. Take care."

Baker and Odell walked down the hallway and headed for the exit door. While walking, Lyle patted his suit jacket pockets, then his shirt pocket and then the pockets of his pants, in search of his pack of cigarettes, and after not finding the pack, the detective finally stopped walking and threw his arms up in vain at the loss of his cigarettes.

Officer Baker pointed at the rear pocket of his pants, where Lyle stashed a now very flat pack of cigarettes, and Officer Baker said, "Left back pocket, Detective Odell. So, Doctor Barken. Is he a suspect? Or did Harry have something to do with the car keys?"

Odell found the pack of cigarettes, pulled them out and

fished one cigarette out of the flattened pack. The cigarette was flat on one side and Lyle shook his head at the sad condition of the cigarette. Then he carefully examined it before placing it into his mouth. Odell stuck the cigarette in his mouth and waved to Baker to follow him outside.

Odell plucked his cigarette lighter from his suit jacket pocket while mumbling something about, "Strange how it is always easy to find the lighter," and he lit the cigarette up as they were a step or two from exiting the building and Odell pulled a drag, but he held it until they hit the cold air outside. It was late in the day now on Friday and after a long exhale and with the smoke hanging in the air and floating all around them, Lyle Odell answered the question.

"Back pocket, huh? Interesting, Baker. Stop me from stashing my cigarettes there. Please. Doctor Barken, huh? Interesting fellow. He is involved. For sure. I am confident that the doctor is in this very deep. Perhaps, over his head and stethoscope. Harry? No way! A good man that Harry is. He is another key to all of this. No pun intended. Are you off tomorrow?" Lyle asked as he drew a long pull on the cigarette, faced away from Officer Baker, and Lyle blew the smoke into the air.

"I am. Unless you need me. It has been a long week. In fact, I have been ten days on with some doubles in there too."

Lyle Odell waved in the air, took another drag on the cigarette, and then, after realizing the potential repercussions of unauthorized overtime for the young police officer, proclaimed, "Oh, shit! Tucker will have my ass for the overtime. Please, take the day off. Pick me up on Monday morning at my house. Call me first and bring coffee. I work Sundays, but Sunday nights usually don't go too well for me, Baker. Thanks. Have a nice weekend and be safe out there. Be sure to check in on the protective detail for Mack. I can drive back. You take your car. I am good. Just going to smoke a few."

Officer Baker carefully studied Detective Lyle Odell and after a few moments of study, the young officer spoke, "I will check in on Mack. For sure. I just want to say thank you, Lyle. For giving me a chance here. I have already learned a great deal, sir."

Odell frowned and then smiled before saying, "Not learned to bag the sir stuff. Yeah, well, rook, ya got miles to go. However, you are welcome. See ya."

Officer Baker waved goodbye. Odell watched while he walked away, climbed into his patrol car, and the young officer drove away into the darkening sky of the late afternoon. Detective Odell stood for a long time, enjoying the cigarette and watching the taillights on Officer Baker's patrol car disappear into the distance. The daylight was quickly disappearing, and it was giving way to the darkness. The air grew colder. Spring was being cagey and staging its arrival.

Odell finished off the cigarette; he tossed the spent butt on the sidewalk and ground it out with his heel. He then reached down, picked up the butt, and tossed it into the waste can next to the door. Odell turned on his heels and headed for the door of the morgue. He had a hunch, and he needed to speak with Harry O'Shea.

The door slowly closed behind Detective Lyle Odell, and he made his way down the hallway to find Harry.

Odell was doing just what he always did. He knew what he had to do now. The picture was very clear in his brilliant mind. Once more, the good detective needed to venture where phantoms tread.

After all, it was what he did.

Chapter Six

The Best-Grilled Cheese in the World

"Okay . . . Odell, don't keep me waiting here. If ya got sumthin' to say about it . . . then spill ya guts on it. I have been doin' this too long," Sergeant George Grundy spoke rather harshly while the police sergeant leaned in and carefully studied Detective Lyle Odell for his reaction and a response.

Lyle Odell nodded, and he slowly chewed and savored the food in his mouth. While Grundy tapped his fingers anxiously upon the bar counter, Lyle finally swallowed and nodded his head. The old gumshoe picked up the pint glass of ice-cold beer, tilted the glass, and took a long sip of the brew. Odell smacked his lips, leaned back on the bar stool and ran his fingers across his unshaven face, and then gave another nod of his head.

"Oh geezzzz, for the love of food, Odell, geez, it ain't filet minion! Damn! Tell me if I am right or not!" Sergeant Grundy grew impatient with the waiting for the opinion of Odell on the quality of the grilled cheese sandwich washed down with the daily special of beer. The two men sat at the bar at Gulliver's Bar and Grille on Fifth Street and Main Street in downtown Mohawk City, New York, on Saturday afternoon around two in the afternoon. Grundy was off duty and Odell, well; it was always difficult to determine when he was on duty or off duty. Most of the popular consensus amongst the Mohawk City Police Department and the career criminals in and around the city was that Homicide Detective Lyle Odell was never off duty.

"You are correct, George. Best damn grilled cheese in the city. Perhaps, in the entire world," Odell pronounced as he picked the grilled cheese sandwich off the plate and took another bite. As another testimony of the skills of the great detective of which he is, Lyle Odell scanned the sandwich while he chewed, and after a swallow, pointed to the evidence.

"The grille is at just the right temperature. The cheese melted perfectly and the crispy burnt edges are amazing. This is an amazing contributor to a middle-aged person's waistline, and I am sure it tips the cholesterol levels in one's blood to borderline heart attack range. This might make me take up eating again in lieu of whiskey." Odell lifted an eyebrow at Grundy and added, "It might. I emphasize, the word, might."

George Grundy slapped his hand upon the bar counter and most of the nearby patrons jumped in his response. "Hot damn! Told ya so. Now, I am having a'nudder brew cuz, I was right. Annie, please, a refill. By the way, this is all on Odell's tab."

Annie the bartender smiled. She pulled another pint glass out of the cooler and proceeded to fill the glass from the beer tap, pouring out the daily special. Annie looked as if she had poured a few million beers in her career. She was ancient but effective. Odell took a sip of his beer and set the glass down, and when Annie delivered George his refill, Odell struck into a casual conversation between two long-time veteran police officers.

"So, George, how much longer are you going to keep working? I think you have me beat by a year or two. I will hit twenty-nine years in July."

Grundy swallowed the beer and set the pint glass upon the beer counter. It was his third beer and by now, some liquid enhancement floated through the big man's veins.

"Yeah. I have ya beat by a few. Thirty-two last month. 'Fraid that I gotta keep at it, Lyle. Too many bills dragging me down to consider packing it in. As much as I want to retire . . . it ain't in the cards right now." George Grundy reached out and picked up the pint glass while Odell finished off his sandwich. He spun the beer around and around in the glass and studied it in silence.

"That crazy son of ours. We saved up our pennies and sent his ass to some fancy college down south in Carolina. Let me tell you that those college savings plans are total bullshit. They pay for a few textbooks and a box of pencils, and that is all. Even with a partial free ride on a scholarship, we had to borrow mountains of dough. The dumb-ass partied hard, flunked out in his second year and blew a partial scholarship in baseball and they sent him home as a loser. Sucked down every penny of the parent-student loans we took, and now, I eat the bills every month."

Grundy picked up the beer and took a long sip and then set the glass down upon the counter with a thud.

"I am swimming in debt, Odell. Swimming. The wife never worked outside the house, so let me tell ya, those bills don't taste so good at my age. He is doing okay now. He retooled and went off to tech school, did a two-year gig with auto technology and has a solid job with auto repairs in the repair department at the Chevy dealership out on Route Five. Union job. Solid pay, benefits, and a pension. The really sucky part is that the tech school was on my wallet too. It sucks to have worked so hard and after all these years, not be ahead."

Sergeant Grundy turned and looked at his afternoon drinking partner, and the old sergeant focused some weary eyes on Detective Odell. The joy of a simple grilled cheese sandwich and a few ice-cold beers faded into spent glory. Sadness and reality replaced the joy.

"The daughter . . . she always had it together. She went to beautician school, nailed a nice job right out of training and now, she manages a joint on the west end. Fancy joint.

When the owner packs it in, I am sure she will take over and buy the place. She is sweet on some guy too. Decent guy. He has a solid job on the state highway maintenance crew. Makes tons of overtime on taxpayer's dough. She picked a solid guy, and she is enuff of a looker to have picked any man." Grundy studied Odell's face for a reaction, and before Lyle could comment, Grundy beat him to the words.

"Yeah, Odell, the daughter took after her mom. Anyway, it is so strange. How could two kids be so different?"

Odell nodded and then shrugged his shoulders and said, "Dunno. Never had any children and never had a woman fancy me enough to consider marriage. I am a loner, anyway. Probably for the best. What was your son studying when he went off to college down south?"

"Ha! Besides, how to get into as many short skirts as he possibly could with as many young women as he could and play baseball?"

"Yes, I guess that short skirts were a tricky subject to manage. Especially, every nine months or thereabouts after careful . . . study."

"Political Science. He wanted to be a homicide detective. Like you."

"No one wants to be like I am, George. No one should be, either. I am sorry for your troubles. Ya need a taste of the heritage."

Odell waved to Annie, and the old bartender wobbled over, stopped, and stared at Lyle Odell.

"Please, Annie, when you can. A shot of Irish for George and me. Top-shelf. That one." Odell leaned over the bar counter and pointed to a bottle of Irish whiskey on the top shelf of the bar. Annie's eyes widened, and then she followed with a nod.

"It's eighteen bucks a shot, guys," Annie added with a suspicious left of her eyebrows and a sideways glance out of her eyes for confirmation of the order. Odell simply waved to indicate that he still wanted the two shots.

"So much for me being a cheap date, Odell," Grundy added with a laugh. "Thanks."

"Hey, no sweat. Don't beat yourself up, George. You love your children and do your best for them. It will come around. Eventually."

Annie dropped the shots, and in one motion, she scooped up the men's spent lunch plates and she was on her way. The two men lifted the shot glasses and made a toast in the air, and down the whisky went. Odell's inners thanked him for the familiar burn, and Grundy's inners protested the stronger than beer feeling. After leaning back onto the stool and crossing his arms along his chest, Grundy shook his head to offset the burn and the ensuing warmth of the whiskey a little, and then he spoke with a whiff of whiskey drifting in the air.

"I do love them. I would do anything for them. Anything. No matter what the cost is. Even if our son was and might still be a dumb-ass. That whiskey works some magic. My lips are loose. I can see your attraction, Lyle. Now, this is where I should ask you about how long you are going to work, and we can be all cozy and concerned for each other, but I already know the answer to that question. Instead, I know this is where you are going to probe for some more details on the night when Baker and I responded to the call at the Mohawk City Conference Center and Luxury Hotel. Even if we are drinkin' buds, and if we are on a case together, the notorious, loner known as the eccentric Detective Lyle Odell does not invite my old ass for beers and lunch or spend dough on top-shelf whiskey to an old, washed-up police sergeant without milking him for information. Sympathy or not for my drowning in debt. Your reputation precedes you, Odell." Grundy's eyes snuck over to the now almost-empty glass of beer and he reached for the pint glass, picked it up and while the glass hovered a few inches off the counter of the bar, Grundy added, "Speaking of Baker. How is the rook doing? By the way, I got my ass chewed by Captain Tucker for working the deal with pawning the kid off on ya, without asking Cap first. Ya owe me a'nudder beer for taking a hit for you. Captain Tucker said the same thing that I thought, that Baker is a kind of unusual police officer for you to take under your wing. He is so neat and uptight with his Marine Corps bullshit—the rook must take one look at your hair, your uniform and, well, you, and cringe."

With those words, Grundy tilted the pint glass and allowed the rest of the beer to escape the confines of the glass and empty into his throat. Odell remained silent as Grundy downed the rest of the beer. He knew that the old police sergeant was cagey enough to predict his next move, or perhaps his overall motive for the meeting.

Odell also knew that Grundy was softened up due to his liquid intake. . ..

"So, buy me a beer or maybe two or even three more and ask away, Lyle. I can take a cab home and come back tomorrow to pick up my car. And . . . so can you," Grundy said as he peered out of the corner of his eyes and with an air of curiosity hidden within his voice at detecting, or perhaps, knowing all along that Detective Lyle Odell wanted to ask him about that now fateful night and his response and actions. "We don't want to make the newspapers or six o'clock news reports as the dumb-ass cops who broke the drunken driving rules."

Lyle motioned to Annie, and he gently smiled and casually pointed at the empty pint glasses in front of them and then finished with a point at the shot glass. Annie nodded, held one finger up to indicate that it would be a minute or two before she poured the drinks.

While shifting gears, Odell quickly addressed the business at hand and in his mind, "Baker is tricky to read. He is a little uptight, but smart. He is learning quickly. In small steps and small bounds. No leaps, yet, there is some progress. He now knows not to show up early at my house, beating the hell out of my door and waking me up without bringing coffee. My apologies for the ass chewing from Tucker. If it is any consolation, Cap, let me know his displeasure too, and I took responsibility for the actions and split-second decision to bring the rook under my wing."

Grundy held his hand up and interrupted Odell.

"Of which is a mystery, Odell. Why, the rook, Odell? Not that I mind. The last thing that I want to do at this point in my career is to have to train a rook. Not sure why Captain Tucker stuck him with me to begin with. I am not interested in training. Even a smart and military trained and experienced officer such as Baker is. It is a pain-in-my-ass and does not allow me to do what I need to do. Cramps my style and makes me take one-hour official lunches."

Odell did not comment or answer Grundy's question as to why, however; he leaned back as Annie dropped the pint glasses and shot in front of Odell. Odell slid one beer glass over to Sergeant Grundy and mumbled, "Thanks," in the direction of Annie, who had already moved down the bar to sling some more beers to thirsty patrons. The gin-joint was growing crowded with late afternoon patrons.

"You worked a double-shift on Thursday night as well as on Wednesday night, George. Hence, sleeping in the patrol car. Which, I assure you, is just between us." George nodded and took a sip of the beer while studying Odell. "As is my whiskey-laden breath and my shaky condition when I showed up."

Another nod from George, followed by another sip.

"I know the staffing sucks and we have major issues. It is not fair to a thirty-year veteran and a patrol sergeant to work consecutive doubles. My opinion. Tell me, George, I already checked the shift logs, listened to the dispatch recordings when the call came into headquarters for the report of Ms. Murdock's demise, and I carefully noted the times, but I need you to answer three questions. When did you break for chow on Wednesday night?"

Without any hesitation, Sergeant Grundy answered, "Eleven O'clock."

"Was it your suggestion to go at that time, or Baker's suggestion?"

"Baker's, idea, Lyle. His phone beeped with a text, he glanced at it and then suggested we break for chow."

"Did he say who texted him?"

"No, I assumed it was his gal pal. She beeps him a lot."

"Did you eat together?"

"No. Baker went off by himself. Said he forgot his chow bucket, and he needed to head to his apartment to eat. Took his car. I ate in the patrol car parked in the lot at headquarters."

"That is a little unusual."

Grundy took a sip and he overreacted to Odell's comment. The old sergeant slammed his glass down hard on the bar counter. Some beer splashed over the edge of the glass.

"What the hell, Odell! Are ya makin' me vouch for my whereabouts? Bullshit. I already told ya, I ate in the patrol car. In the parking lot. Had a ham and cheese sandwich that the wife packed. A cup of applesauce and a cup of yogurt. I washed it down with bottled water. That was a whole lot better than you did that night, with the whiskey sucking. Baker went home. The kid came back ten minutes late, and I did not log it because I fell asleep in the patrol car and missed the exact time to log, anyway. It was not too cold that night. I wanted alone time. The kid made me uptight and cramped my style. We go way back, Lyle, if ya got sumthin' to say and want to accuse me of sumthin' out of line, or if ya implying that I had sumthin' to do with that druggie's death, which by the way is an overdose and not a homicide . . . then damn well say it!"

Odell picked up the shot glass, waved it under his nose, and took a sip.

"Easy, George. All is well. I meant unusual about the rook slipping off to eat alone. Not you. Please, no hard feelings. You have been most helpful," Odell said, just above a whisper. He downed the shot in one quick motion and smacked his lips. "What position?"

"Huh? What the hell do ya mean? What position? Where did I park my patrol car? This is such bullshit, Lyle. Ya can check the cameras monitoring the lot and watch the damn video and figure out what position that I parked the car. You and your Sherlock Holmes investigation riddles and bullshit are really friggin' annoying. No wonder only O'Malley, Cap, and me can stand to even drink with ya ass. This might be the last time that I drink with ya, by the way. Cuz, ya really pissin' me off now." Grundy's eyes narrowed and his nostrils flared in anger.

"Take a sip of the beer, George, and then finish it off. I will buy you another," Odell said while he picked up his beer glass and took a sip. "Taking cabs seems like a predetermination tonight. I already checked the camera and videotape at headquarters. I did not mean the position of where you parked the patrol car. You always park your patrol car in the third row from the rear of the lot, first space inside of the row . . . on the left. Always, in the same place. Every police officer and the civilian employees in the police department all know not to park in your spot, George. You parked your patrol car there forever and then some. My third question about position was in reference to what position that your son played in baseball."

George's face broke into a smile, and he shook his head. Grundy mumbled as he tilted the glass and finished off the last drop, "Should've known. Ya did say three questions. Damn, ya always twenty steps in front of everyone else. Ya always choose ya words so carefully. Ya using me to put the parts and pieces of the case together in ya mind. I get it.

Ya knew everything already, even that the kid was late, and I fell asleep. I am a soundin' board for ya. My apologies, Lyle. He played centerfield. Damn fine arm . . . he could peg out a runner at home plate from deep center. Kid was a ball hawk out there with great speed on the base paths and he could hit a curveball. I love the kid, but he blew it. I could've seen the kid sign a big-league contract and kissed retirement on the ass and all those damn bills paid for, but no . . . he had to bang every chick in the school, smoke weed, and drink like you and party like a fool." Grundy held his hand up and added, "No offense about the drinkin' comparison."

Odell laughed, ran his hand through his messy hair, messed it up more, leaned back, and said, "None taken. It sounds to me as if your son has some keen potential. I will order another round. Say, George, before I order us another round, please, let's bump outside for a puff or two on some cancer rods. There is something that I want to discuss with you. Out of earshot of any probing ears around here. Not that I know anyone here to be particularly untrustworthy."

"Odell, ya don't trust anyone. Ya wouldn't trust the Holy Father, or Jesus, or Moses."

"True, George. My career has tainted me. But I do trust you, George. Very much so. My good drinkin' bud, Sergeant Grundy, I might need your assistance. Yes, indeed, there will be a time in this investigation when I might need your invaluable assistance. . .."

Detective Odell sat in a chair in the kitchen of the Mackie family. Timothy Mackie sat in a chair opposite Odell, and Timothy's father, Jay Mackie, sat on a chair in the middle of the table. A uniformed police officer stood guard at the rear door of the home, just outside the door and out of earshot of the conversation. Another uniformed patrol officer stood watch in front of the home. The house was located in a difficult part of town, and the house displayed some serious signs of neglect. Unfortunately, the home defined dark, dingy, and dirty.

Jay Mackie was gently puffing on a cigarette and Odell mumbled, "Right-side suit jacket pocket," tapped his own cigarette pack in his suit jacket pocket and pulled out the pack.

He tapped out a cigarette, held it in the air, and asked, "Do you mind if I join ya?"

"Go 'head, Detective Odell. A little more nicotine hanging on the ceiling and walls ain't gonna hurt anything in here. Not like we are entering a home beautiful contest 'round here."

Odell stuck the cigarette in his mouth and began his search for a lighter. After tapping, mumbling, feeling, and poking and prodding all the pockets in his pants, shirt, and suit jacket, Jay picked up his lighter, flipped the flame on, and held it out for Odell to lean into the flame.

"Thanks. Never can find the damn thing."

Timothy Mackie leaned in over the table and asked, "Where is your sidekick today? Uptight and square, officer what-was-his-name?"

Odell exhaled a long drag of smoke and the smoke combined with the smoke from Jay's cigarette and created a whirlwind of smoke that spiraled upwards toward the smoky brown, sad light fixture hanging above the kitchen table. The nicotine stains hung on the glass of the light fixture as if they were icicles.

"Officer Dennis Baker. He is off today. The kid worked a number of doubles last week, and the bean counters in the department severely restrict overtime and give my captain grief when we run over on the budget. I am on salary. Does Baker not give you the warm and fuzzies, Mack?"

"Let's just say that we would not go bowling together and leave it at that, Detective Odell. By the way, you smell like a whiskey distillery. I saw ya drive up in a cab. You must have had an enjoyable Saturday afternoon. Nothing 'bout you is really 'bout being a police detective, Odell. Nothing . . . except that you are a damn genius and have kept me alive so far during this mess. I thank you for that." Mack pointed a thumb in the direction of the kitchen sink and cupboards near it. "We have some Irish in the cupboard next to the sink. I could use a hit or two. Dad? You too?"

Jay Mackie nodded and took another drag on his cigarette.

"Let's have a few hits. This protection situation is getting on my nerves. It is a little tough to deal with having these officers follow me everywhere that I go. They stand in the hotel lobby as if they are silent sentries. At least, they hide in dark corners and try not to unnerve the hotel guests. My boss is not happy. Baker sends the officers with personalities like rocks. Just like he is. Drink, Odell?"

Lyle waved at the young man to indicate that he was in. He took a few last drags on his cigarette, looked at Jay with a lift of his eyes for the ashtray, and Jay slid the ashtray and the lighter over the table to Odell. Odell ground out the cigarette, tapped out another from his pack and lit up another smoke.

Mack pushed away from the table, stood up, and walked over to the cupboard. He opened it and removed three glasses and a bottle of Irish whiskey from the deep depths of the confines of the cupboard. Odell's eyes caught the brand label on the bottle.

It was cheap Irish.

Paupers could not be fussy.

After returning to the table and pouring three glasses of whiskey, and an air toast and a few sips from all the men, Mack asked, "How much longer, do I need this twenty-four-seven protection, Odell? Are you making progress? I would think that you foiled their plans to wipe me out and pin it all on me. I think. Delilah's funeral is on Monday and I would like to pay my respects."

Mack lowered his eyes, toyed with the whiskey glass, picked it up, and swirled the whiskey around in the glass while Odell and Jay studied his actions in silence.

"I loved her, Detective Odell. Dad. She was extremely special, and I was very lucky to have shared her love and our love. Our time together will stay with me until my last breath."

Odell ran his hand through his messy hair, messed it up more, leaned back, and said, "I get it, Mack. Yes, you can attend the funeral. I plan to be there too. As far as foiling their plans goes . . . yes. The initial plans might be history, but please keep in mind that you still would be better dead than alive. Sorry, Mack. Progress? Oh, yes. After this weekend, I have some direction and can make some predictions in the case and with the players involved, but I need your help, Mack. I need the exact motive. I think that I know the players, but without an exact motive and proof thereof, all my theories are bullshit. The attorney general and the prosecutors will laugh at me. Already had some phony and corrupt federal clowns tell me that my theory of homicide was Sherlock Holmes bullshit tidbits. In many ways—they are correct. It is obvious to me that Ms. Delilah Murdock knew something that she should not have known, and she wanted to divulge it. No one murders a beautiful, young party gal, who enjoys sex and love and some recreational weed and copious amounts of wine and all that goes with it unless she becomes a huge liability. Sorry, Mack, all my gut instincts point to the senator. Only a taste of power and glory and greed and position trumps the taste of a beautiful young woman. Delilah shared her body and her love. I am sorry if that hurts you."

Odell carefully watched Mack for a reaction, as did his father. Mack simply remained stoic and emotionless. There was little doubt in Odell's mind that Mack loved the young woman, and while Odell's statement caused Mack pain, the young man was realistic.

"If it is any consolation and I truly hope that it is . . . I feel this came to an emotional as well as a tragic climax because she was falling deeply in love with you and was ready to give it all up and perhaps, spill the beans, to join you and ride off into the world of love and hope somewhere with you." Odell leaned into the table, loosened his already messy necktie, let it dangle free, and placed his hands neatly and calmly down upon the tabletop. "I am sure this is because of something that the senator was and is or will be embroiled in, and I want to nail him . . . and I know that you two men want that, too. I need your help, Mack. I need the smoking gun."

"Hell, yeah, we want to nail him. Even more so now, if he did kill Delilah or ordered someone to do it. Dad and I despise that smiling, phony bastard. My help? I think that I told you most of what I know of it. You gonna bust me for peddling weed?" Mack waved his hands around the kitchen and added, "You can kind of see why I had to make some side money, Odell."

Odell finished his cigarette and ground it out, and proceeded to light up another one.

"Lookie, forget all about the weed peddling. We can work a deal in exchange for your outstanding cooperation on this case. We will wipe that all clean. No one will know except my captain, Officer Baker, and me."

"This Captain Tucker. I assume he is your boss. I guess you call him your commanding officer. Is he the guy that I saw on the news yesterday, stonewalling the press? The reporters were swarming the guy and all he had to say was no comment and we are in the early stages of the investigation."

"That is correct. He is my boss, and he is my chain-of-command, commanding officer. Good guy. Honest man. He will handle the press. He knows what to do. We've been together for a long time. I trust him and you can too."

"Okay, he seems very cool. Thank you for the support."

"Mack, lookie, I need you to think. Really, really, think hard. I need your total concentration and do not leave out any details. Even the smallest detail. Let's continue to pour some Irish and as we sip, I will recap what I know and you stop me if I screw up the facts or go astray. Deal?"

Mack looked over at his father, who nodded affirmatively, and then he downed the rest of his whiskey. Jay Mackie was a man of very few words. Despite his age, the pain of his life and the toils that the man endured, Jay Mackie remained a handsome man. The deep lines of worry and pain manifested around his eyes and in his face, but his facial features left little doubt as to where his son inherited his own good looks.

Jay downed the remainder of the whiskey with a smack of his lips and a glance at the bottle centered in the middle of the table that begged to refill the glasses.

Mack did the same as his father did, as did Odell.

While refilling the glasses, Mack said, "Deal. Go ahead. I am all in for helping you in any way that I can, Odell."

Suddenly, Jay Mackie decided to speak, "Good choice, son. You got to help the detective here. You owe it to your woman. You owe her to be sure that justice is done here."

Mack nodded and leaned back into his chair and mumbled, "I do owe her, Dad. I am all ears, Odell. Go for it."

Another cigarette bit the dust, but Odell did not light up another. Lyle handled the whiskey glass, but he did not take a sip yet. Instead, the good detective began his relation of the case and the facts as he saw them from his side and from his own observations and keen skills and profound judgment.

"Lookie, here, I have spent a ton of thinking time on this as well as digging into the research, and a few bottles of Irish have assisted me to bring me to this point. It will help me to brainstorm this aloud with both of you. Especially, you, Mack, since you knew her so well. So intimately. Please stop me right away if I am too far off kilter. Ms. Delilah Murdock began staying at the hotel and after the initial visits and you always checking her in for the stays, the two of you, sort of, kind of, struck up a relationship of sorts. At first, it was business and small talk, but gradually her good looks and your handsome puss, grew onto each other. Slowly, a mutual attraction occurred. She shared a little more each time, and so did you. Finally, there was an invitation for drinks, some social interaction. The two of you met after your shift, and you talked and talked and talked. Both of you dug each other. A deep connection began. It was a nice time. She was profoundly beautiful, super-intelligent, engaging and, of course, very wealthy. Additionally, she was willing to party too. I spent some time researching her life, connections, and all about Ms. Delilah Murdock late last night into this morning. College and high school yearbooks tell many hidden stories and libraries and the internet reveal so much. It is difficult to hide in this world nowadays, especially so since the internet brought everyone into your computer hard drives. When you are a Murdock and in the public eye, there is no hiding. Hell, no one can hide. Even regular folks. Anyway, Delilah was ultra-liberal in her ways, loved the environment, the flowers and the trees and music and the arts. I would say she was Bohemian in nature, a carefree hippie chick, and she pissed her already mean and nasty father off by shunning the family business. It led to a brutal estrangement and rift between the two of them, and Delilah's sister moved into the family business while Delilah did her own thing with her life. Delilah did not care. Originally, she went to Washington, D.C. to save the world, as all of them do. Senator White Choppers was the logical senator to latch onto . . . the new senator from her home state, an ultra-liberal, save the world guy, still young at fifty years of age, and a guy who is Robin Hood. He will steal from the rich and give away everything to the poor. The large, evil corporations will pay for everything. Everything is free! The only trouble is the high taxes already drove out all those large corporations from the state, and sooner or later, White Choppers will come after our wallets. The media loves him, movie star good looks, he supplanted an old, washed-up ugly conservative guy and Monger tells the young people what they want to hear. They can obtain everything for free without any effort on their part. He must have flipped over his luck when Delilah Murdock glided into his office to apply as an intern. All he could do was drool and figure out from day one how to get her to drop her panties for him. There she was . . . a Murdock. Wealth and power and connections and campaign donors and her beauty and body were a side bonus. In addition, she was free-spirited and open-minded. Ole White Choppers hit the jackpot . . . all he had to do was to turn on the charm and she was his. He must have ordered more cans of spray tan and ran out to have his teeth whitened. It all seemed so easy."

"I like you more and more, Odell. If you ran for office, I would vote for you," Jay Mackie said as he sipped his whiskey. "Ya tell it as it is."

Odell tapped out another cigarette and lit it up and while the cigarette balanced on his lower lip like a tightrope walker on a high wire, Odell spoke, "I try, but I am not running for any offices. Besides, I am not electable. Too honest and too ugly. Granted, there might be some elements of educated guesses here on my part, not assumptions, but educated guesses based upon research as well as my experience, but for the most part, I think that I am right on target. I apologize if some of this is a little rough, Mack."

Mack only nodded, but his eyes weighed a little heavier with his sorrow as Odell continued to relate his story. His theories mired in mountains of truth.

"There she was, and she arrived in your world too, Mack. She was close to her mother, perhaps, her sister, but I am not sure yet. I need to probe a bit more into that relationship. Delilah visited her home here in Mohawk City to spend time with her mother, maybe when the evil father was away. Not sure yet. You were the poor guy from Mohawk City, from the wrong side of the railroad tracks, the guy struggling to make it in an obscene world, and you did not hold back with relating to Delilah, your tales of sorrow and hardship. All factual . . . I might add. However, it added to your softening her up . . . to get her into your bed. It was a great angle to sympathize with the poor, lowly, Timothy Mackie scoring with the super-hot, wealthy chick. Especially, when you realized that her father's greed and power in closing the factory led to your own family's hardships with your dad here . . . losing his long-time position and the loss of quality jobs hitting Mohawk City so hard. The political talk gave you an in with Delilah. Common ground. When you gradually became more comfortable with her, and discovered she liked to dabble in a little weed, you found a solid little side gig of making a few extra bucks. You knew some guys around town that could supply a little smoke, and you saw an angle and scored a few ounces here and there and sold them to Delilah Murdock. Maximum markup. She could afford it. She smoked the blunts in her room, with your blessing and your assurances that you could cover it all up and not only did you make a few bucks, but after some copious amounts of intake on the wine and some smoking of the weed, the stunning Ms. Murdock dropped her panties all too willingly and Mack moved in. At full attention. The sex was great. Amazing. Beyond words or description. On both sides. Her body was heavenly, and it sent shivers down your spine and nearly cracked the walls of the hotel room."

Odell stopped speaking, finished the cigarette, and

ground it out into the ashtray. He picked up the glass of whiskey and took a long sip while studying, first, Timothy Mackie over the rim of the glass, and then his father. At first, they had no immediate reaction to the words of Detective Lyle Odell. Then the two men picked up their own glasses and took sips, too.

Timothy spoke first.

"As I said before, Detective Odell . . . you are simply amazing. Please, there is no doubt that I can take it. Continue on."

Jay Mackie remained typically silent but deep in the study of the words and testimony. The man carefully followed every word through shipwrecked eyes and a growing haze induced from the intake of the Irish whiskey.

Odell nodded and continued, "The relationship progressed over a few years, to the point where, you skirted the rules and she did too. You both fell in love. You, first, more so than she did, and you were head over heels infatuated with Delilah Murdock. She fell in love a little slower, however—you both fell in love. It became more than just wine and whiskey and weed and amazing sex. It became something wonderful and magical and profound. More and more and after you realized your love and her position of potential influence with Senator White Choppers, phony-baloney, you pushed past the lust of the relationship and focused on each other. Perhaps, you could have a future together. Perhaps, she could influence the senator and her father to assist with the plight of Mohawk City, reopen the factory, pull back the work from Mexico, be a true American, and bring jobs back and prosperity to lowly Mohawk City. Delilah promised to help with pressure on her father, even if they were estranged, and to utilize the lure of her love for the wretched senator. She was a kind soul. A caring soul and she loved you deeply, Mack. You two were soul mates. She gave into his demands and invitations and finally slept with the senator, lent her gorgeous body to him in hopes of enlisting his aid. But it was for you. In the end, I believe that it was all for you. I truly do. Somewhere along the line, poor Delilah learned something that she needed not to know. A deep secret. A dark tale that led to her unfortunate and tragic demise."

Odell's words hit hard and finally Mack buried his head in his hands and the tears erupted. His sobs shook his entire body and his tears dripped upon the table. Jay Mackie stood up, walked over to his son, and wrapped his arms around Timothy as he provided comfort.

Lyle Odell fought back the tears and emotions too. Odell often felt pain, but he tried very hard to hide it. Sometimes he succeeded; other times, he did not.

He could only take another drink, pour a refill and think, 'Damn those phantoms.'

It was his only defense against the continual haunting. To acknowledge their presence.

After a few moments of comfort and a few refills and a now nearly empty bottle of Irish staring at them, Odell spoke once more, "I am so sorry, for your pain, Mack. I think that, unfortunately, I have hit the nails all on the heads and in doing so, caused you much pain. Sometimes, we walk through Hell to get to Heaven. The field of flowers turns to iron and then back to heavenly scents of roses and sweet peas and golden sunshine. Let's get you there."

"I am okay, Odell. Please, I want to help. I think that you are right on so far. Continue. Please."

"Senator Monger serves on many committees in the senate. Generally, he gets nothing done, but his good looks and white teeth and the media backing him push him toward a White House run. In digging around, I found that his most prominent position is on the Appropriations Committee. There, he does try to push and manipulate purchases, and overall, promote the use of New York State businesses. As all the senators on the committee, do for their home states. No doubt that they all push their home states. That is where I feel there could be a connection with Murdock and his business."

Odell turned to Jay Mackie and asked, "Jay. You worked there for years upon years. What could they manufacture in Mexico that the United States Government would need?"

Jay answered without hesitation, "Military clothing. Uniforms, boots, shoes, hats, vests, gloves. We were working on retooling from civilian to military goods when Murdock pulled the plug on the operation. He claimed that the government contracts were going to be more profitable than supplying retailers with civilian goods. We could no longer compete with cheap overseas goods and pay union wages and benefits. In order to retain the business, and have contracts awarded and do business with the government, Murdock would need to do some form of business in the states though. That makes sense. I have an idea cuz, I know that heartless, greedy bastard, Murdock, and I knew his old man too. His old man was even worse than this son-of-a-bitch is. I also know that business and the rules and regulations. I was a foreman there for over twenty-five years. He needs to manufacture the basic product in Mexico, ship it here, do the final inspection of the goods here, box them up, label them, and then distribute the product through the warehouse on Division Street. That way, ya conform to the government guidelines. Murdock broke the back of the garment union when he closed us down, but he utilizes some non-union workers in the warehouse. Only 'bout fifty jobs there. Over two-thousand employees worked at the factory in the hey-day. Easy to do the math there. The word is that his other daughter runs that show. But here is the ace in that deck, Odell," Jay Mackie leaned in and waved for both of the men to join him in the testimony. The two men did so as Jay continued, "ship through the Port of Albany and who knows what the hell else ya can hide inside of crates from Mexico. Especially so, when ya name is Murdock and ya got all the union business leaders of the dock workers in ya pocket and ya got the backing of Senator Monger. Oh lord, the shit can run deep there. Mighty deep. As in organized crime, deep. Everyone gets a cut of the pie."

Detective Lyle Odell leaned back in his chair and his face told both Jay and Timothy Mackie that he was deep in thought over the recent observation made by Jay Mackie. Jay looked at the nearly empty bottle of Irish whiskey on the table; he picked the bottle up and poured the last remaining amount of whiskey into Odell's glass, then slid back from the table, stood up, carried the empty bottle and dumped it into a trash can near the back door of the kitchen.

Jay then opened the cupboard while mumbling to everyone, "Don't worry. I have another bottle."

Odell had already leaned into the refilled whiskey glass when Jay spoke, and a smile almost formed on Odell's mouth and his eyes widened. The good detective was a mess now, deep in a haze of Irish whiskey from an all-day-marathon of drinking, nicotine flowed through his veins while competing for space with the alcohol and his mind whirled with endless clue crashing. Despite the influences, Odell's spirit remained powerful and his mind remained razor sharp.

Odell spoke while he fumbled for yet another cigarette and then he spoke, "You worked there at the factory for over twenty-five years, so I think you might know Officer Baker's father. Ya know, Baker . . . he is my sidekick on this investigation. Officer Dennis Baker. Your son mentioned how uptight and square he is. Did you know Alex Baker? I think I read or heard somewhere that he was in charge of security for the entire factory, the warehouse and the Murdock shipping and receiving business."

Jay answered as he uncorked the whiskey bottle, "Sure. I

knew Alex. He was the manager of all the security. Yes, he was. Alex was ex-military. Uptight kind of guy. Kinda dark. I guess, like father and like son in that manner. From what Timothy told me about your sidekick, anyway. I never dealt with Baker too much. Our paths really never crossed too much. Just a wave, a nod, and some small talk. He is retired now. He lost his position when the factory closed. Family fell on hard times . . . like us all. I think that is why the son joined the Marine Corps. No work. No money. No jobs. Join the military in order to escape this shitty city."

Odell nodded and said, "He did lose his position there at the factory, but I think he crawled his way back into the mix. I think there still are some assignments that Alex takes on now for Murdock. Here and there. I need to dig into that a little more. Anyway, the United States Coast Guard ultimately oversees the Port of Albany and can easily be involved there. I have friends there. I served fifteen years active and then ten years in the reserves for the Coast Guard. I will make some phone calls in the morning." Odell blew a long puff of smoke out and it circled above the table and drifted toward the light fixture. More icicles of nicotine.

"This has been a most productive afternoon. Thank you both, for your amazing input and ideas. I have much to ponder and much to work on now. Jay, please, can I circle back tomorrow with you and pick your brain about Murdock Enterprises? I need to know everything about that company, both past and present. I dug into things a little earlier today and here and there, but in light of your knowledge and certain statements, it is obvious that I need to dig some more."

Jay nodded and answered, "Sure, Detective Odell. Tomorrow works. It is not as if I have a ton of things going on in my life right now. I will be happy to help you in any way that I can."

Odell ran his hand through his hair and then tried in vain to smooth it out. It was a habit. Not a fashion statement.

"Did I miss something? Mack, please, think. Did I miss anything?"

Timothy Mackie stared at his whiskey glass; he slid the unopened bottle over, twisted the top off and poured a generous pour into his glass, then did the same for his father's glass and then finally, he topped off Odell's glass.

"Just that Delilah played the violin and the piano. Oh yes, she loved dogs and animals. Especially dogs. She has or had two Siberian huskies. Freda and Tundra. Male and female. They loved her. Never left her side when she returned home to Mohawk City. She could not keep them in her apartment in D.C. so they stayed here. That was another reason that she came home. To see her dogs. The male dog, Tundra, was very close to Delilah and protective of her. He could get downright mean if he did not know you, and you came too close to Delilah. I met them a few times. She brought them to the hotel and once they knew I was a good guy and that Delilah loved me – they would be fine with me. She did love her mother, and they were very close. She not only returned home whenever she could to visit with her mom, but to play some super-expensive grand piano that the Murdock's have in their home. In their sitting room, as Delilah called it. A sitting room. Can you imagine? Delilah always wrote notes in this leather-bound journal thingy that never left her side. She told me she wrote musical lyrics, bits, and pieces of music that floated in her head. Delilah could read and write music. She said that she also wrote notes and daily diary sort of things. Events."

Detective Lyle Odell, generally, was not inclined to show any reactions. He always tried to remain cool and calm, albeit . . . messy. Odell tried hard, but he was not always successful in those endeavors. Except for the messy part. Upon hearing the testimony from Timothy Mackie, Odell leaned in over the table and his eyes opened wide. As wide as they could give, all the outside influences weighing upon them at his point.

"She played the piano in a sitting room and wrote in a journal! Two dogs! Siberian huskies! My goodness! These are vital and fantastic pieces of news! Thank you, Mack. Right now, I need to focus on what you know about the journal. Our investigation teams never found a journal. I am sure it was not in the hotel room and it was not listed on the investigator's report as found in her apartment. I requested through my chain of command for the local investigators in Washington, D.C. to conduct a search and compile an inventory of Ms. Murdock's apartment. They did so and I read that report earlier today. There is no dairy or journal listed. No writings, no books, nothing. That makes sense since you say that it never left her side. Are you sure that it never left her side?"

Mack remained adamant. "Never left her side. We would make love, wild and passionate love, and when we were finished, she would find that damn journal and write in it. It seemed so weird. I would question her and she would giggle and say that she recorded everything."

Odell then struck at the heart of his theories and slipped in the tidbit that he was already sure of but, still, deep in his mind desired confirmation of, "She was left-handed, right Mack? She wrote lefty."

"Yes, she was. Another amazing observation, Odell. Amazing. How did you know that?" Mack asked, as he seemed amazed once more at the observation skills of Detective Odell. Odell picked up the whiskey glass and since the day and now the night both disappeared, he tilted the glass over to take another sip and lose it some more.

"Despite my appearance, I am a detective and once in a blue moon, I find a clue and get it right. Even the blind squirrel finds an acorn. One thing to ponder, though, Mack, and once you take another long sip of that whiskey, I will explain, but please recall carefully the woman who waved to you from the front door of the lobby. The woman that you said was Delilah, and I asked you to think really, really hard about . . . and after a careful and deep thought, you said that she waved with her right hand. Now, I ask you, Mack, would Delilah have waved with her right hand?"

Now it was Timothy Mackie's eyes that opened wide, Jay Mackie looked over at both Odell and his son, and since Jay was not privy to all the details, he was somewhat lost in the conversation.

Odell stuck another cigarette in his mouth and picked up the whiskey glass while saying, "Don't worry. It looks like another long night. I can call a cab. We need a plan. Together. All of us. Please, let me explain. . ..."

Doctor Mikhail Barken slowly walked to his car that he parked on the second level of the parking garage in downtown Albany. His belly was full; it was an exceptional meal at his favorite restaurant. An exceptional meal of the finest cut of filet mignon, fantastic vegetables all steamed to perfection, top-shelf cocktails mixed with the finest top-shelf whiskey, and the dessert was incredible—all served by his newest favorite restaurant. A few weeks earlier, there was no way that Doctor Barken would eat at such an expensive restaurant.

Now, money was not really an obstacle.

The night was cold and the sky overcast, and growing colder and darker by the minute.

Doctor Barken spotted his brand-new sports car parked in the corner of the second level. In a dark corner, and for a fleeting second or two, Barken looked in, around, and over his shoulder. It was late on Sunday night and the parking garage was empty now. A few hours ago, the garage had been almost full, but restaurants and nightlife were now winding down as the weekend ended. Doctor Barken stayed later at the restaurant than he had anticipated. He was enjoying the atmosphere and throwing some money around. He thought for a moment that he had a chance of bringing the beautiful young redhead home with him for a night of lovemaking, especially so after, he showed her a picture of his new sports car, and boasted of his job as a pathologist and medical examiner, but she backed out with some lame excuse. No problem, Doctor Barken was sure he would run into her again at the same restaurant and score on the next meeting.

While walking to the dark corner where he parked the car, he second-guessed his previous decision to park the expensive vehicle in such a remote location, but quickly dismissed the thought. This area of downtown Albany was a safe area, and there were surveillance cameras in the garage and security officers on patrol and watching the cameras. After all, he was not going to risk dents, nicks and marks on the paint of his amazing car and tolerate any joy riding of his new precious vehicle to some valet car junkies. Doctor Barken pulled his collar up around his neck as the cold air whistled through the concrete garage and he reached into his coat pocket, pulled out the key fob to the car, pointed it at the vehicle, and pressed the button.

The bullet blew most of the side of Doctor Barken's head apart when it struck his skull. The pieces of his skull and brain splattered into the cold air.

He never felt a thing.

The doctor's dead body crumbled in a heap next to the door of his brand-new sports car, and his warm blood spilled out into a pool on the cold concrete. From a few feet away, from around the side of a concrete support pillar for the garage's structure, a man emerged. A man dressed in black, a black balaclava mask pulled over his head, black gloves on his hands, and black low-quarter shoes on his feet. The man unscrewed the silencer from his handgun and dropped the silencer and handgun into the left pocket of his overcoat. He looked around, and upon seeing no one around, the killer quickly ran to where the body fell. The killer rifled through the pockets of Doctor Barken, found his wallet and his house keys, as well as the entrance ticket to the parking garage. He pocketed the keys and the ticket into the right pocket of his overcoat, removed cash from the wallet and a few credit cards as well as his driver's license, and stuffed it all into the right pocket of his overcoat. He tossed the wallet a few feet away, toward the rear of the vehicle. The wallet hit the concrete wall behind the vehicle and dropped at the base of the wall.

Then, he pulled the car key fob out of the fingers of the dead body of Doctor Mikhail Barken, opened the car door of the sports car, jumped into the driver's seat, and started the engine of the car. He placed the car into gear, popped the clutch, and sped off into the night.

Into the cold, overcast evening.

In the brand-new sports car.

There were no marks or dents on the paint.

Anywhere.

Chapter Seven

Cold April Winds

Detective Lyle Odell slowly opened his left eye, and then, as if his eyelid was a rusty hinge on an ancient barn door, he slowly pried open his right eye. He strategically used a combination of his thumb and his forefinger in order to pry open his eye.

Right now, in Detective Lyle Odell's world, everything was painful. Very painful. It felt as if the entire Third Division of the United States Marine Corps was marching through his head. A quick march of elite infantry marines followed by tanks. Lots and lots of tanks with loud and rumbly treads upon the ground.

Odell moved his eyes slowly around his living room and with his feet; he kicked at a pizza box and an empty Irish whiskey bottle to move them away from the foot of his easy chair. He almost anticipated the frantic banging on the front door of his home. It had been a very difficult night. Sunday nights after work always were. Saturday afternoon and early evening with Sergeant George Grundy did not rank very high on the happy list either. Grundy took a cab home, and most likely, felt the wrath of his wife for having a little too much to drink. Odell had taken cab rides all weekend. He lost track of where his car actually was, but he thought it was in the parking lot at Gulliver's Bar and Grille. Eventually, he would track it down. Odell worked on Sunday in the office at headquarters. When he returned home, the phantoms followed him to his doorstep.

They always did.

"Okay, okay, Baker. Hold on and please stop your damn banging on the door! I hear you. I am coming. Slowly. Very slowly."

The sound of his own voice caused an eruption of incredible pain in Odell's head. It felt as if his ears would melt off the sides of his head. Odell made his way to the front door of the home, spun the locks and slid the deadbolt open, and when the door swung open, Officer Dennis Baker immediately stuck out his hand and offered a container of coffee to Detective Lyle Odell.

"Here you go, Detective Odell! I am gaining in my training!"

Odell took the coffee and painfully and slowly waved Officer Baker into the house.

"Loud, but gaining. Yes. Thank you for the coffee."

Baker gently and carefully closed the door behind him and went to speak, "Ah, Lyle, I needed to rush over and tell you. . ..

Odell cut him off, held one finger in the air while lifting the drink door in the plastic lid of the coffee cup.

"Please, first a sip of heavenly brew. Have to rely on the caffeine to reboot my functions."

Baker nodded and watched as Odell placed the cup to his lips and took a long sip of the coffee. He smiled and stared at the cup and swallowed.

Before Baker could pick up on his conversation, Detective Lyle Odell spoke, "You rushed over here with coffee in hand to inform me that the Albany Police found Doctor Mikhail Barken dead of a gunshot wound to his head. Most of his head is gone now. He was a victim of what seems to have been a robbery in a deserted parking garage late last night. A night, when the good doctor tipped too many drinks in a fancy restaurant, struck out with a beautiful young woman that he had the hoochie-coochies for and then unfortunately, parked his brand-new expensive sports car in a secluded corner of the same parking garage. A corner where the evil killer or killers, supposedly trailed him from the restaurant, along the city streets, then confronted the doctor, shot him, stole his wallet and his car too." Baker stood silently and slightly dumbfounded that as usual, Odell was seemingly a hundred steps ahead of anyone else. Odell took another sip of the coffee and with his free hand; he attempted to smooth out his messy hair. He was still dressed in the same suit.

"Was the beautiful chick in the restaurant bar a set-up chick for luring high-rolling businessmen and then baiting them for her thug friends to rob and assault? That does come to mind, Baker. However, in this case . . . no. It is not the case, although the young woman will be questioned. On Saturday morning, I alerted a detective friend of mine in Albany Homicide to the fact that I felt Doctor Barken would meet an ill-fated demise, but they were too late in finding him. Well, they found him, but most of his head is missing as well as his car. The robbery is another staged scene. How ironic that the doctor met his own demise within a staged scene. The Troy, New York Police Department found the fancy sports car across the river. We have a CIS team combing that for clues and evidence, as well as his fancy apartment in an exclusive section of Albany."

Baker still stood silently while carefully listening to Odell relating the events of last night. His face was emotionless and expressionless.

Odell took another sip and then continued, "I am sure we will have some key pieces of the puzzle by tomorrow. When the CSI team reports in with the results. Funny, apparently, the doctor recently came into a ton of dough. A brand-new sports car, he leased a fancy-ass apartment overlooking the city," Odell waved in the air with his free hand and for a second, Baker thought that he would drop the coffee cup but Odell held onto it, "one of those penthouse jobbers. Nice view of the city. Especially at night. You can see The Egg and the Corning Tower and Empire State Plaza. Beautiful lights. I enjoyed the view. He paid for everything in cash. A year of rental and association fees in advance, the leasing agent said. Until a few weeks ago, the doctor was deep in debt. He lived alone, his wife ditched him years ago, and he had no children. Life is a funny thing, Baker. A very funny thing."

Odell finished speaking and while taking another sip, he peered over the lid of the coffee cup at Officer Dennis Baker. Odell seemed to be studying the reaction of the young police officer.

Officer Baker removed his patrol cap, tucked it under his arm, adjusted his necktie, and checked his police badge position before speaking, "Yes, it is, Odell. No doubt. I see that all of your window shades are down, so I need to tell you that there are a few television and radio and newspaper reporters and their crews hanging out on the sidewalk in front of your house. They rushed me when I pulled up and jumped out of the patrol car. Assaulted me with questions on the progress of the case and why did Detective Odell declare this death a homicide when it appears that Ms. Murdock was just into the recreational use of drugs, made an error and mixed the drugs with alcohol and accidentally overdosed? A bunch of other questions too."

"What did you say, Baker?"

"Exactly what you told me to say. No comment. Captain Tucker is the only officer releasing information on this case."

"Good work, Baker. Very nice."

"So, I guess we are picking up some travel vouchers and permission from Captain Tucker to drive to Albany today?"

Odell walked over and set the coffee down up on the only end table in the living room and he kicked at an empty pizza box at his feet and then slid it closer to the wastebasket, while using his foot to slide and empty Irish whiskey bottle and nudge that a little closer to the wastebasket too.

"I gotta clean up here a little bit. Nah, I was there until about two in the morning. Only slept for a few hours until you came banging and hollering at my door." Odell turned quickly, pointed at Baker, and added, "With coffee. And a loud volume too."

"So, Lyle, you feel as if Doctor Barken had something to do with the death of Ms. Murdock?"

"Yes, of course. I knew it as soon as I saw him in the hotel room with his bedroom slippers on his feet and wearing the white coat too, while spouting off about other overdoses and rushing around from home and the other bullshit he spouted off. Good thing that he went into medicine and not acting. On the other hand, actually, it turned out to be a bad poor career choice for him and many others, too. Anyway, I cannot wait to see what the CSI team finds in the way of his shoes and what evidence of substances are on that white coat too. I hope that the doctor did not wash it yet. We will see. He wore the white coat to appear as a doctor would appear and not to get certain evidence onto his suit. Suits are expensive to clean. White coats . . . not so much. I am quite sure one of his pairs of shoes will match the imprints on that fancy carpet. The imprints close to the sliding door of the hotel room. And the white coat will have some telltale clues stuck on it, too. By the way, there was only one other drug-related death in our good city that week, other than Ms. Murdock's demise. I was on the scene for that death. Doctor Barken was not there. A young man with a long history of drug abuse mixed into some of those lethal opioids hitting the streets these days. I have to find out where that poison is coming from. Anyway, all of that drama and that scene in the hotel . . . that was a phony act of nonsense. Barken had no way of knowing that over three weeks ago, I left orders with the police dispatch desk to receive notifications of all drug-related deaths. Technically, Doctor Barken was her killer. At least, he was by actually mixing and technically delivering the lethal mix of drugs. However, he had an accomplice. Of course, he did, as well as indirect accomplices that preyed upon his poor situation and recruited him for the evil deed. Doctor Barken simply mixed the lethal dosages up and monitored her reactions. After all, he was a pathologist."

Odell stopped speaking and caught his words. It was as if he was very carefully releasing information to Baker and needed to stop at a certain point.

Odell pointed at the disorderly appearance of his living room and commented, "It was a rough weekend, Baker. As you can see, life around here over the past few days has been kind of bumpy. I worked a ton of hours, both in the field and at the station and the library and with my head and mind in research. I tipped a few sips of Irish last night in order to chase the phantoms away."

Officer Baker did not comment on Odell's release of the evidence and progress of the case. Instead, the young officer chose to focus on the condition of Odell's house.

"I see. Honestly, it actually looks a little neater than it did in here last week," Baker said while searching for honesty and delivering gentle words and while scratching his high and tight haircut.

"Thanks, Baker. I try. Anyway, we are going to Delilah Murdock's funeral this morning. We will stand a long way away and observe every single detail and you will take copious amounts of notes, Baker. Then we will try to ask Senator Austin Monger a few key questions, but his guard-dog attorney will chase us away. Then, we will pay a visit to the Murdock crew and that will become even messier. Anyway, I will be right back. I have to change my suit, clean myself up, and maybe I need a shave. Even Detective

Lyle Odell, respects a funeral."

Odell waved in the direction of his disheveled living room and added while he walked to the staircase to head for the second floor, "Please, it is hardly inviting, but feel free to sit and relax, Baker. Maybe check out my new cellphone that Captain Tucker finally acquired for me. It is there on the end table. It is much more advanced than my old one was. These things seem to be advancing more and more into complexity. It will not power up. Perhaps, you can help me out with it?"

Baker nodded and walked over to the end table where the new phone sat.

Baker explained, "That explains why you did not answer the phone. I tried calling you, but of course, you did not answer."

Odell ignored the fact that he did not answer the phone, mostly because he did not know how to work on it.

The detective took a few steps up the staircase, turned around, and said, "I need a cigarette. I think there is a pack in my bedroom. By the way, where did you go in order to get it?"

Baker held the phone in his hands and he was fiddling with the buttons when Odell asked the question.

Baker's eyes narrowed, and he looked very puzzled and slightly alarmed by the question. His body posture tightened.

The young officer answered, "Go? Get what? I am not sure, sir, what you mean."

Odell smiled and waved while ignoring the slip up into the "sir" title. After all, the young officer was very uptight.

"The coffee, Baker. The coffee. Where did you go in order to get it? It is very good."

Officer Baker relaxed his posture, nodded, picked up the coffee from the end table, and studied it before setting it down.

"Believe it or not. The gas station down on the corner of

where headquarters is. On the left corner as you hit the main drag. Grundy told me that they make outstanding coffee."

Odell nodded and said while climbing the steps and with a fading voice, "Grundy ought to know. He has been around for a very long time. Good choice, Baker, to consult the veterans and utilize your training resources. Good choice."

The April wind blew cold, and it blew strong. Even on the warmest of days, cemeteries are cold places.

Detective Lyle Odell's hair blew all over the top of his head and he reached up to smooth it out, only to have the wind disturb it once again. Detective Odell cleaned up rather nicely . . . not great, but his present appearance was an improvement over his usual appearance. Most anything is and would be. His suit jacket was open, his shirt slightly untucked from his waistline, and he did not tie his necktie in a perfect knot, nor was it a color or pattern match to the color of his shirt or his jacket and it did not hang straight. However, he was almost clean-shaven, and this was a suit jacket, pants, and a shirt that he had not worn in the last few days or thereabouts. The only indication that Lyle Odell was a police officer was the detective badge, clipped slightly askew to his belt. If his jacket did not move, you could not even see the badge. That was typical for Lyle Odell; he did his best to remain hidden and preferred to operate in the shadows and out of the limelight.

Where the phantoms tread.

Odell stood on the outskirts of where a clergyman performed the graveside funeral service for Ms. Delilah Murdock. On his right side stood Officer Dennis Baker, all decked out in his perfect police patrolman's uniform. Nothing out of place. On his left side stood Captain

Lawrence Tucker and next to Tucker stood Sergeant George Grundy. Both Grundy and Tucker wore dress uniforms, and all stood in respect of the tragedy of the demise of the young, lovely, and in the eyes of Detective Lyle Odell, innocent Ms. Delilah Murdock.

Odell whispered just above the roar of the wind, "You never get used to this, Baker. Never. Ever. This is why I do this bullshit. To bring justice to the victims. To mourn them, to honor them, and to make sure that those responsible for their deaths are brought to justice. It is more than upholding the law. It is a badge of honor that we all need to carry. What we all should carry on our chests and within our hearts. You would think that the trail of dead bodies created by vile evil would harden your heart—but it doesn't. It only makes you dig in deeper."

Detective Lyle Odell bit his lip and his mouth quivered with the words that he spoke. His eyebrows narrowed and his eyes darkened as he broadcasted his determination.

Officer Baker only blinked away the water in his eyes that the wind caused, and gave a slight nod. His emotions answered without words. Grundy and Captain Tucker carefully listened to Odell's words, but they chose not to comment.

The wind blew colder and stronger, and it whipped around the trees. It touched the gentle wisps of the edges of the grass, a grass still brown with the lingering grip of winter. A grass that spring had not yet touched with warmth to turn it green with growth. A grass that remained dormant with the depths of the cold and the bitterness of the moment. The wind whipped around the persons in attendance and it chased across their bodies while capturing their grief and their pain, and then it gently drifted into the air. It worked hard at the hearts of the persons in attendance. It worked to broadcast the evil in the world, and it chilled the spirits of the good persons . . . such as Detective Lyle Odell. A few feet away from where the police officers stood while simultaneously mourning and doing their jobs at the same time, Timothy Mackie and his father stood silently with a police officer standing a few feet away watching their every move and the moves of all those in attendance. Timothy Mackie softly wept, and his father placed his arm around the shoulder of his son in a vain effort to comfort him. The wind had no grip upon Timothy Mackie's grief. Some human emotions overcome even cold and bitter winds because they are powerful, real, and deep.

"Please, take very careful notes of everything that you see, Baker. It is very critical to this case. Even the facial expressions of the mourners and of the pretend mourners, too. I will record what escapes your eye as well as your pen, as will a police photographer zooming into the scene with his telescopic lens. He is far off in the distance. On that little knoll over there. No need to cause more pain to those in attendance here who actually care that Ms. Murdock is gone. Even, the so-called callous and perpetually inebriated, Detective Lyle Odell respects the situation. Anyway, the pretenders always turn out here at funerals to fake their mourning and pain, they wring their hands, contort their faces and pretend. Our accomplices and planners in the homicide are here, right now, Baker. All the actors aren't in Hollywood."

Odell still spoke in a whisper; he gently lifted his hands and pointed as he identified the various persons attending the funeral.

"There," Odell pointed, "the Murdock family. Father, mother, sister, the ever-present bodyguard also known as Mr. Muscles, cousins, aunts, uncles, friends. For some of them . . . the grief is painful, profound, and real. For others, not so much. Over there, the tall, handsome man with the perfect hair that even the strongest wind cannot move out of place, I am sure that you recognize, Senator Austin Monger. Movie star good looks and the extra-solemn, worked-up and contrived expression . . . unbeatable combination for the media."

Odell turned and pointed at the array of reporters and camera crews, all pointed and focused upon the service and particularly focused upon Senator Monger. Even the media held back and stayed under control, out of respect for the funeral service and for the dead. A team of Mohawk City uniformed police officers formed a line of barricade and established the perimeter while following Captain Tucker's orders, and they helped keep the media's position on the outskirts of the funeral service.

"Lookie there. The media eats it all up. They have become more influential than the government is in our lives. By the way, the man standing next to Senator Monger—that cannot stand still on his feet without shifting his feet or checking out every aspect of everyone and everything around him . . . the man with beady eyes and angry eyebrows, is his personal attorney. Attorney Rexford Covington. The guard dog. All crooked attorneys have angry eyebrows. He protects the senator because he rides his coattails. So many do. We have already locked eyes a number of times. He knows that as soon as the funeral service is over, we will intercept him and the handsome senator at their limousine." Baker nodded and jotted notes in his notepad. Still, neither Officer Baker nor Grundy, or Captain Tucker spoke a single word. The law enforcement team stood silently for the rest of the funeral service. Motionless and silent amongst the cold wind and underneath the ominous sky with only the keen eyes of Odell slowly moving to scan every detail of the service while Office Baker continued to scrawl notes into his notepad with his pen.

The clergyman completed the service, and the sound of weeping floated in the air. Its mournful dirge cut through the sound of the wind as it rose in unison to Heaven. It was time for the cemetery workers to do their job in privacy.

The air was cold. The ground was colder.

Mourners wiped at their eyes and they tried to comfort each other. As the service ended and the group of family, friends and assorted mourners and attendees slowly left the graveside and made their way to their cars, Odell made a slight motion with his hand for Officer Baker to follow him. Detective Odell had his eyes set upon Senator Monger and his attorney, who now had stopped to express condolences to Mr. and Mrs. Murdock and Ireland Murdock.

Sergeant Grundy apparently knew of Odell's plan, as did Captain Tucker, because Grundy leaned into Odell as they broke away and said, "Go get 'em, Lyle. Cap and I will fend off the media with the officers for as long as we can. It is gonna be a mad rush now that the service is over. Freedom of the Press, ya know. Ya gonna take long with the senator?"

Odell turned, smiled, and answered Grundy in a low whisper. "Not too long. I hope. Once, I stand down his pet bulldog of an attorney who is going to grab my pants leg and try to rip my leg apart. The actual questions for white choppers will not take too long. Six or seven questions are all that I have, for Senator Monger, George. Six or seven questions."

Grundy nodded and as Odell and Baker made their way in the direction of Senator Monger and Attorney Rexford Covington, Captain Tucker gently grabbed the arm of Detective Odell and said, "Detective Odell, try not to piss them off too much. However, do what you need to do. Do you still want to meet the media afterwards? Is that your plan?"

"I will do my best not to piss them both off, I always do my job and yes to the media."

Odell and Baker made their way in the direction of Senator Monger and Attorney Covington, and Baker turned and glanced in the direction of the Murdock family as they made their way to a waiting limousine. Ireland had her arm around her mother and they comforted each other as they made the long walk to the vehicle. Walks away from gravesites are some of the coldest walks that humans can ever experience. Especially so when cold April winds blow so hard and so strong. Mr. Murdock walked ahead of his wife and his daughter. He walked quickly and strongly. His head was up, and his eyes focused upon the vehicle's rear doors where bodyguards and the driver awaited. The rear door of the limousine was open, and the driver held it open against the wind. It was apparent that Mr. Murdock wanted nothing more than to escape the grips of the cemetery and the potential onslaught of the media.

Odell carefully watched Officer Baker's eyes and commented as Odell tried in vain to smooth out his mussed hair from the work of the wind while saying, "Uncanny, huh? Her resemblance to her sister, huh, Baker? Uncanny. You are checking out, Ireland, huh? Never seen her before, huh?"

Officer Baker adjusted his patrol cap and pulled it down tightly so that the wind could not work at it.

He seemed to fumble at his words and then catch his voice with a mumble of an answer while seemingly to answer only one of the questions, "Yes, Detective Odell. Uncanny is a good word."

Odell made a careful mental note of the answer.

He studied Officer Baker and then said, "Take careful notes, Baker. Follow my lead. This is critical, Baker. Critical." Odell spoke, and then he fumbled at his suit jacket pocket in search of his cigarettes. Of course, they were not there, and Odell began the now familiar routine of tapping and feeling every pocket of his suit and garments in search of them.

"I think you should check the left pocket of your pants, Detective Odell. Just a suggestion here . . . perhaps, you should not smoke here." Baker glanced at Odell out of the corner of his eyes and added, "Out of respect."

Odell nodded and found the cigarette pack and without breaking stride, he tapped out a single cigarette, stuck it into his mouth and let it dangle upon his lower lip.

"Thanks, Baker. I always lose them. Good observation skills, Baker. Not going to smoke it. Just taste it. Well, maybe. Maybe, I will light it up to annoy some of these weasels. The dead around here will forgive me. It is all in the interest of justice. Damn well sure to be another adventure to try to find the lighter. . .."

Senator Monger almost made it to the waiting limousine when Odell and Baker closed in on them. Two black suited, dark sunglasses attired bodyguards who were undoubtedly special federal agents assigned to the senator moved in aggressively into a protection formation, despite Officer Baker wearing his police uniform. The agents, along with the driver of the limo, gathered into a protective circle and protected the senator and his attorney.

"Relax, men. It is just us two lowly law enforcement types from the Mohawk City Police Department. I am Detective Lyle Odell. This is Officer Baker."

After the introductions, Odell carefully studied the eyes and interactions of each person, while the group studied Odell and Baker. Detective Lyle Odell did not miss anything. Not a single thing.

With the dangling cigarette dancing upon his lower lip, Odell fumbled with his suit jacket, bent over and searched for his badge. It was clipped to the side of his belt and after pulling his already unkempt shirt even further out of his pants; Odell found the badge, unclipped it from its belt holder, and held it up for display.

While the wind blew his hair into wild circles above and all around his head, Odell added, "Homicide Detective Lyle Odell. I need to ask you, Senator Monger, some questions. About the homicide of Ms. Delilah Murdock."

Upon hearing the words and the title of Detective Odell,

the driver of the limo abandoned the security detail, ran to the front of the limo, and jumped into the driver's seat to prepare to move the vehicle for a hasty escape. The one agent next to the scene glanced toward Rexford Covington in a pleading look for direction for the situation. Covington quickly motioned with his right hand for them to move Senator Monger into the back of the limo. The attorney moved in front of Odell and Baker and blocked their path. Odell's eyes glanced up and down at the face of the attorney and then he studied the suit of Attorney Rexford Covington. Nothing was out of place on the man. Despite the wind, not a single hair on his head moved. Covington was tall, muscular, and slightly imposing. His suit clung to his physique and proudly displayed his wealth, as well as his muscles. He wore a perfect haircut and a very expensive watch on his wrist.

"Nice watch, there Attorney Covington."

"You know who I am?"

"I know many things. It is my job to do so. I have an empty life and poke around dark corners to kill time. That is where I found you. In a dark corner. So yes, I know who you are. Do you represent Senator Monger?"

"I do."

"On all matters?"

"Yes, on all matters."

Odell's slightly squeaky voice rose just above the roar of the wind while he clipped his police detective badge back onto his belt. "That is what I thought. Thank you for the confirmation. I kind of thought that was the case. Yeah, I know who you are. I study things. In fact, I study everything and everyone. This new-fangled internet has made my searching effort a helluva lot easier. Kind of amazing how you can find out stuff in a stroke of a keyboard click whereas it used to take me hours of research time and pavement striking to find the facts. Anyway, let me jump in here and save you a few words. Save us both some time. Senator Monger is very busy, he has to catch a flight out of Albany back to Washington, D.C., he was only here for the funeral, yakity-smackity. Oh, yes, he has nothing to say about the demise of Ms. Murdock other than it is a terrible tragedy and he feels awful about the tragic loss of such a fine, young woman," Odell said while the cigarette held on for dear life to Odell's lower lip. Officer Baker marveled at the resiliency of the cigarette hanging on for dear life to the lip of Detective Odell, and Baker swore that he glued the cigarette to his lip. Odell then dug his foot in the ground, removed the cigarette from his lips and held it between his fingers in his right hand while he waved into the air with his left.

"Here is where you can also add your own smart-ass opinion about how you cannot believe that I am a detective, how messy I am and how I smell, since you are a little downwind of me, like whiskey. And how, in my right mind, can I rule this death as a homicide? Then again, I am a raging drunken fool, who could not find a clue in the pocket of my own pants. So . . . how did I do, there Covington? Did I nail it?" Odell said as he replaced the cigarette into his mouth. Senator Monger sighed loudly. The agents held onto the senator as he hovered between terra firma and the rear seat of the limousine, and Covington narrowed his eyebrows even more than they previously were.

"Ah yes, the infamous and unruly and messy, Detective Lyle Odell," Attorney Covington began to speak, "it is not a pleasure to meet you. Not at all. Not in the least. Your disrespect at intercepting us in this time of mourning is despicable. I must say you are the smart-ass around here, not I. Yes, you nailed my words and speech. Exactly. I must say that your reputation for unprofessionalism and for being rather messy and sloppy and a drunken stumblebum did not do you justice. You are even worse in person."

"Thank you. You think that you smell whisky now—you

need to wait until around five this afternoon. The way this day is going, maybe around seven tonight. Time will tell. Then, you might not want to light a match around my exhales. One fact that I will dispute. I am not a smart-ass, nor do I have one . . . my ass cannot sit on ice cream and tell you what flavor it is, but some people seem to think that I am good at my job. As in, very, very good. As far as my appearance in person goes . . . I would not want to disappoint you. Despicable. Maybe, but you know something? So is murder. I let God sort it all out after I solve the cases, and I ensure human justice. That is what I do. I walk where phantoms tread. Lookie here, I only want to ask, Senator Monger, six questions or, perhaps, seven questions. The seventh is dependent upon one of the answers provided. Baker here, who I might add, makes up for my horrible appearance, with his picture-perfect police officer appearance, will take careful notes of every word. Every. Single. Word."

Rexford Covington nervously shifted his feet on the ground. It seemed to be a habit of his when he was uncomfortable in a situation. He stood up tall and his height towered over the bent and tilted frame of Detective Lyle Odell. Covington adjusted his necktie and looked over at Senator Austin Monger, who now motioned for his bodyguards to release their grip on his arms. Senator Monger then stood up and took a step or two out of the door of the limousine.

Attorney Covington, in a slightly wobbly voice, said, "Senator Monger has no comment. Above what you already said, Odell, in your eccentric and wild mind, you should have your minion here simply jot down your own words. Go back to your desk in police headquarters and play with the words and suck down whiskey from a flask and gallons of black coffee. We are catching a plane. Goodbye and good luck chasing a homicide that only exists in your own mind and in the bottom of those empty whiskey bottles."

"We can do this here . . . or we can do this down at police headquarters, Attorney Covington. Your choice." Odell said, while patting his suit jacket and pockets in a frantic search for his cigarette lighter. Odell mumbled while Covington fumed, "If I am going to be despicable, then I might as well go for the brass ring of despicability."

Officer Dennis Baker held his pen out and pointed at Odell's suit jacket while saying, "Check the inside of the left side of your suit jacket."

Odell nodded, reached inside the jacket, pulled out the lighter and with a gentle sigh of relief, he flicked the lighter, leaned into the flame and lit the cigarette. A long pull on the cigarette brought a long exhale of smoke and resulted in a swirl of smoke that blended into the wind and quickly disappeared into the cold air.

Odell asked as he blew the smoke into the wind, "Did anyone ever tell you, Attorney Covington, that you have angry eyebrows?"

Covington took a few steps in front of Detective Odell as Baker carefully watched and said in a lower and more threatening voice, "This is outrageous for even a low-life detective such as you obviously are. To think that Senator Monger, a highly respected senator, one of the leaders of our country and the United States Senate is somehow involved in the supposed homicide of his personal assistant is not only ludicrous but it only enhances the fact that you are a crazed, drunken fool with a badge. To top it all off, only you, in your wild, drunken mind, think this was a homicide. The poor woman had a drug habit. She dabbled in the wrong thing, mixed it with some prescription drugs and alcohol, and she died when she passed out and choked on her own vomit. Tragic? Yes. Murder? No. Only in your mind, so you can whip up drama and bullshit. You are indeed, a fool."

Odell stood and pondered the words of Rexford

Covington for a few seconds; he stuck the cigarette in his mouth and adjusted his belt to glance down at his badge. It seemed as if he required confirmation that he replaced it on the belt.

"You know something, Covington?" Odell took a long drag on the cigarette and blew the smoke into the air. "Many people accused me of being many things over thirty years of homicide detective work, yet being a fool is not one of them. A drunk, yes, crazy, sure. In fact, every single day, people tell me that I am crazy, but a fool, no. I only want to ask Senator Monger six or seven questions. I did not even suggest any involvement of Senator Monger in any despicable shenanigans. You just brought that up. Not me. Ms. Delilah Murdock was the senator's assistant. They had a close relationship. He might give me some ideas. What are ya hidin' Attorney Covington? Why ya so defensive? Until I solve this case, everyone who knew the victim, interacted with the victim, spoke to her and generally walked in some close or not so close circles with the victim, is a suspect. It is my nature. I am cynical. Chasing phantoms and clues and staring at dead bodies kinda makes you that way. My ancestors came from a pile of rocks known as Ireland with nothing but their clothes on their back, and they made a new life here in America. Stubbornness flows in my veins."

Odell paused with his words for a few moments, he kicked at the grass with his right foot, attempted to fix his wind-blown hair with his free hand, took a small drag on his cigarette and he looked down at the ground while pausing in his speech. Odell lifted his head, and it seemed as if the detective now had a direction that he wanted to go in the interaction and that he found the exact words to speak.

"As far as this not being a homicide, well, I can assure you that it was. Right now, I have enough evidence to prove that it was a planned homicide and staged death scene in the hotel room. My crime scene team is outstanding and so is the one in Albany too. I received the results earlier today. Amazing stuff, those men and women do. Peering into microscopes at a hidden world. Behind the scenes heroes and heroines," Odell spoke the words and then immediately studied the face of Rexford Covington, and then he glanced at Office Baker and finally, Senator Monger. Covington's face grew ashen and Baker jotted frantically in his notepad while Senator Monger stood silently, still in the same location with his two agent bodyguards supporting him. The senator was in limbo. Half in an escape and half into the world of Detective Lyle Odell.

Odell pointed with the cigarette at Covington and spoke, "Don't play poker or try to convince a jury of your case with that face, Covington. Seems my words ran through you a little. Better, stick to political law, stay away from playing detective and stay the hell out of the courtroom. You're not convincing and makin' mistakes too."

Covington's face recovered the color and now, it grew red with anger as his words rose in volume high above the wind, "I will make sure that I strip you of that badge, throw it on the ground and spit on it. I will have your badge and what is left of your career for this, you drunken, stupid, son-of-a-bitch. Austin Monger is the senior federal senator from the state of New York, and his destiny is to occupy the White House. You are a drunken, loser of a detective, making, what? Sixty grand a year, in this hellhole of a city here in the middle of nowhere, New York. You will be sorry that you did this, Odell. Very sorry."

Odell took another drag on the cigarette and said, "Yup. I will be sorry. Drunken loser with a mediocre salary. Okay. So, noted. Baker, please note those words of Attorney Covington. By the way, the question about your eyebrows is not one of the six or seven questions. Your client is a United States federal senator for New York, and I am sure he is a very important man. The media loves him, everyone falls all over him, his movie-star good looks, young, powerful, dynamic. Must be great to be Senator Austin Monger and be on top of the world Anyway, I am, well, just a homicide detective. Right now, unfortunately for you, my rank trumps yours. Too bad for your side. I will take your words as a non-threat to a police detective, because, right now I still have a trickle of Irish whiskey in my veins from my recent shenanigans, you have angry eyebrows and I don't really care nor do I really give a shit what is stuck up your ass or what you say. As far as feeling sorry. Ah, no. Not at all. My captain is right over there," Odell pointed in the direction of the media where Captain Tucker stood while answering countless media questions, "you can go and speak with him now and face the media yourself. Now, we can stand here and trade insults and coy barbs all day or I can ask your client a few questions and you can make your flight. Or you will need to return to answer my questions at police headquarters. I assure you that you will . . . because drunken fool or not, you were correct when you said that I have a badge and guess what, Attorney Covington . . . I am in charge and you are not."

Covington glared at Detective Odell then; Covington shook his head and waved in the general direction of the vehicle and Senator Monger.

Odell smiled and took a few steps in the direction of Senator Monger while adding, "I thought that would be what you would say and do. Nothing. Baker, please take careful notes. First note is that I rather unsuccessfully did not follow Captain Tucker's orders of not pissing anyone off."

Baker nodded while Detective Odell turned toward Senator Monger.

"Senator Monger. Sir, just six or seven questions and we will be out of your way. Thank you for your time."

Senator Austin Monger looked past Odell, while looking

over at his attorney, and Covington quickly said, "Austin. You do not have to say a word. Nothing."

The senator waved in the air and put on his best face while smiling with his perfectly formed and pure white teeth fully exposed, "I understand, but I have nothing to hide, Rexford. Nothing. Please, Detective Odell, I understand that you have a job to do and I hope you appreciate that, so do I. Please, ask me what you need to ask me so that I can get back to the people's business in Washington. Foremost, it is an awful tragedy about Ms. Murdock. I echo your words."

Odell took a long drag on the cigarette, blew the smoke in the opposite direction of the senator, nodded and mumbled, "Yes, indeed. Terrible. Sure. The work of the people. Okay, only six or seven questions. That is, it. First, did you ever see Ms. Murdock socially outside of work-related events or work-related social outings?"

Senator Monger took a breath; he narrowed his eyes and answered, "No. Only social events that were work-related or at work. We worked very closely together. On a daily basis. She was my assistant. My right-hand person. We would socialize during work hours . . . you know, take a break from work and go to lunch or dinner if sessions ran late. That sort of thing."

Odell simply nodded and looked at Baker to make sure the words were in the notepad.

Satisfied, Odell launched into the second question, "Did you ever see Ms. Murdock write notes in a daily journal?"

Senator Monger looked over at Rexford Covington, and the attorney stood stoically without saying a single word.

"No, I don't ever recall, Delilah . . . writing in a journal. Not specifically. I mean, obviously, I saw her write. I never asked if it was in a daily journal of sorts. Did she?"

"Sorry, Senator Monger, but, at this point in our discussion, I get to ask the questions on this one. Not you. No offense meant." Odell finished his cigarette and while the group looked on, he tossed the butt on the ground, then ground it out with his foot, reached down and picked the cigarette butt up, examined it carefully and then placed it into the pocket of his pants.

Attorney Covington shook his head at Odell's actions.

With a wave of his hand over his windblown hair, Odell said, "You serve on the senate committees for Appropriations and on the Committee on Armed Forces. In fact, you are a co-chairperson on the Appropriations Committee."

Senator Monger stood up taller and prouder and flashed his million-dollar smile as the words of Odell, proclaiming his status in the senate, propped up his already considerable ego. "That is correct, Detective Odell. I am very proud of my record there on both committees. Just last week, we managed to. . .."

Odell interrupted the senator with a wave of his hand and said, "Yeah, great work, Senator Monger, but save it for the campaign trail. I ain't interested. The question is that did you know that because of your sponsoring legislature and the passing of the same in both committees, Murdock Enterprises Limited, of right here in good old, Mohawk City, received multi-million dollars contracts to provide clothing and garments such as hats, socks, gloves and such, for our military serving in the Middle East?"

"Yes, of course, as I said before you cut me off, I am very proud of my record of serving the good people of New York and bringing jobs back here to Mohawk City is part of my mission. As you can see, I am quite successful at that mission," Senator Monger said while once more flashing his perfect teeth at Detective Odell.

"Great choppers, there Senator Monger. Perfect teeth. Right on about the jobs. Only trouble is that Murdock Enterprises Limited makes most of the goods in Mexico and ships them here to the Port of Albany. Most of the jobs, about two thousand or so of them, maybe even more, went south a few years back when old man Murdock refocused on military contracts and pulled the plug on manufacturing domestic garments here in America. In reality, the facts are there are only about fifty jobs in a warehouse here in Mohawk City and another thirty or so working at the Port of Albany in receiving the goods. You can do the addition and the subtraction. So much for jobs and success, Senator Monger. Sorry, but I am a detective and I tend to deal with facts. Those are the facts. Politicians deal in razzle-dazzle and yakity-smackity and detectives deal in facts."

Senator Monger's smile faded, and so did his flashy display of teeth. Through a now clenched mouth, the words came out of his mouth just above a whisper and they strained in the wind, "Murdock Enterprises Limited meets the stringent requirements for making some goods here in New York and for providing American jobs to qualify for the contracts."

"Yeah, sure he does. He makes a few token cardboard shipping cartons in an outsourced factory in Brooklyn, New York and if you include old man Murdock and his daughter, Ireland, and the board of directors, as employees then they qualify," Odell said as he waved in the air and added, "I spent quite a bit of time as of late studying Murdock Enterprises Limited. It is fascinating how these American corporations can spin things and fly under the radar with rules and regulations. Lots of evil there. Tons of evil. My old man used to tell me that money makes money and ain't that a fact."

Odell finished speaking. He turned to Officer Baker and waved again in the air with his hands and asked, "You getting all of this, Baker?"

"I am, Detective Odell. I am," Baker answered as his eyes flashed glances first at Senator Monger and then to Attorney Covington. "I am not missing a word. Taking copious notes."

"Good work, Baker. Officer Dennis Baker is learning the

ropes on this case. His presence has been insightful and rewarding," Odell said as he pointed at the limousine parked in front of them. The limousine that Senator Monger still stood in front of the open rear door of and a limousine that, by the look upon the senator's face, he would love to dive into and speed away in right now.

"You maintain close ties with old man Murdock. It makes sense, the old guy is a very large supporter, a huge campaign contributor, his daughter worked for you, and the old boy even gives you his prize limo to ride in to attend his daughter's funeral and to use when you are here in Mohawk City and upstate. I had one of the patrol officers run the license plate. The limousine registration is under Murdock Enterprises Limited. Nice rig." Senator Monger did not answer Odell, but the glare in his eyes made his movie star good looks seem as they were on fire.

Through clenched teeth, Monger spoke, "We are friends. As you just said, his daughter works for me and he supports my political views and platform."

"Sure, thing, Senator Monger. Nice to have support from elite and powerful and mega-wealthy persons. One correction, though, his daughter used to work for you. Now, she is dead. Murdered."

Covington stepped closer to the group and angrily proclaimed, "Stop badgering my client, Odell! Or we will end this questioning and we will return with a herd of attorneys and continue these questions in a formal setting in your police headquarters and you will begin to regret the day that you became a police detective. We will trample you and snuff you out forever!"

"A herd of attorneys, huh? Now, that would invoke serious regrets, Attorney Covington. Facing a herd of frantic attorneys, especially, if they have angry eyebrows as you do. Trample and snuff. A threat? Was that a threat? Bad enough that you want to stomp and spit on my badge. Now, you are issuing actions to force regrets. Tsk, tsk, not exactly proper behavior for an officer of the court. And to think that you accused me of being unprofessional. I think that I am getting underneath your skin, Attorney Covington. Why is that? Presenting facts is not qualifying as badgering. No one here offered a correction. Did they? Baker, did you hear any correction to my presenting of the facts?"

Officer Baker did not speak, but he looked up from his notepad and shook his head to indicate no. His eyes danced from Odell to Covington, and over to Senator Monger, and then he returned to jotting down notes.

Odell walked closer to Attorney Covington. His slumped appearance straightened, and his wind-blown hair stuck out in all directions. His suit jacket was askew and his pants wrinkled and his shoes were muddy, but even through his red eyes, you could feel the burn of the pain and the passion of his mission. Odell's voice was strong and forceful. Some of the squeakiness was missing.

"That aforementioned trickle of whiskey in my system just ran out, and now I am feeling very police-like. Don't threaten me, Attorney Covington. I am a police detective and I am warning you right now, don't threaten me. Both you and your client already agreed to these questions. I will have Officer Baker arrest your ass, and slap you with an obstruction of a police detective's investigation charge and you will miss your flight. I will do it just to piss you off and then drop the charge later this afternoon. Just. To. Piss. You. Off. Now, stand down and shut the hell up. Are we clear now? I ain't waiting for an answer . . . Senator Monger," Odell quickly turned and faced the senator, "another question. Did you know that Ms. Murdock suffered from panic attacks?"

Senator Monger immediately answered, "Rexford, I appreciate the defense, but please, we, ah, ah, I have nothing to hide here. Let the detective do his job so we can all move on from here and through this horrible mess. Yes,

I did know that she suffered from panic attacks. She unfortunately suffered one on the senate floor one day during a highly stressful day of senate debate, while running information for me during an intense debate on the floor. Delilah did not enjoy being in and amongst crowds. That is why I moved her into the office to work as my assistant and away from the duties of an aide. It helped her to work alone and stay out of the limelight."

"I see," Odell said, while fumbling for another cigarette from the pack and lighting it with the lighter that was close at hand now. "See there, Covington, you forget to mention in your disparaging remarks about me that I am a chain smoker."

Covington folded his arms across his chest and simply stared down at Odell without commenting.

"Do you or did you know a Doctor Mikhail Barken? He was a forensic pathologist working out of Albany County. Primarily, he performed autopsies and medical examinations. Apparently, the doctor dabbled in other things, too." Senator Monger's eyes narrowed, and he put his hand to his chin in thought while Detective Odell carefully studied his every move. It was easy to tell that Senator Monger felt the burn in Odell's eyes.

"No, the name does not ring any bells, Detective Odell. Why . . . should I know him? I meet many, many people."

"Once more, I ask the questions. I will answer yours . . . eventually. I understand that an important man, such as you are, meets tons of peeps. Here, perhaps, this photocopy of a newspaper clipping from the Albany Union newspaper will refresh your memory. I found it while doing research. It is from the social section. From a year or so ago, some fancy cocktail party in downtown Albany. A fundraiser for your reelection campaign. I think. I am sure you know the type of joint and those kinds of gatherings," Odell stuck the cigarette in his mouth and puffed at it and exhaled the smoke from the side of his mouth as he fumbled through all of his packets until he produced a wrinkled and excessively folded piece of paper. "I think it is a safe bet that you will never see me in one of these photos in the social section. Too messy and ugly. Here take a lookie, Senator Monger."

Monger reached out and took the paper from Detective Odell and he waved in the air at the exhaled cigarette smoke in an effort to push it away from his face. It was obvious that his previous calm and cooperative behavior and senator-like behavior were slowly fading.

"Honestly, Detective Odell, must you smoke so damn much? It is a disgusting habit."

"Honestly, yes," Odell answered.

Monger shook his head and took the paper, unfolded it and stared at it. It was a photo of Senator Monger with the now deceased Doctor Barken. Both men were shaking hands and smiling at the camera.

Senator Monger glanced at it, narrowed his eyes and then shook his head and handed it off to Attorney Covington while saying, "I am sorry, Detective Odell. As I already said, I meet many, many people. I do not recall ever meeting this Doctor Barken fellow."

Without commenting, Attorney Covington handed the paper back to Odell, who took it and forced the paper into his pocket and managed to crumble it even more than it was already crumbled and wrinkled.

"I understand. Many, many people. The good doctor was a supporter of yours, he contributed a few baubles and trinkets to your campaign and then the doctor fell upon hard times. Silly investments. He was a sugar daddy to some young gal, who took him for a ride, he lost a bunch of dough and it is a sad story." Odell took a long drag on the cigarette and while exhaling the detective added, "In a remarkable twist of good fortune, he really rebounded as of late. He suddenly came into some dough. Big dough. Major dough. A new fancy penthouse, a fancy sports car, working the edges for the pretty young ladies, and then." Odell stuck the cigarette in his mouth, and while it dangled in his mouth with his words, he clapped his hands together and everyone jumped.

Even Officer Baker dropped his pen and mumbled, "Sorry," while the young officer bent over and reached into the grass to retrieve it. Odell glanced at Baker, and it appeared as he almost smiled at the young officer's nervous reaction.

"Bang! It all came to a tragic end this weekend. The poor doctor met his demise with an unfortunate gunshot wound to his head. His fancy sports car . . . gone. His wallet . . . gone. A victim of a supposed robbery in downtown Albany. Kind of sad."

Monger mumbled, "I am sorry to hear that. I am not sure what that incident has to do with these questions in reference to Ms. Murdock, but whatever."

"Well, you see, just by a coincidence, or by design, or by what was the word you just used, Senator Monger? Whatever. Well, Doctor Barken was covering for Mohawk City's regular medical examiner last week, and he responded to the hotel room and declared Ms. Murdock dead. He also visited the morgue, but that is another story. It is so interesting how everything seems to come together in cases such as these. So complex, so much digging to do, but perhaps, this drunken detective is not such a fool after all."

Covington shifted nervously on his feet. Senator Monger blinked and Officer Baker wrote feverishly in his notepad. Even the two bodyguard types exchanged glances with each other.

"Did you know that Ms. Murdock had two Siberian huskies, and that she was a dog lover?"

"Well, she did mention the dogs, and it does not surprise me. Delilah was a very caring, carefree, young woman. She loved trees and plants and music and animals.

It is a tragedy that she had to become mixed up in a world of drugs and too much alcohol to drink. Such a shame. She was an amazing person."

"She was. Carefree, happy, loving and beautiful and gorgeous, with a knockout body that she loved to share. Apparently. Kind of a hippie chick. Bohemian. I like that word."

Senator Monger bordered on exploding at the words and hidden implication of Detective Lyle Odell.

He managed to keep it together as the words rolled from his lips, "I would not know about that, Detective Odell. Your implications are horrible and not welcome. I am a happily married man. My wife is gorgeous and my two daughters are the pride of my life."

"Yeah, I am sure they are, Senator Monger. When did you last speak, email with, communicate with, or see, Ms. Murdock?"

"Last Tuesday before she left for Mohawk City."

Odell nodded, and he rushed over, extended his hand out and shook it while waving to Baker to follow him. "Thank you. Senator Monger. I will not keep you any longer. If I have more questions, then we will be in contact with your office. Come along, Baker. We need to meet with the press. Attorney Covington, see you around. Keep on narrowing those angry eyebrows. Muscles," Odell said, while patting one of the agent's shoulders, "have a great day and keep your head on a swivel. Not everyone is a good guy."

Senator Monger looked rather puzzled as he stood in the same spot and finished the handshake with Detective Odell.

"That's it?" Senator Monger asked.

Odell turned around and answered, "That's it . . . except for the fact that you need a lint brush." Odell walked over to the senator. He peered in with his eyes and then while putting two fingers together; he reached for the suit jacket of Senator Monger and carefully plucked something off the jacket and held it between his fingers. Odell held the object in the air and studied it.

"Ha! Dog hair. Silver with black edges. Siberian huskies often have silver hairs with black edges on the hairs. Do you have a dog, Senator Monger?"

Before the senator could answer, Odell said, "Don't answer that." Odell stood straight up and closed his eyes for a brief second or two. He opened his eyes and said, "That would make it eight questions and I am many things, but one thing that I am is a man of my word."

Odell reached in his suit jacket pocket, with one hand, he held the hair in his other hand and he removed the pack of cigarettes. Odell then nodded in the direction of Officer Baker. "Baker, here. Please, go ahead and peel the metal foil out of the pack and tear off a piece."

Baker took the pack, lifted the lid, and tore off a small section of the foil.

"Please, Baker, hold it out flat."

When Officer Baker did so, Odell carefully avoided the wind. He placed the dog hair inside the metal foil, and then he took it from Baker and carefully folded the foil up to contain the hair with the foil. He stuck the foil inside of his shirt pocket and tapped the pocket to make sure it was there.

"Top shirt pocket," Odell mumbled and then he added, "Right side. I knew smoking those cancer sticks would come in handy someday." Odell said, and then he turned to face the dumbfounded Senator Monger and his attorney and his bodyguard agents. "Oh, by the way, I didn't," Odell said.

Senator Monger's eyes narrowed as he directed his gaze upon Odell.

"Didn't what, Detective Odell?" Senator Monger asked as Odell turned back around and smiled, and then began to walk away.

"Vote for you. I think you are liberal, phony loser and a fake son-of-a-bitch. Almost as fake as those white choppers of yours are. Almost," Odell answered as his voice floated into the cold air and mixed in with the wind.

Chapter Eight

A Crumbling Plan

"Damn it! You totally screwed up! You stupid-ass bastard! I should never have listened to you!" Senator Monger screamed in anguish and anger at Attorney Rexford Covington. "Get me a brandy! Pour it four fingers deep. Now!" Senator Monger had lost his usual polished politician's demeanor and moved into full anger and attack mode. He slammed his hand down on the rear seat of the limousine as it pulled away from the curb at the cemetery. Rexford Covington reached into the portable bar mounted on the divider wall of the rear area of the limousine. He poured Monger a straight brandy, and he poured one for himself too.

"Our world is crumbling all around us! Friggin' Odell." Senator Austin Monger changed his voice tone to mimic the voice of Rexford Covington, "Oh, don't worry, Austin. Calm down. This is a cakewalk. Drunken detective! Washed up! HAS-BEEN! Those were your words, Rex! YOUR EXACT WORDS! The guy is a damn super-genius, and he walked up your ass, stomped all over you and spit you out. You let him get to you. Now, we are up shit's creek without a paddle. Tell me, Covington, what is the plan? You had better have a damn good one because right now, our very lives depend upon it!"

Rexford Covington took a long sip of the brandy as the engine on the limousine roared and the vehicle merged onto the New York State Thruway and made its way to the Albany airport.

"Are you finished with your little tantrum now, Austin? You need to relax and take it down a few notches. You answered the questions perfectly. Even when he pulled out that photo of you and Barken. After all, you do meet many, many people. Odell has nothing to pin us to anything. Yes, he figured out some parts and pieces, but there is nothing to tie us to anything. Nothing. Regardless, I am invoking the contingency plan. The plan is to use our resources and eliminate Detective Odell and old man Murdock, too. Now. Today."

"What about the journal that Delilah kept? Where the hell is it?"

"Don't worry about that. No one can find it. Odell included. If Odell, had it, and it contains what you feel it contains, then we would have known a few minutes ago. We would be in deep shit right now. We will eliminate Odell before he finds out anything more. The case will die without him pushing it because everyone thinks he is out of his mind by ruling it a homicide, anyway."

Senator Monger wrung his hands, and he lamented in loud shrieks of anguish.

"More death! More murders! Oh, how this awful mess just becomes more horrible! Rexford, won't killing them cause even more suspicion?"

Covington pondered the question for a few seconds and then answered, "It might cause a helluva mess. But with Odell gone, there will be no one left to figure it all out. I doubt anyone in the police department even understands how that eccentric nutcase of a detective thinks to pick up the case after he croaks. Then, after Odell is gone and the old man is history, we will eliminate the last person with any ties to us and the details. I have connections ready for that. Ultimately, we can set it up so that our hired gun will be the fall guy for the murders."

Monger narrowed his eyes at his attorney. The senator sensed that Covington was scrambling now and making the plan up in desperation.

Covington continued to explain, "As far as the journal goes, maybe Doctor Barken grabbed the journal and disposed of it when he drugged her. I don't know, but our best people could not find it . . . therefore, I am confident that it is gone forever."

"Well, we sure as hell can't ask Barken now. Can we? You had better be correct, Rexford. If she wrote down all we discussed and did, then I am cooked, and honestly, I am taking you down with me."

"That is so good to know, Austin. Such a friend you are to me. After all, you did come to me for assistance," Rexford Covington said with a sarcastic air.

"Assistance that you have been extremely well paid for, Rexford. Extremely. Don't forget that I paid for your little island retreat all snuggly and comfortable for your retirement plans with that little Spanish chickee that you keep company with and in a few weeks when this madness is over, I am sure you will be basking in the sun there. Anyway, forget all that. What about old man Murdock? How will you kill him? How will you kill Odell?"

"Oh, Odell will be a head shot. One bullet. Our hired gun is an expert marksman. As far as the old man goes, I think he might just have to commit suicide over his profound grief at the loss of his daughter. That might take some pressure off the suspicions. Eventually, once we silence whom we need to silence, then we will eliminate the eliminator. Eventually. I will make the call now to begin the action plan, Austin. Drink your drink and relax. I have it all under control."

Covington leaned into his brandy as the vehicle sped to the airport. He smiled over the rim of the glass and whispered, as he reached for his cellphone, "Under control."

Odell tapped his suit jacket and pulled out the cigarette pack and without breaking a quick pace; Odell shook a cigarette free from the pack. He stuck it in his mouth and without much searching, found his lighter, snapped off a flame, and leaned into the flame and lit the cigarette.

"Did you get it all down, Baker?" Odell asked between puffs and exhales of the cigarette.

"I did, Detective Odell. Yes, I did."

"Good. Thank you. Please let me have your notepad." Odell held his hand out, and he studied Baker's face as they walked and as the young officer seemingly became hesitant and slightly surprised at Odell's request.

"I, ah, ah, write a little sloppy. I thought that I might translate it and type the notes up in an outline format."

"Not necessary, Baker. Thank you. No need for that military perfection in this particular case." Baker nodded. He unfastened his uniform shirt pocket and handed Odell the notepad. Odell slipped it in his suit jacket. And as he did so Odell mumbled aloud, "Suit jacket. Inside pocket. Left side."

"Am I not taking any more notes, Detective Odell?"

"Most likely not, Baker. We only have one more stop to make and this case will reach a conclusion. I only need three or four more pieces of the puzzle. The biggest prize we will find very shortly in the Murdock mansion. We are on our way there right now. Thank you for your assistance. I hope you have learned a great deal by tagging along."

Officer Dennis Baker did not comment.

The duo reached the media madness; Odell leaned into Grundy and asked, "Is it all in place to intercept the limousine at Albany airport?"

Grundy looked at Captain Tucker, who nodded to affirm the answer to Odell's question. Sergeant Grundy's cellphone went off and simultaneously, Captain Tucker's phone beeped too.

The sergeant reached into his uniform pocket and

glanced at the phone and nodded his head, while explaining, "Text message. Confirmed the officers and crime scene crew are in place at the airport. By the way, one of our police officers stopped by with the keys from the Coast Guard officer at the port and this paper. They could not reach you by your cell number, so they dispatched the findings of the inspection to Cap and to me," Gundry explained as he handed a set of keys to Odell, along with the paper.

Odell mumbled, "I left that stupid cellphone home. Battery is dead, anyway. Can't figure the blasted thing out or remember to charge it. Thank you," while glancing at the paper. Odell's eyes scanned the paper, and the group stood in silence while Odell read the note. "No surprises here," Odell said while nodding and then stuffing the keys and the paper in his pants pocket. He added, "Left front pants. Did you read the note and the Coast Guard's official report, George?"

"I did."

"Good. Is it clear to you?"

"Perfectly. As usual, you were right on in your details and your investigation. The container is now secured and under surveillance by the Coast Guard. It is out of our hands. All under federal jurisdiction."

"Great. Thank you so much, Grundy. You have been of great assistance to me. Lieutenant Commander Nelson is a solid man. Back in the days when we Coasties used row boats out of Cape May, I served with him and we swallowed a lot of seawater together."

Captain Tucker read the screen on his cellphone and added, "Odell, I am so happy to hear that you utilize the new cellphone that I bought for you in such a strategic manner. Anyway, it is the same message on my phone. The team is at the airport. We are set to go, Odell. Lord knows all of our careers hang on you being right on this one, Lyle. Lord knows. Here is the search warrant paperwork. I had to beg for this one, Lyle. Beg. I do not need all this stress so close to my retirement. The Coast Guard report on their findings at the port today is impressive. It takes tremendous pressure off. Now, we just need a link. Good Luck, Odell."

Captain Tucker handed the paperwork off to Lyle Odell and Odell handed it off to Baker and said, "Thanks, Cap. Baker, here, you keep this. My pockets are full. Cap, did hear back from the federal boys? Are the accounting folks in place on the federal level?"

"I did hear. Everything is ready and they are skeptical, but for now, cooperating. Once more, there is Heaven and Hell hanging over us, Lyle. Heaven and Hell."

As soon as Captain Tucker finished speaking, another cellphone beeped and Officer Baker unbuttoned his uniform shirt pocket button, pulled out a cellphone and he quickly read the text on the screen. His brow furrowed and his eyes grew narrow while he studied the screen.

"Is it trouble, Baker?" Odell asked as the other police officers waited for his reply.

Officer Baker took a breath, forced a smile, waved his hand dismissively and spoke rather sheepishly, "No trouble. Sorry. Just my gal checking in. She wants to know if we are going out tonight." Officer Baker tucked the cellphone back into his uniform pocket and added with a chuckle, "I guess she is in love."

Odell quickly answered, "Love, huh? Love is for chumps, Baker. That gal ya been looking at, the not so steady one is becoming steadier, huh? Are you following all of this, Baker, or are you too love struck to think straight? Ya seem nervous."

Baker seemed disturbed by the observation of Detective Odell and he nervously shifted his weight on his feet and then stood up a little taller while admitting, "I am not nervous. But I admit that I am rather lost in all that is going on here. What is going on with the Coast Guard? How do they fit into all of this? What did they find?"

Odell narrowed his eyes and glared toward Baker, but with great willpower, he opened his eyes and held his demeanor.

The detective answered Officer Baker's questions rather loosely, with a monotone voice, "They intercepted a container in the Port of Albany that I tracked, and I asked them to check out very carefully. They found illegal stuff in it that was obviously not on the shipping manifest. Very illegal."

Officer Baker blinked a number of times and then asked, "What exactly did you do in the Coast Guard, Detective Odell? What was your billet?"

"I did investigations, Baker. Investigations. Anyway, well, let's all pay attention. It is about to get a little dicey. Tell her that you will be busy. Going to be a long night, Baker. I will bring you up to speed very shortly. Keep that phone under wraps and use it for police work only. Damn all these beeping phones. No one ever calls or sends me a text," Odell said as his eyes studied the situation. "Cap, George, thank you for the update and invaluable assistance. Anyway, I am right. Don't worry. The crime scene crew will find some type of evidence. Delilah Murdock began ingestion of that lethal cocktail mix in that limousine when they picked her up from the airport. Doctor Barken was there, too. He had an appointment with Murdock. Funny thing, they both came in on the same flight from Washington, D.C. and never met until they sat together in the limo. They both flew first-class. They didn't know each other. Correction, I should say that Ms. Murdock did not know who Barken was. Barken sure as hell knew her, though," Odell said while he reached into his suit jacket, then he tapped his shirt pocket, and finally, after lifting a finger in the air in a display of recognition, he reached into the rear pocket of his pants and pulled out a wrinkled piece of paper. "It is getting very difficult to keep track of all these papers. Here, Cap, read this listing. I obtained it from the airline company this morning. They sent it over and I printed it out for you. I hope that it will help to settle your nerves. It is the passenger list on the flight from Washington, D.C. into Albany airport. The crime scene crew in Albany found the old ticket in his apartment. They confirmed the booking as well as many other things upon examination of his laptop. It was a treasure trove of clues, potential indictments and information. Doctor Barken was not a professional murderer or criminal. He did not cover his tracks too well. Those crime scene guys down there in Albany were amazing. Big help to this case. Huge."

Odell handed Captain Tucker the paper and Captain Tucker unfolded the paper, slipped his eyeglasses on, and carefully studied the paper.

"Brilliant work, Odell. As usual, you are amazing at putting these pieces together so quickly. It does help to settle my nerves a little. Just a little. It seems as if for certain there was a connection. Can I keep this? It will help to alleviate your rather poorly organized filing system that you have on your person."

"Sure, thanks, Cap. I am running out of pockets and have to keep reminding myself of where stuff is," Odell said as he pulled at his pants at the beltline. The pants still drooped. "I already spoke with Mr. Cortland McNealy. Once known to us as Mr. Muscles. Bodyguard, driver and right-hand person for the Murdock family. He proved to be quite a cooperative and professional man. A top-notch guy. Very interesting background and training. He confirmed many, many things. One of them is that he did indeed pick up Delilah and Doctor Barken in the limo that is on loan to Senator White Choppers today. The driver today is a hired gun by the agents with Covington and Monger. Poor Delilah rode in luxury with her murderer. By the way, sorry, Cap. I really pissed those two bananas off. Chances are very good that your cellphone will be lighting up any minute now. Your chain of command is going to be livid at the perceived mistreatment of the beloved senator. Oh, well. Please forgive me. Okay, I am ready to plant some seeds and face the music," Odell said as he walked under the yellow tape that cordoned off the restricted area. Odell stepped into the midst of the media frenzy. Odell faced an immediate onslaught of media reporters, microphones and cameras.

One reporter, a stout man working for the local newspaper, and a veteran of maneuvering within fellow media types for the first scoop, pushed his way to the front and asked with the microphone stuck in Odell's face, "I saw you speaking with Senator Austin Monger. Detective Odell . . . is Senator Monger a suspect in your homicide case and investigation into the death of Ms. Delilah Murdock?"

While the media world took a long gasp of air and silence floated over the entire group, Detective Lyle Odell took a long drag of his cigarette and then blew the smoke into the air.

His words echoed into every microphone, into the trees and into the air, "Right now, everyone is a suspect. Everyone. Senator Monger, yes. Everyone else, yes. I suspect that we should wrap this case up very shortly. As within a few hours. By the way, does anyone have any extra cigarettes? I think this is my last one."

Captain Tucker shook his head, leaned into George Grundy and asked in a low whisper, "Odell did not just say what I think that he said. Did he, George?"

"He did."

"Do you think he has a flask of Irish whiskey with him and he was nipping at it during the funeral service?"

"I don't think so, Cap. Nope. I hate to say it, but, unfortunately, I think he is sober."

"Damn," Captain Tucker whispered underneath his

breath and the wind.

"Of course, he did tell you that this was going to be horrible. Didn't he?"

"He did. Yes, he did," Captain Tucker said, as the cellphone within his uniform pocket began to ring.

The April wind blew cold, and it blew strong. Even on the warmest of days, cemeteries are cold places.

Detective Lyle Odell's hair blew all over the top of his head and he reached up to smooth it out, only to have the wind mess it up once again. His efforts to keep his hair in order were in vain. He stuck the last cigarette in his mouth as the cameras flashed and the reporters shouted questions in a mad frenzy of interviewing.

Yet, despite his disorganized and disheveled appearance, Detective Lyle Odell was good at his job.

Very, very good.

As in exceptional.

Chapter Nine

Endgame

Detective Lyle Odell could not help but to think of the rather bold injustice of it all. He was a conservative man, a sound thinker and a supporter of the American way of life. Capitalism included. Yet, as the Mohawk City police patrol car driven by Officer Dennis Baker pulled into the property and passed through the majestic wrought-iron gates of the estate leading to the mansion that was the Murdock family home, Detective Odell, could not help but to think of his lowly little twelve hundred square foot Cape Cod home. The lowly home that was set on a side street in a so-so section of Mohawk City, New York. The kitchen of this mansion alone must be twelve hundred square feet. . ..

Odell shook off the thoughts and as the patrol car slowly made its way up the driveway and it slipped by the fine-trimmed lawn, still dormant before the spring flush and it glided by the shrubs and the rose garden beds and other assorted broadcasts of the seemingly endless wealth looming herein, Detective Odell realized that he had a mission. Above all, the good detective was going to stick to that mission. Because that is what he did.

An impeccably dressed man in a custom-fitted, all-black suit that strategically displayed his bulging muscles stood in the driveway to meet them. He stood right at the base of the sidewalk leading to the front door of the mansion. Odell tapped Baker on the arm and pointed at the man as Baker pulled the patrol car to a stop in front of the man.

Odell said, "Mr. Cortland McNealy. Also known as Mr.

Muscles. The bodyguard. The limo driver. The right-hand man. The anchor. By the way, he is totally innocent in all of this horrible mess. He is a great man. Former special ops guy. Air Force Vet. Saw some horrible shit in his military career. Very honorable and trustworthy. Very loyal to the Murdock family. Very loyal. Especially so to the sisters."

Officer Baker nodded, but did not comment.

"We are going to meet with the Murdock family. Explain the reason for our visit. Try to avoid stepping on their pain and carry out the search warrant. I wish it did not have to go down like this . . . so soon after the funeral, but time is of the essence now. No use in prolonging this madness. Please, stick close by me, Baker, and follow my lead. McNealy here has plowed the road for us." Odell glanced over at Baker and he studied the young officer for a few seconds before asking, "You okay, there Baker? You seem very quiet."

"I am fine, Detective Odell. Just working hard at taking it all in. I am only picking up parts and pieces of what you have found out over the weekend. I guess that I should have stuck with you. I know, the overtime. Anyway, I am doing my best. Honestly, today and the last few days of this investigation have been very stressful. I have been in tight spots in country, in combat, seen death and pain, but this is different. It is intense, and it builds and works at you. I have developed an admiration for your remarkable skills and being able to do this for as long as you have. You are quite . . . intense and very thorough in your investigative skills. Very efficient. How do you manage to gather so much information and evidence and clues in such short periods of time?"

"I only sleep a few hours a night. I work about fifteen to eighteen hours each day, then go home and drink, and when I am half-in-the bag, answers become clearer to me. Then, I sleep and my dreams haunt me and the phantoms arrive to provide me with more clues and directions. I am good on three to four hours of sleep and then good to go again. I don't recommend the lifestyle."

"I can see why. You tore that nasty attorney to shreds. He deserved it. He seemed as if he was a smug jerk. If I might ask, what exactly are you looking for here at the Murdock's mansion?"

"I will know it when I see it, Baker. We are only going to one room in the mansion."

Officer Baker shrugged his shoulders. But it was easy to see by his facial expression that the elusive answer from Detective Odell perturbed the young police officer. Baker's eye quickly glanced at the search warrant paperback sitting on the front console of the patrol car, and then his eyes darted away and refocused upon his driving. The facial expression, his eyes, and shoulder shrug did not go unnoticed by Odell. The detective's keen eyes and observation skills of everything and everyone never missed anything. Instead of commenting further, Odell shifted gears in the conversation.

"Do you drink alcohol, Baker?"

"A few beers. Never whiskey."

Odell nodded and reached for the handle of the door as Baker stopped the patrol car and the cagey old detective said, "If you stick around this business long enough, you will drink. I recommend whiskey. Gets you where you need to be a helluva lot quicker. Makes you forget most of what you have seen and recall only what you think you need to have seen. Before you get out of the car, please grab that search warrant paperwork, Baker. And Baker . . . no matter what happens, make wise decisions and do try to stick around."

Baker did not answer.

The door opened and Lyle Odell stepped out of the patrol car and Mr. McNealy immediately met him. Odell spoke right away as the huge man loomed over the top of him.

"McNealy . . . nice to meet you in person," Odell said while he opened his suit jacket and pointed to the police detective's badge clipped onto his belt. Cortland McNealy gave it a passing glance but did not focus upon it. "Thank you for taking my phone call last night and for the long discussion, and for the invaluable information. Most of all, thank you for allowing us the visit and to act upon the search warrant without all that unnecessary drama and foot stomping bullshit. As you are now well aware of, but . . . in order to keep it formal and proper, I am Police Detective Lyle Odell. Homicide. Some say my voice is unforgettable, but when we spoke, I had been up for almost twenty-four hours straight and into a little touch of the Irish whiskey. The whiskey affects my voice, or so they say. This is Patrol Officer Dennis Baker. Baker, please, hand to Mr. McNealy the search warrant paperwork."

Baker nodded and handed the paperwork off to Cortland McNealy while Baker explained, "Here is the search warrant paperwork. Please examine it carefully, sir."

Odell watched as the paperwork exchanged hands and the detective added, "I trust that you will find it in order. As you can see there in the paperwork and as I explained on the telephone call, there is only one area of focus. One room based upon the information that you, Mr. McNealy, provided to me in our discussion. I am confident that I will not need to go back to the bench for additional search warrants covering other areas or locations. I expect this case to conclude shortly and in fact, right here."

Cortland McNealy nodded at Officer Baker, and then he read the paperwork carefully for a few minutes while he flipped through the papers and checked each one. After he finished his study of the search warrant, McNealy nodded and then handed the paperwork back to Detective Odell while reaching out his hand to shake Detective Lyle Odell's hand. Odell grasped the huge man's hand, and Odell's hand disappeared within his grasp.

Mr. Cortland McNealy growled, "The search warrant is in order. It is my pleasure to serve the police department as they try to find out who is responsible for Ms. Delilah's murder. You have my full support. She was an outstanding and amazing person. Ms. Delilah was beautiful on the outside and on the inside too. I fully support you, Detective Odell. No question. Ms. Delilah would not have overdosed. No way. She enjoyed her wine and some recreational partying, but she was always responsible for her actions and remained under control. Ms. Delilah was a free spirit who enjoyed life. I will greatly miss her. In some way, I feel as if I failed her. It was my duty to protect her." McNealy delivered the words in a bland monotone voice. A voice that was unaffected by the emotional proclamation. The big man quickly gathered his thoughts, gave a little wave of his hand and spoke once more, "Please, come this way, Odell and Baker. Follow me. Warning, Mr. Murdock is spitting nails at this visit and the news of the search warrant and Mrs. Murdock and Ms. Ireland are both very upset. They are both emotional disasters. I did my best to explain the timing, and I truly wish that you could have picked a different day for this visit and not requested to have all the family members present in the room. However, this is official police business and that business must carry on despite the circumstances."

McNealy, despite his huge size, moved effortlessly and his large feet hardly made a sound as his polished boots struck along the concrete pavement leading to the front entrance to the opulent mansion. McNealy's presence loomed like a thunderstorm in the distance. The huge man caused large shadows to form on the sidewalk in front of Odell and Baker.

McNealy suddenly stopped short on the sidewalk. He turned to face Odell and Baker as they both braked to a stop behind Cortland McNealy.

"Woahhhh, drop anchor," Odell said as he stopped in

his tracks and Baker did the same.

"Oh yes, sorry. Full disclosure," Cortland McNealy opened his suit jacket and revealed the fact that he wore a shoulder holster with a handgun neatly tucked inside of it. McNealy added, "Private property. People's lives. I defend it and them at all costs."

Odell waved in the direction of the weapon and mumbled, "Gotcha, McNealy. Thank you for that display of firepower. I would expect nothing less from an honorable man entrusted with what you have to safeguard in both valuable properties and in lives. I seldom carry a weapon. I have found out over the years that I don't usually have a need for it. The bad guys usually surrender by the time that I corner them. Officer Baker is the primary weapon man for today. Nevertheless, you never know these days. Anyway, thank you for the ground rules."

"You are welcome. This way, men."

Odell and Baker followed Cortland McNealy. By his mere presence, McNealy commanded authority. It was obvious that Mr. Cortland McNealy was a no-nonsense type of guy. The three men walked in through the front door of the mansion, and McNealy led them through the foyer and into a grand entrance hallway of the home. A crystal chandelier hung from the ceiling and its lights sparkled with a dazzling display of light that danced along the polished marble floor. An oak-cased floor clock stood proudly, but not silently, in the corner of the entrance hall. Its distinct sound of timekeeping seemed to echo throughout the spacious room as its swinging pendulum kept careful time. There were a few red-velvet covered chairs, a number of attractive potted live plants, and the centerpiece of the entrance area was a grand entrance staircase. Curving, twisting, full of dark oak wood, the treads and risers perfectly covered in a plush red carpet and the stairs seemed as if they led to forever. The walls of the entrance hall were white, the trim was a gentle hue of red, and the woodwork and fixtures were dark oak.

"Wait here. Please. I have the family assembled here in the sitting room. I smell the smoke from Mr. Murdock's cigar. It is floating this way. I am sure that he is in the sitting room waiting for our arrival, along with his wife and daughter," McNealy said as he disappeared through two large oak double doors and into the room located off to the right side of the entrance hallway. The doors closed with a hard and resounding, "thud."

Odell turned to Officer Baker. He attempted to tuck his shirt into his pants, and to straighten his necktie, and then after realizing those efforts were rather fruitless, he tried to smooth his hair out and then quickly gave up on that effort too.

Odell's squeaky and soft voice echoed in the large entrance hallway.

"Geez, this is some joint, huh, Baker? I could use a shot of Irish right now. Since old man Murdock is smoking a cigar, I am dying to light up a ciggy butt, but I am afraid that McNealy will either shoot me or stomp me into dust."

"Might be a good idea, Detective Odell. The dude is like a man-mountain. What do you think? Six-six or thereabouts? Two-seventy-five?"

Odell mussed with his hair and made it messier. His eyes focused upon something and he walked over to an elegant chair sitting in the corner of the entrance hall near the clock and ran his fingers over the red velvet padding.

Odell then leaned in while studying the padding.

He fumbled around in the seemingly bottomless pocket of his suit jacket while mumbling, "Right-side suit jacket." After some fumbling, while Officer Baker stood silently watching, Odell finally produced his magnifying lens, leaned over the chair, and focused on the padding.

"At least that large. Something tells me that he is anything but a gentle giant when he needs to be. Lookie here, Baker, fancy red velvet padding on this beautiful chair and it has dog hairs on it. Silver with black edges. The housekeepers must have missed cleaning the chair. McNealy confirmed to me last night that the Murdock household has two dogs. Freda and Tundra. A female Siberian husky and a male husky. Both are purebreds. That particular breed sheds a ton of hair. Might be the worst shedders of all the breeds. The dogs must love to curl up in this chair. It is big enough and gives them a good view of the front door. They can wait for their favorite master to arrive from here. Most likely the male doggie, Tundra. McNealy reports that Tundra was very fond of Delilah. This is very interesting," Odell said as he lifted one hair from the padding and held it between his fingers and studied it carefully through his lens.

"The family will see you now, men," the voice of Cortland McNealy thundered throughout the entrance hall as the doors to the sitting room flew open and the immense man stepped within the threshold of the doorway.

Detective Odell seemed to forget all about his spontaneous dog hair investigation, and he quickly spun around when he heard McNealy's voice and stuffed his trusty magnifying lens into the suit jacket pocket and mumbled, "Right-side suit jacket pocket," and then waved to Officer Baker. "Let's go, Baker. Thank you, McNealy. Your cooperation is very much appreciated."

Odell followed Cortland McNealy into the sitting room with Officer Baker in tow. When all three men stood inside the doors of the sitting room, McNealy turned around and tugged the massive oak doors closed behind them. Officer Baker coughed and cleared his throat. Odell glanced at the young police officer out of the corner of his eyes, and just a shadow of concern quickly moved across the face of the detective. After closing the doors, Cortland McNealy stood stoically and silently in front of the doors and crossed his arms in front of his body. The man was beyond imposing; his mere presence filled the entire room.

And what a glorious room it was!

It was a huge room, with large windows on three sides that afforded a fantastic view of the manicured landscape and grounds beyond the walls. The décor was once more dark oak, with white walls and plush carpeting. The color of this carpet was more of a burgundy color than it was red, but indeed, it was plush. Odell studied the room, and he bounced on his heels as if he was testing the depth of the carpet underneath his shoes. The furniture was more of the same as found in the grand entrance hallway, with beautiful ornate wooden structures and carvings on the backs and legs and the red velvet pads and seats. The walls were full of oil paintings and photography, and plants lined the perimeter. The room seemed more of a museum display than it was a room within a residence. Then again, this was no ordinary residence; it was the Murdock mansion. An elegant light fixture hung from the ceiling in the center of the room, its soft glow muted by a dimmer control, and the light competed effortlessly with some table lamps glowing on the tables in the room and with the light chiming in through the windows. A wet-bar stood in the far-left corner of the room. Solid oak doors remained half-opened, but even with the doors only opened a little bit; the lights of the bar illuminated the various colors of the bottles contained within the bar.

Detective Lyle Odell carefully scanned all the contents of the room, and then he focused upon the most majestic piece in the entire room of displayed majesty. A grand piano sat in the far-right corner of the room with a violin case sitting on the piano bench. It sat right next to one of the windows that allowed the best view of the sprawling landscape. A garden sat within a few feet of the window, sleeping until the spring fully blossomed. The piano was a perfect white color, the lights of the room reflected in the finish of the piano, and they glowed in the polish and grandeur. The piano was a remarkable instrument that most likely cost more than three years of paychecks for Detective Lyle Odell. The good detective, allowed his mind to wander as he pictured the beautiful, Delilah Murdock seated at the piano, playing the glorious and amazing instrument, creating beautiful music to fill the room, while gazing out at the garden through the window, taking in flowers and colors and the beauty of the world. A world of which the young woman appreciated and loved. The horror of her murder ran through Odell. His spine shivered, and he clenched his fists in a rare display of anger.

Odell caught his emotions, and he focused on the Murdock family members in the room. Mr. Murdock stood behind his wife and his daughter, who both sat upon the sofa. He puffed a large cigar and his white hair offset the redness of his face. His anger at the visit, the intrusion, and the situation remained readily apparent and on full display. A quick glaze at Mrs. Evelyn Murdock told where the two twin daughters obtained their beauty from; and Odell quickly noted that it was not from Mr. Murdock. Even while in grief and displaying watery and tear-filled eyes, Mrs. Murdock was a captivating beauty. Flowing and glowing brunette hair tumbled around her shoulders; her perfect facial features displayed by a black dress of mourning. Ireland sat next to her mother, the spitting image of her sister, and Ireland, held her mother's hand while sitting close to her in a show of comfort. Ireland, too, was dressed in black. The grief of these two women hung in the air as if they were black clouds of a summer thunderstorm, preparing to burst.

Mr. Connor Murdock's voice burst out of his mouth, "Odell! It is not bad enough that you invade our privacy on the day that we buried our daughter, but now, you pull this stunt to obtain a search warrant to invade our home too! You drunken, red-eyed, idiot! You look more as if you are a derelict panhandler than you are a police detective!

Believe me, I have already run this all the way up the flagpole with judges, and the attorney general, and even the governor. You are not only wrong about Delilah's murder, but you are wrong that you will find anything of evidence here! After today, you will be stocking shelves in a supermarket. Perfect job for a drunken fool!"

Murdock's long nose pointed in the direction of Odell and his clear blue eyes erupted in anger and glowed with the blue color, then shifted to an overcast gray color. He pointed a finger in the air and the direction of Odell, while he shouted and his anger overflowed. After his rant finished, Mr. Murdock stuck his cigar back into his mouth as he banged his hand down hard upon the rear seat of the sofa, where his wife and daughter sat silently and motionless.

"Well, perhaps," Odell ran his hand through his hair while speaking. "Stocking shelves in the local market is not such a bad job. After all, it is an honest job. Might be low stress except for the occasional store manager who might be a frantic mess to deal with as a boss. Low wages, but usually great benefits and a solid pension plan too. First off, I understand about the grief and the intrusion. I am not heartless. I feel grief too. Especially so, when investigating horrible cases such as this one is. I wish to express our sincere condolences on the loss of your daughter, and I apologize for the intrusion. If time were not so critical, then it would not occur as it has. I will explain in a moment, but first, I assure you that I am correct in my judgment, and my sole mission is to bring justice to your daughter's murder. That is my sole purpose. Justice and a restoration of honor."

Mrs. Murdock carefully listened to Odell's words. She gave a weak nod of her head, and she began to weep and buried her head into her hands while Connor Murdock glared at Odell. Ireland remained silent and emotionless while she hugged her mother and supported her.

"Yes, I am, Detective Lyle Odell. Homicide detective. I am messy, slightly wobbly, here and in the flesh, and this police officer . . . well, everyone, except perhaps, Mrs. Murdock and Mr. McNealy already know, is Officer Dennis Baker."

Upon hearing Odell's words, Officer Baker's head swung around and he glared at Odell in a display of stunned surprise. "That's, of course, from you working at the Port of Albany for Murdock Enterprises Limited as a security officer protecting shipments of goods. You know . . . Baker, when you returned home after your discharge from the Marine Corps and a year working as a private contractor in the Middle East, as, well, sort of a mercenary. For lack of any other description. Not to mention that your father worked in security for Mr. Murdock for over twenty-five years." Odell waved his hand in the air, and added, "It is all in your human resource records, Baker, and the Mackie family filled me in on the rest. As I mentioned in the patrol car on the ride over here. I seldom sleep." Baker's facial expression changed to aghast. Without dwelling upon his surprise news and his statements or studying Baker for very long, Odell quickly turned to Connor Murdock and said, "You do know the Mackie family, Mr. Murdock? You should. Mr. Mackie was a loyal employee for your company for twenty-seven years until you sent his job and thousands of others to Mexico. Timothy Mackie was Delilah's lover and best friend and boyfriend. They were deeply in love, and Mack is a great guy. He loved your daughter with all his heart and soul, and this tragedy runs deep and hard in all avenues of many lives."

"You son-of-a-bitch, Odell!" Mr. Murdock's anger exploded as he pounded his fists on the top edge of the sofa and snuffed his cigar out on the wooden ledge of the back of the furniture and then tossed it in the direction of Odell. "Timothy Mackie! A damn loser hotel clerk who peddled drugs on the side and he is most likely the person who sold Delilah the drugs that killed her! And you protected him! You stupid-ass bastard! I will make sure you end up regretting this until the last breath that you take!" Murdock was beyond angry; he was erupting. His face was as red as a thermometer is on a July afternoon. Cortland McNealy took a few steps forward while Officer Baker stood motionless and in shock at Odell's testimony.

McNealy attempted to diffuse the tension and the anger of Mr. Murdock.

"Mr. Murdock, please, Detective Odell is on official police business. Threats will get us nowhere, sir."

"Shut up, McNealy! I am going to fire your ass, too! You were supposed to protect Delilah! From where I stand right now, you did a shitty job of it!" Connor Murdock shouted.

Odell reached down and picked up the spent cigar. He calmly looked around and spotted an ashtray on an end table, walked over and placed the cigar on the tray.

"This does not have to go on very much longer. There is no need to prolong the pain. Baker, please, the search warrant. Tear out the pink copy and leave it on the table there. No need for further discussion or study of the paperwork. McNealy plowed the road for us already. I will wrap this up, we can all move on, and where it falls, it will fall. Evil never sleeps," Odell said as he tapped his various pockets and different areas of his attire. He then mumbled, "Right rear pants pocket." He reached into that pocket and after some fumbling; he produced a pair of rubber gloves and a plastic bag. As everyone stood in silence and watched, Detective Odell slipped the rubber gloves carefully on each hand and tugged at his hands in order to make sure they were secure on his hands and fingers.

He mumbled, "Right-side suit jacket," reached in, and produced his trusty magnifying lens. Odell walked over to the piano and leaned in while carefully studying the polished finish on the piano, and then, after spotting something of interest, Odell zoomed in to examine it closely through his lens. "Mr. McNealy, I know we discussed details of the fateful day yesterday when we spoke on the telephone, but please, I need some expansion of the details as I study this area." Odell waved his hand over the top of the piano and the floor around it, as if to proclaim his entire area of investigation. Odell spoke again after staking out the area, "Please, to the best of your recollection, Ms. Delilah played the piano last on the day that she arrived from Washington, D.C. and I am sure housekeeping has polished and dusted the instrument since then. Is that correct?"

McNealy answered in his usual monotone voice, "It is, Detective Odell. Correct."

"And Doctor Barken waited where for Mr. Murdock to arrive for their meeting?" Murdock's eyes glowed with anger at Odell's words, and Officer Baker's mouth hung open.

"He waited while sitting right there on the sofa where Ms. Ireland and Mrs. Murdock are now sitting," Cortland McNealy explained and added, "Ms. Delilah only played the piano for a few brief minutes. She was out of sorts. Not feeling up to snuff, so she did not play for too long."

"Gotcha. Thank you. That is of course, because she was already feeling the adverse reactions to the drugs covertly and horribly given to her by the evil Doctor Barken. Mr. Murdock. You were where, sir? No offense, meant, I deal in facts, not judgment, but Ms. Delilah would not be here if you were in the house. You did not see eye-to-eye on many things."

Murdock's trumpet-like voice lowered. His voice was softer, laced with some elements of sadness, as he nodded to affirm Odell's words and the reality of them.

"I was downtown in my corporate office. I was running late from another meeting. McNealy was going to pick me up to meet Doctor Barken, but I told him to stay here and I would have one of the persons that I was meeting with, drive me home. I do not drive myself around. It did not work out that way, because the meeting ran late and the person who was going to drive me home, had something come up that required immediate attention"

"Yes, of course, you are too important to drive yourself and you were running late and the airplane flight was early. Tailwinds do that when you fly south to north on the east coast of America," Odell said while focusing on the finish of the piano. "Looks as if the coaster with the wine glass sat right about here." Odell said while placing his finger on a faint ring that he detected through his lens. "Mr. McNealy, please confirm for me that Ms. Delilah and Doctor Barken brought the already opened bottle of wine from the limousine in here and did not open another bottle of wine from the wet-bar over there." Odell pointed at the luxurious wet-bar tucked behind half-opened oak doors in the corner of the room.

McNealy remained rigid and stoic in his answers while remaining a few feet away from where Officer Baker stood. Ms. Ireland Murdock and Mrs. Murdock still huddled close together and neither of them spoke a single word. Even the weeping of Mrs. Murdock was now lost in the riveting testimony and remarkable piecing together of the day's events by the uncanny abilities of Detective Lyle Odell.

"Of course. Yes, you are correct in every detail, Detective Odell. Ms. Delilah set the glass of wine there where you pointed to, and it was the wine poured from the bottle in the limousine. Yes, indeed, she sat the glass right about there where you focus your lens and Doctor Barken drank Scotch. Neat. From the bar," McNealy confirmed Odell's testimony with an uncharacteristic look of surprise at Odell's magical abilities on full display. Yet, the tone of McNealy's voice remained the same. Odell ran his hand through his hair; he tugged his necktie loose and then focused his attention on the violin case. After scanning the surface of the case through his lens, Odell carefully flipped the latches open and then slowly opened the lid.

Everyone in the room could hear Odell mumble, "Glorious instrument. Worth a fortune." After scanning the inside of the case, Odell calmly moved the instrument and pulled out a music book full of violin music to play. He opened the book, scanned the contents and spoke with just an increase of volume and without any surprise in his voice at all, "Here it is. The elusive daily journal. It is, of course, as I knew, not a myth. Its existence is very real. Thank you, Mr. McNealy, for advising me that Ms. Delilah carried the violin with her from her home in Washington, D.C. to here. She loved the piano, but the violin was her favorite musical instrument. It is my favorite instrument, too. Especially the cascading string arrangements. The journal is right where I thought it would be. Good. Of course, Ms. Delilah would keep the journal within her violin case. Mixed with her music. Her heart kept with her music. This should wrap this entire wretched mess up. This should move us rather quickly to the endgame. Left-side rear-pocket."

He plucked a leather-bound journal out of the midst of the musical notes, and then reached into his left side rear pants pocket and produced a plastic evidence bag and after carefully snapping the plastic bag open, Odell dropped the journal into the bag and with a run of his fingers along the zipper strip, Odell, closed the bag tightly. He reached down and closed the violin case, flipped the latch levers closed and stood up and blinked a few times while stuffing the plastic bag inside his right-side suit jacket pocket and scanning the stunned faces of every person in the room. Officer Baker shifted his feet nervously while he locked eyes with Odell for a few seconds. The two men locked eyes in a cold stare that displayed that the two men both knew where this was heading next.

The endgame was near now.

"I will feel that one," Odell mumbled while tapping the pocket. "Let me finish the rest of that awful day's events.

Ms. Delilah grew faint and felt strange due to the ghastly influences of the drugs in her wine, placed there by the evil Doctor Barken. After all, she already took her anti-anxiety drug in order to fly, so the super-charged opioids that Doctor Barken strategically dumped into her wine glass were already brewing into a lethal and wretched mixture of death. After all, opioids were the subject of the meeting between Mr. Murdock and Doctor Barken."

Mrs. Murdock gasped in shock at Odell's words, as did Ireland, and they both quickly turned their heads to study Mr. Murdock.

Odell stood in the room next to the piano and continued to explain. His rumpled appearance, messy hair, loose pants and his suit jacket bulging with evidence and various gizmos and gadgets suddenly was not the area of focus.

"Illegal and smuggled opioids and fentanyl from China that are shipped in through Mexico and hidden within the garments, socks, and other military gear that is packed in America and then shipped to military contractors and our own military. Those contracts to provide the military goods are awarded to Murdock Enterprises Limited and are somewhat legitimate, except that the goods are shipped with extra stuff. And of course, bribes paid to Senator Austin Monger sealed delivery of this said contract to Murdock Enterprises Limited."

"Liar! Liar, Odell! I swear that I will kill you with my bare hands!" Connor Murdock screamed while Cortland McNealy acknowledged the nods of Detective Odell and moved into the restraint of his boss. Officer Baker stood silently in shock as the words and testimony continued. It was as if he was frozen in his steps and unsure of what to do next.

"Easy now, Murdock. There is no use in denying it. We have all the evidence needed. Your life of power and riches and stepping on the poor people of this world is ending. With you rich clowns, there is never enough money. Never.

It has to be a sickness. Greed, that is. Anyway, I assure you that I am not the liar here. My Coast Guard connections at The Port of Albany already seized the latest container shipment to Murdock Enterprises Limited last night, and it contains all of the military goods listed on the shipping manifest and a few side goodies too. I will add a side note to that fact in a minute or two. Doctor Barken's former lover, of which he was a sugar daddy to, and his little side chickie-poo, a little dish named, Amy Wolfe, turned the doctor onto the illegal connections for the drugs and she played the good doctor as well as Ms. Delilah played the violin. He fell hard for the beautiful Ms. Wolfe who by the way, along with her kingpin that she worked for, was arrested by Sergeant Grundy and Captain Tucker of the Mohawk City Police Department in conjunction with the Albany, New York Police Department about one hour ago."

Odell took a few steps toward the sofa, and he reached out and attempted to smooth out his hair. It was to no avail.

Odell blinked and added, "Ms. Wolfe is indeed quite captivating. It is easy to see how an ugly mug like Doctor Barken was, fell for her act. Anyway, the connections here are deep, but none of these want-to-be criminals covered their tracks too well. Murdock, you should have teamed up with professionals to pull illegal stunts. These clowns were a bunch of amateurs."

Murdock fumed while the hug of Mr. McNealy held Murdock tightly in his grasp.

Murdock growled in anger, "I swear, Odell. I swear that you will die right now in front of my eyes."

"Maybe. Maybe not. No bets on anything. I am not afraid. Death brings peace. Might be better than my life is. All subject to debate. Anyway, Doctor Barken pushed his side gig to everyone's favorite New York State federal senator, America's darling, Senator Austin Monger.

Monger knew everyone, and the circle was complete. Huge side money for everyone. The bank accounts of all concerned in this mess, both overseas and here, are remarkably overflowing. Federal accountants have those under control now. Monger and his angry eye-browed attorney and the mastermind of most of this mess, Mr. Rexford Covington, should be in police custody right now. The Murdock limousine will turn up fingerprints and evidence to confirm all of this. And dog hairs. Always, lots of dog hairs and they all are a direct match to the Murdock's doggies. Mostly Tundra's hairs. The dog was quite fond of Delilah. Monger also was a lover of Ms. Delilah, yet Ms. Murdock was on to his evil ways. Delilah fell into bed with the handsome senator to milk him for information, since her true love, Timothy Mackie and his family were a victim of Murdock abuse and their lives as well as thousands of others, were left in ruins when the factory closed."

Odell lowered his voice, and his eyes darted around the room while he studied everyone for reactions. He particularly focused his attention upon Officer Baker, first his face, then his feet, and then his hands. Baker was intense, but motionless. It seemed as if Odell was gauging reactions, but that the old detective was also determining everyone's position in the room. Odell spoke again, and while he spoke, Odell took a few steps in the direction of Baker.

"Ms. Delilah was a compassionate soul and a wonderful woman and she vowed to right the wrongs of her family and she was about to turn the tide on the senator and his cohorts in the evil scheme. A scheme she was aware of because, Senator Austin Monger was a loose-lipped jaw-flapper, and pillow talk while drunk and in the arms of a gorgeous young woman can come back to bite you in the ass. Ms. Delilah wrote it all down. It is in here. The final pieces of the puzzle that I required."

Odell proudly tapped the journal inside his suit jacket.

"Unfortunately, when Senator Monger sobered up from the lust-fest and booze-fest and he became aware of his excessive jaw-flapping and the fact that Ms. Murdock recorded it all and was about to turn the tide on this awful mess, she needed to leave this world. Quickly. What better cover than her recreational drug use, her love of wine, the convenient access to an evil doctor, the poor-boyfriend-true love-hotel-desk-clerk, and a very occasional drug-peddler, Timothy Mackie and the usual medical examiner out on vacation at the perfect time? It all seemed to work to perfection. Even more so, when Timothy Mackie would commit suicide over his grief that he accidentally fed his lover a lethal overdose of bad stuff, be framed as the fall guy for her death and be silenced forever."

Mrs. Murdock once again gasped at the words, and Ireland buried her mother in her arms.

"Evelyn, I swear, I knew nothing of the plan to drug Delilah. I loved her dearly!" Connor Murdock screamed, as McNealy held him within his powerful arms. His wife and daughter ignored his pleas and his confession of sorts, and they sobbed uncontrollably while seeking comfort in each other.

Odell continued, "I am so sorry, Mrs. Murdock. Please, Ireland, provide comfort to your dear mother because the rest of this testimony is not pleasant. Not that any of it has been pleasant, but as I said, evil never rests. It keeps me employed. I often wish that I did stock supermarket shelves. Delilah asked to head to her hotel room early, and since Mr. McNealy, had to go and pick up Mr. Murdock because his other driver could not drive him when other business came up, Cortland agreed to the evil doctor's suggestion to allow Doctor Barken to drive Ms. Delilah's car to the hotel room. After all, he was a medical doctor and he would make sure she was okay and settled into the room. It was the best plan because, even in her drugged state, Ms. Delilah was able to convey that she wanted her car to use for when she and Timothy Mackie went out later in the day. Timothy Mackie knew that Delilah was on her way, and he prepped the usual room and left the sliding door unlocked. This was all standard procedure. Mr. McNealy would follow up and check in Ms. Delilah, as he usually did when she stayed in the hotel. Mr. McNealy did that after he drove Mr. Murdock back here to the mansion. The only trouble is that poor Delilah went comatose due to the lethal overdose concoction on the way to the hotel and died when she choked on her own vomit. All while a doctor drove the car and allowed her to die in the back seat of her own vehicle. Evil knows no boundaries."

Ireland spoke for the first time, as she continued to hold on to her mother and her voice was barely a whisper, "It is true that Delilah loved Mack with all of her heart and soul. They planned to be together. She told me so. She also told me that she fell into bed with Senator Monger because she needed information. She refused to tell me what it was that she needed, but she told me so. All of that is true. My sister and I shared special things. Very special things."

"Thank you, Ms. Ireland. I initially miss-judged you and your character during my initial investigation. I corrected that error. My sincere apologies. I should have known that twins always bond tightly. Forever." After a slight pause, Odell continued, "Ms. Ireland panicked and called her secret lover, who is, of course, you, Officer Baker, and she reported the situation and asked you if you thought everything was okay or should she check on her sister. Of course, because you were lovers, Ms. Ireland already shared many insights of her sister to you, Baker. Insights that unknown to poor Ireland, you used to plan the evil with your associates in evil. Insights such as Delilah's intense love for Timothy Mackie, her itinerary, and her recreational use of some smoke, drink and the medication she used to offset the panic attacks."

Now, Baker reacted, and he stepped closer to Odell and his face turned from ashen at hearing of the previous testimony to a red face flush with anger.

"Easy now, Baker. The truth is on the threshold now. Hold your ground and remain steady. You, Baker, reassured her that you would check in on the situation, and Ms. Ireland felt that all was well. After all, you were or are her lover and you are a police officer! Of course, you already received the text from the evil Doctor Barken informing you of what was happening. He required your muscles to drag the dead body of Miss Murdock into the hotel room and stage the scene. You took your chow break with Sergeant Grundy and were on your way to assist Barken. Oh my! Yes, the good doctor would check on her sister and be sure that she was all right. Some damn doctor. All too convenient a plan, huh? Ms. Ireland drove along with McNealy to pick up, Mr. Murdock, as well as to fill him in on what happened with Delilah falling ill at the house. Ms. Ireland checked in with a wave to Timothy Mackie when she watched the check-in process at the hotel. You, Baker, are the muscles and the weapons man in all of this mess. You are the informant, the person who obtained the vacation information from the city manager of when Doctor Kent was going on vacation that locked the date in for Doctor Barken to fill-in and fed the info on Delilah that you milked from Ireland while you were making passionate love. You are the inside man for all of this madness."

Baker's face twisted in hearing the truth and in anger, and he looked at Ireland, and then he turned quickly to face his accuser.

"Oh, yes, I might add that the shipment seized by the United States Coast Guard, in addition to disgusting illegal opioids, also had illegal knockoff military weapons buried inside. Chinese stuff. Junk by our standards, but still lethal. Made from stolen blueprints. Weapons to sell overseas to our enemies. Enemy connections that you, Baker, made while working as a military contractor there. You responded to Ireland's call, took your dinner break off your tour with Sergeant Grundy in order to head to the hotel, all of which of course, you knew was going down anyway, because you are the hired gun in all of this, and you helped Doctor Barken drag Ms. Murdock's dead body into the hotel room and stage the scene. When you realized the screw up with the car keys, you were able to sneak away while on an official training visit to the morgue with Sergeant Grundy, disable the video system and allow Doctor Barken to plant the missing car keys on Delilah's body. Joining the police department in your home city worked as a perfect cover. Everything matches, Baker, your shoes match the carpet imprints near the door of the hotel room, the dog hairs that I lifted from the lint brush you used at my house when you met the supposed dog outside the diner, those dog hairs are from Tundra. Hairs that littered your uniform because you dragged the dead body of Delilah Murdock under her arms and placed her into the chair at the desk in the hotel room. The same dog hairs are inside of Doctor Barken's sports car. He had them on his white coat and you have them all over your uniforms. I had the CSI team examine the dog hair samples as well as your shoe imprints from your locker at police headquarters. The white coat came in handy because vomit traces are hell to remove and leave some serious DNA for crime scene wizards to pick up. You had some traces on your shoes too, Baker. There are traces of vomit all over the back seat of Delilah's vehicle. Your clean-up efforts there sucked. Maybe you picked the traces up when we were investigating in the hotel room, except for the fact that you told me you never touched or went near the body."

Baker held his ground, but now his body posture changed from defensive to offensive. He was ready to make a move, but Odell was not complete in his testimony.

The old detective knew that he needed to spill the details of the case in front of as many witnesses as possible. McNealy was armed, Baker knew that, and despite the evil, Baker did love Ireland. Odell was betting many things here in order to minimize the events of the rapidly approaching endgame.

"The morgue tech, Harry O'Shea, testified to your slipping off during the visit. That damn weak bladder or tricky bowels or a combination thereof of yours, Baker, is a nuisance. He also told me about the fact that you had access to the room where the electronics are located with your police visitor's access badge and that you even tested it a few times during the tour when Grundy explained how it worked to you. That was just a ploy to disguise the access card reads for when you really required access. Funny, though, the card access system times the card that it records, and it reads. Yes, I just had to run the times of access. One, two, and then one about fifteen minutes late. When you supposedly had to go to the restroom."

Odell stared intently at Baker, who glared back at the detective. The tension was mounting to a crescendo.

"I first knew that you were involved when you snuck off to make a phone call to Rexford Covington under the false pretense of using the restroom when we left the hotel room to interview Mack. There are those tricky bodily functions again, Baker. A phone call recorded on each end and confirmed by telephone company records, and a phone call, in order to warn angry eyebrows that this drunken fool of a detective, might not be such a pushover after all. Dumb move by calling. Nowadays, these fancy cellphones are both a blessing and a curse. Too bad about the left-handed thingy, tough one for you and Doctor Barken. By the way, that is some bank account for a retired Marine Corps veteran and rookie police officer. Not as much dough as Senator Monger and Covington's overseas account has, but, from what the accounting-types told me, overall, not too shabby."

It was now the endgame. Without any further words or hesitation, Baker made his choice.

Baker quickly drew his weapon and Ireland screamed, "Dennis! No! Please!"

Baker shook his head as tears brimmed in his eyes.

"I did this for you, Ireland. For you! No rich, gorgeous woman such as you would want a poor police officer as a husband. I did it all for you. So that we could be together. Wealthy and on our own. Away from all of this. Away from this disgusting city and your family. I love you, Ireland. I did this for you."

Odell stood motionless a few feet in front of Baker and the old detective remained fearless as he continued to speak details of the investigation, "Including killing Doctor Barken with a head shot? You are an expert sharpshooter, Baker. One shot. One kill. I reviewed all of your military records as well as your police records. Even the mileage on your car to and from Albany to Mohawk City matches and video from the parking garage in Albany on Sunday night matches. After all, you had to take those days off, Baker. Over time, you know. We have you clearly recorded on video parking your car, exiting, and taking the staircase to the upper level where Doctor Barken parked. Nice try with the hoodie and by parking two levels away from the murder scene. Should have rented a car. The Troy, New York detectives tracked a taxi call made a few blocks away from where the killer of Doctor Barken ditched the sports car. Funny, how the description by the taxi driver of the rider matched you perfectly, and the fare brought the taxi right back to that Albany parking garage. Those detectives down in Albany and Troy are solid, and they helped me out within a few hours. So, did you kill Barken for Ireland too? Mind you, Doctor Barken is feeling the flames of Hell right now, so his death is not going to produce any tears from me."

"I had no choice, Odell."

"There is always a choice, Baker. You still have a choice. Please make a smart choice. That was my advice before, and it is the same advice now. Please."

"No. No choice. Covington pulls the strings here. I was and am in too deep. And, you are going to be the next dead person. Honestly, I do not want to do that and I could not do that until you found the journal. Covington kind of thought that your genius mind would find the journal, and now that little book is worth a fortune to me. I needed to stick with you until then. It did not turn out too well for killing you. Too many witnesses now, so I will take the journal and bail. The payoff will be huge and I will disappear. I actually admire you. Give me that journal. Now. No one could find it, and you did. Friggin' amazing. You really are. You are this mess of man, a walking friggin' drunk and smokin' mess of a man, but you are a damn super genius. Shit, man, you need to mumble reminders of where you put things so that you can remember where they are. You are a pickled mess. Yet, I give you credit. You figured it all out in a few days. Unreal." Baker shook his head and waved the weapon that he pointed at Odell a little to emphasize his point. "After I realized your skills, I tried to stop it. To warn them. However, we were all too smart for our own good and into this horrible mess too deep. I never wanted any of this to happen, but now—I have no choice."

"You have a choice, Baker. I advised you before, when we first arrived, to try to stick around. I meant it."

For a second or two, while Baker spoke, he lowered the barrel of the weapon toward the floor as emotions captured his voice.

"What? Advice? Now in the midst of this horror you want to give me advice! C'mon, Odell, prison is not gonna be a ton of fun. No, no, no. Nice try, but I am out of here. Give me the journal, Odell. I will run out of here and destroy it, and all of this will disappear along with me. No one else has to die," Baker said while he once again aimed the weapon at Odell and when he did so, McNealy drew his weapon, and pointed it to shoot Baker, but the sharpshooter abilities of Baker were too skilled and Baker beat him to the draw. A single shot rang out. Connor Murdock ducked and fell to the floor, while tumbling head over heels and flat out on his back, and the women screamed. The shot hit McNealy in the hand; he dropped the weapon, and he fell to the floor in pain and then realizing that his weapon was close at hand, McNealy dove for the weapon but he fell short. Because of the defensive maneuvers by McNealy, the next bullet struck McNealy in the shoulder and the big man became motionless on the floor while he screamed in pain. Baker ran over, kicked the weapon away and grabbed Mrs. Murdock around the neck and pointed his weapon at Mrs. Murdock's head while he kept her in a headlock.

Ireland fell over screaming and yelling, "No! Dennis. We were to be together forever! I never needed money! Only you. Please stop all of this madness. There is a way out!"

"There is no way out, Ireland. I am so sorry, my love. So, so, sorry, now, Odell! The book! Now! Or the blood of her splattered head will be all over this room and will be on your hands."

Baker cocked the trigger, and his eyes grew in intensity. Baker killed before and he would kill again. He already pulled off two shots, and the trigger stood ready for another squeeze. His eyes filled with evil intent, and the old detective knew the look. It was the look of a killer.

Baker's voice screamed out, "This is one time that you should have been smart enough to carry your service weapon. As brilliant as you are, now, you look awfully stupid! Now!"

Odell nodded, mumbled, "Wish it could be different, but you, Baker, made the choice. I see the look in your eyes.

You will not kill Mrs. Murdock, but you will kill Mr. Murdock, McNealy, and me, too. I can't allow any more death. Left-side suit jacket pocket," reached into his jacket, and in a flash, Odell produced a service revolver and . . . the shot echoed into the air and into the world.

Screams of horror filled the air.

Dennis Baker instantly dropped when the bullet hit him squarely between his eyes, and he tumbled into a heap.

The smell of the shots filled the air; blood spilled onto the fine carpet, and the screams of horror and terror mixed with agony.

Odell's eyes filled with tears, and he shook his head as he placed his weapon back into his suit jacket.

"You were not the only expert marksman on the police force. I never said that I *never* carry a service weapon, Baker. I specifically used words such as seldom when I described my habits in carrying my service weapon. I never said the word, never. Too bad, Baker. You should have paid more attention to my words and actions. I put the journal in my right-side suit jacket pocket. Weapon on the left side. I always choose my words very carefully. Always."

Chapter Ten

One Year Later

One year later. . ..

"Okay . . . Cap, don't keep us waiting here. If ya got sumthin' to say about it . . . then spill ya guts on it. I've been coming here for too long to endure any pussy-footing around," Sergeant George Grundy spoke rather harshly while the police sergeant leaned in and carefully studied retired Police Captain Lawrence Tucker for his reaction and a response. Detective Lyle Odell nodded, and he watched while Captain Tucker slowly chewed and savored the food in his mouth. While Grundy tapped his fingers anxiously upon the bar counter, and Lyle carefully studied Captain Tucker's face for clues, Tucker finally swallowed and nodded his head. Tucker picked up the pint glass of ice-cold beer, tilted the glass, and took a long sip of the brew. Lawrence Tucker smacked his lips, leaned back on the bar stool and ran his fingers across his cleanshaven face and then gave another nod of his head.

"Oh geezzzz, c'mon, Cap! What the hell? It ain't filet minion! Damn! Tell us if we are right or not!" Sergeant Grundy grew impatient with the waiting for the opinion of Captain Tucker on the quality of the grilled cheese sandwich washed down with the daily special of beer. The three men sat at the bar at Gulliver's Bar and Grille on Fifth Street and Main Street in downtown Mohawk City, New York, on Saturday afternoon around two in the afternoon. Grundy was off duty and Odell, well; it was always difficult to determine when he was on duty or off duty.

Most of the popular consensus amongst the Mohawk City Police Department and the career criminals in and around the city was that Homicide Detective Lyle Odell was never off duty.

"You are correct, George and Lyle. Best damn grilled cheese in the city. Perhaps, in the entire world," Captain Tucker pronounced as he picked the grilled cheese sandwich off the plate and took another bite. "The cheese melted perfectly and the crispy burnt edges are amazing."

George Grundy slapped his hand upon the bar counter and most of the nearby patrons jumped in his response. "Hot damn! Told ya so. Now, I am having a'nudder brew cuz, I was right. Annie, please, refills all around for us. By the way, this is all on Captain Tucker's tab. He is retired."

Captain Tucker was now retired for eight months.

"Ah yeah, Annie, retired as on a fixed income. Oh well, what the hell, go ahead. Another round on my tab. You only live once and when you go to war with the same guys for over thirty years, the least we can do is to share grilled cheese sandwiches and beer together."

Annie the bartender smiled. She pulled pint glasses out of the cooler and proceeded to fill the glass from the beer tap, pouring out the daily special. Annie looked as if she had poured a few million beers in her career. She was ancient but effective.

Annie set the beers in front of the three men and Odell stared at the full glass of beer and mumbled, "Time to shift to Irish." He looked up and caught the concerned look in Captain Tucker's eyes, and Odell added, "Relax. Irish whiskey on my tab, Cap. My tab." Captain Tucker nodded and picked up his pint glass and held it in the air. His companions did the same. "Here is to the convictions of Covington, Monger, and Murdock. Could not happen to a nicer bunch of weasels."

"Here! Here!"

The three men leaned into their individual beers and

after hearty sips and swallows, their beer glasses were sitting on the bar counter and the three men sat and stared into the foam. They were pensive, contemplating the details of the case that turned into a national scandal as well as a local scandal.

The courts sentenced Senator Austin Monger to life in federal prison; he was found guilty of multiple charges, all tried and convicted in federal court. He also received convictions at the state level; however, since he was heading to prison for life, at a federal level, the state sentences became irrelevant. Monger was found guilty of assorted charges such as guilty for conspiracy to commit murder, accepting bribes while a federal senator, guilty of overseas money laundering, and for trafficking illegal weapons and drugs. The courts and prosecutors mentioned treason as potential charge, since the weapons went to foreign enemies of the United States, but he pleaded out of that charge. Rexford Covington sang like a bird and he pleaded guilty in return for lesser charges and decreased sentences for turning evidence and revealing all the details of the sordid mess, but Covington still received a sentence of fifty years. No parole in sight. The courts convicted Mr. Connor Murdock of bribery, but he was innocent of the charges of having anything to do with the murder of his daughter. Detective Odell stressed that fact to the attorney general and the prosecutors. The courts also found Murdock guilty of aiding in the illegal drug trafficking and weapons, as well as some other employees within the Murdock Empire who worked with Dennis Baker. Some low-level organized crime bosses took the fall and received convictions, but the high-level crime bosses remained unscathed. Ireland Murdock was innocent; she actually was oblivious as to what was going on under her nose at Murdock Enterprises Limited. Poor Ireland was only guilty of falling in love with the distorted, but handsome and dashing, Dennis Baker and since Baker was a poor boy from the other side of the city; they kept their romance secret from the volatile Mr. Murdock. He would never approve of their romance.

George Grundy broke the silence first, "How does it feel, Odell, to see all those convictions? Did you see it all sticking or did you think some of them would walk?"

"Nah, I figured that none of those evil bastards would walk. Too much evidence against them all. Monger and Covington were too cocky. Too egotistical and, mind you, very poor at covering their tracks. They were amateurs who simply thought because of their status that they were above the law. Those dog hairs all over everything and traced back to Freda and Tundra. Phone records, emails, overflowing bank accounts in overseas' accounts, hotel stays at the best hotels with Ms. Murdock for covert liaisons, dinner reservations at fancy restaurants with her, physical evidence, too much, too overwhelming. Besides, the journal had too many details that collaborated with actual events and dates. It was easy to track. The fact that Delilah wrote the notes by hand was a huge bonus. If she typed the notes . . . it might have been tricky. The handwriting expert was a key. Verifying that all of those notes were, indeed, in the distinctive left-hand script handwriting of Delilah Murdock. She took wonderful notes."

Captain Tucker nodded in agreement and took a sip of his beer. He studied Lyle Odell. His hair was just as messy as it always was, his eyes were red and glassy, he needed a shave, and he looked as if he had not slept in a few days. He looked as he usually did. Yet Tucker admired the man more than words could ever describe.

"The various gizmos and gadgets that you carry around with you certainly helped too. Glad that you had room for your service weapon. Tell me, Odell, how the hell do you fit all that stuff in all your pockets and inside that general mess, you carry around? I mean, is that part of the plan? Is that why you always look so disheveled, because you carry around a crime lab with you?"

Odell smiled and tilted the glass over and sipped the last drop out of it while waving down Annie and ordering an Irish whiskey that he asked to go on his tab.

"No, no, Annie! Please," Captain Tucker interrupted the order, "please on my tab. It is the least that I can do."

Annie nodded, smiled, poured the glass of Irish whiskey, and slid it over in front of Lyle Odell.

"So . . . Odell? You did not answer my question," Captain Tucker prodded.

Odell handled the glass of Irish and pondered it. He did not drink it yet.

"It might be part of the plan. Yes, it might, Cap. Maybe. Maybe not."

"You know, you are a damn hero, Odell. You not only locked up all those evil and corrupt bastards, but you took a ton of really nasty drugs off the streets and stopped the weapons' flow to our enemies. Saved a ton of lives. It was my pleasure as one of my last official duties before retirement to pin more ribbons on you and a few on George too."

Grundy nodded and mumbled a "Thank you," while Odell shook his head.

"Yeah, okay, thank you, Cap. I put the ribbons in my drawer with the others. As far as a hero goes—nah. The real heroes in all of this are Timothy Mackie, and his dad, and most of all, Mr. Cortland McNealy. McNealy should receive the ribbons. Not me. Mack and his old man gave me all the clues that I needed to turn me onto everything. McNealy went along with my crazy plan to confront Baker in order to obtain a confession of sorts and to turn the final pieces of the puzzle over, and it was at great risk to him and the Murdock family. I trusted him, and he trusted me, too. He thought he could beat Baker to the draw, but Baker was quicker. We spoke at great lengths and worked out a careful plan. We knew that old man Murdock was destined not to come out of there alive. He knew too much. Baker was set to kill him first, then me, after I found the journal. Covington gave Baker those orders and never clued Senator Monger in on the final plan. Baker, if anything, was a good Marine until the end in following orders. When I found out that McNealy served in special operations in the United States Air Force, I went along with the plan. The plan was for McNealy to stare down, and if needed, to disable Baker with a shot-to-wound, maybe in the leg, arm, or hand. That was why McNealy proudly announced that he had a weapon on his person. To plant the seeds with Baker that this was not going down easily. We would both draw our weapons. With no way out and two weapons staring him down from different directions, then Baker would surrender with the confession at hand. It did not work out, but in Baker's defense, his first shot was precision and meant only to dislodge the weapon of McNealy . . . not to kill him. Luckily, McNealy rolled over and all around on the floor when he chose to pursue his lost weapon and the second shot, which was meant to be a kill shot from Baker, missed vital organs and McNealy recovered without any lingering physical issues. Emotionally . . . who knows how he will go onward in his life? I hope that he is okay. He is a strong man. I should have dropped Baker sooner, but, for some reason, I wanted the young man to come out of the madness alive. I really thought that Baker would surrender when he was in a no-win situation, and all the evidence surrounded him. I did not take him for being as cold-blooded a killer as he was. Perhaps, combat made him that way. I dunno. Anyway, it was a miscalculation on my part. Retrospect is a bitch."

Odell shook his head, and his eyes wandered before he spoke once more.

"McNealy is a great man. Brave and courageous. I think that he was deeply in love with Delilah. In retrospect, who could blame him? Very sad. Both Timothy and Cortland lost the love of their lives. Moreover, Baker did wild things for the sake of love. Love is some crazy force and a strange motivator of human actions and emotions. The Mackies, well, I am so glad to hear that Ireland Murdock put them all back to work. She reopened the factory operations here, and I hear that both Timothy Mackie and his father work there. Happy to hear that Ireland put the money and greed aside and she brought those jobs back here to Mohawk City. Smart woman. I apologized to her for my initial miss-judgment of her character. We need to make those Chinese clowns eat our dust. We are Americans and we need those jobs here, for our people and on our soil, and stop giving away jobs for the sake of a few more dollars. When I heard that news, then I knew that Delilah Murdock did not die in vain. She stood up to evil, and she fought hard for the working man."

All three men sipped their drinks, and out of the corner of his eyes, George and Captain Tucker both watched as Odell lifted the whiskey to his lips and took a gentle sip of the liquid Irish. The two drinking companions of the old detective both spotted the tears brimming in the corners of Odell's eyes. Sensing the need for a change of conversation and desiring to close the case off forever, Captain Tucker changed the direction of the conversation.

"So, George, you going to pack it in soon?" Captain Tucker asked.

"Dunno. Still paying off all those crazy student loans. Maybe. We will see. How is retirement, Cap? Is it all it is cracked up to be?"

Captain Tucker shook his head and answered, "No, not really. It becomes a little boring. I am taking Odell's advice and learning to play a musical instrument. It passes the time."

Odell set his glass down and surprise played across his face.

"No kidding, Cap. The violin?"

"Nah, the guitar. I always wanted to play the guitar. I can actually strum three chords. The instructor is very cute, too. I keep missing the fingering of the strings because, well, I tend to stare at her rather than my finger positions. Anyway, it is fun to try. How about you, Odell? Are you going to keep on keeping on?"

Odell did not answer the question right away. He held the whiskey glass in his hands, his fingers wrapped around it, and then he slowly picked it up. Odell then swirled the whiskey around inside the glass before tilting the drink over and downing the rest of the whiskey in one swallow.

Always, the elusive one, Odell spoke a sudden thought that obviously just arrived in his mind. His mind never stopped.

"Say, do you think that your cute musical teacher could play some of the music that Delilah Murdock wrote in her journal? Between her daily notes there are songs written in there. Musical notes and lyrics. I cannot read or play music, but the lyrics are touching. It might be a way to perpetuate her memory and contributions to the world. I bet some of it is great. Just a feeling that I have."

Captain Tucker studied Lyle and answered, "Sure. I can ask her. Bring the music to me and I will see what I can do. You avoided answering my question, Odell. You often do that by diverting. I have known you for too long. So? Retirement?"

Odell still held the glass in his hands and he nodded and set the glass down on the counter.

Odell spoke just above a whisper, "Yup. Going to keep going. I have to. Evil never rests. I need to keep walking where phantoms tread. It is what I do. It is both my curse and my blessing. I guess . . . someone has to do it. Might as well be me."

Odell glanced at his silent companions. He gently slid the glass to the edge of the bar, nodded to Annie, and pointed at the glass.

Annie nodded in return.

"Yup, it might as well be me. After all, guys, my reputation sort of precedes me. I would not want to let anyone down. Especially those phantoms. Oh yes, Cap, George. Please remind me."

The two men looked at Odell and both shrugged their shoulders at Odell's request.

George asked, "Remind you of what, Odell?"

"Remind me that if I ever want to get a dog, to never entertain owning a Siberian husky. Wonderful dogs, but those damn shedding dog hairs sure do get all over everything. And I do mean everything."

THE END

Epilogue

The April wind blew cold, and it blew strong. Even on the warmest of days, cemeteries are cold places.

A Mohawk City police car slowly pulled up to a curb alongside a roadway within the Sacred Heart Cemetery. In the passenger seat, Detective Lyle Odell scanned the graves for the location that his eyes sought to find.

"Sorry, Officer Gardner. It has been one year and my drunken and hazy memory is trying hard to place the location. One year ago, today. Okay, wait," Odell pointed at a spot. "Please, stop here, Gardner. Thank you."

The police cruiser slowed to a stop, and Officer Gardner placed the gearshift lever into the parking gear and looked over at Detective Odell.

"You okay . . . Detective Odell? Do you want me to walk with you?"

Odell smiled and shook his head to indicate no. "I am a little tipsy, but no, I will be fine. Thank you for picking me up, Gardner. I was in no condition to drive, and I had to complete this mission today. In my meager defense . . . it is my day off today."

"No trouble. Sergeant Grundy told me it was okay to pick you up. My lips are sealed. Please, be careful, sir. You are a little wobbly. I will wait here."

Odell nodded, flipped open the passenger door handle, and the door swung open. Odell grabbed the single red rose from the seat, he scooted his legs out the door, stood up and before closing the door, he leaned in and said,

"Thank you, and Gardner," Odell said while staring in at the young police officer.

"Yes, Detective Odell?"

"Please, no sir stuff. Bad memories. Just call me, Odell or Lyle or Detective Odell. Anything, but, sir."

"Yes, Detective Odell. Gotcha."

Odell closed the door, and he slowly walked across the sprawling lawn marked by thousands of grave markers. His messy hair blew all around his head in the cold wind, and he looked even messier than he usually did. He tied his necktie too short, and it was askew. His pants fell around his waist and his suit jacket had a coffee stain on the front of it. His shoes were dull in luster. One shoe had a lace that was loose, and it flapped along as Odell walked.

Odell wobbled while he walked and he tapped his suit jacket and said, "Right-side suit jacket pocket."

After fumbling with one hand while he balanced the rose in his other hand, he pulled out his pack of cigarettes, tapped one out, and stuck it in his mouth. As the cigarette dangled from his lower lips, Odell mumbled, "Just need to taste it."

His eyes scanned the grave markers until he found the one that he wanted, and when he approached it, his keen eyes scanned the grave marker while he mouthed the name inscribed upon the elegant marker stone.

"Delilah Anne Murdock. Forever in our hearts. Reach for the sky and never stop reaching." Odell lowered his head and mumbled a prayer. Yes, indeed, Lyle Odell prayed.

Often.

He finished his prayer, tossed the red rose onto the grave and mumbled, "I feel as if I know you so well, even if we never met. I kept my promise, Ms. Delilah. I kept my promise. I always will. For your honor and for the honor of all the others. It is what I do. I am miserably flawed, but the whiskey dulls the pain of this wretched world. I will always do my best to stand for honor and justice and for what is right. After all, someone has to walk where the phantoms tread. I am not afraid to do so. Thank you for you. I feel this world is a better place for your efforts. I hope you are playing heavenly music somewhere on a grand piano in the clouds. Somewhere where you have joy, where kindness reigns forever, and love rules. Somewhere."

Odell wiped a tear from his eyes. He turned on his heels and as he did so, he tapped his right rear pocket of his pants and muttered, "Right rear pants pocket."

He reached into the pocket and pulled out a small flask. Odell stopped and lifted the flask in the direction of Heaven. He unscrewed the cap and with the dangling cigarette still holding onto his lower lip, Odell put the flask to his lips and took a swallow of the Irish.

"To you, Ms. Delilah. To you."

Odell then turned and slowly walked the rest of the way to the waiting police cruiser. The wind blew hard, and it blew cold. It is always so cold in cemeteries. No matter the season.

It is always so cold.

ABOUT THE AUTHOR

Way back in time, when the dinosaurs first died off, at the ripe old age of sixteen, Paul John Hausleben, wrote three stories for a creative writing class in high school. Enrolled in a vocational school, and immersed in trade courses and apprenticeship, left little time for writing ventures but PJH wrote three exceptional and entertaining stories. Paul John Hausleben's stories caught the eye of two English teachers in the college-preparatory academic programs and they pulled the author out of his basic courses and plopped him in advanced English and writing courses. One of the English teachers had immense faith in Paul's talents, and she took PJH's stories, helped him brush them up and submitted them to a periodical for publication. To PJH's astonishment, the periodical published all three of the stories and sent him a royalty check for fifty dollars and . . . that was it. PJH did not write anymore because life got in his way. Fast forward to 2009 and while living on the road in Atlanta, Georgia (and struggling to communicate with the locals who did not speak New Jersey) for his full-time job, PJH took a part-time job writing music reviews for a progressive rock website, and that gig caused the writing bug to bite PJH once more. He recalled those old stories and found the old manuscripts hiding in a dusty box. After some doodling around with them, PJH decided to revisit them. Two stories became the nucleus for the anthology now known as, *The Time Bomb in The Cupboard and Other Adventures of Harry and Paul.* The other story became the anchor story for collection known as, *The Christmas Tree and Other Christmas Stories, Tales for a Christmas Evening*. Now, many years and over thirty-five published works later, along with countless blogs and other work, PJH continues to write. Where and when it stops, only the author really knows.

On the other hand, does he really know?

If you ask Paul John Hausleben, he will tell you that he is not an author, he is just a storyteller. His mission is to continue to write and tell stories to warm your heart, make you laugh, and sometimes make you cry, just a little. Most of all, he deals in memories, and helping you to remember the good times of your own life, and the special people who touched you along the way. Paul was born and raised in Paterson, and then nearby Haledon, New Jersey, and began writing at an early age. He revisited a writing career later in his life, and he now is the author of a number of novels, compilations, short stories and audio and video works. Most of his work, touches upon nostalgic remembrances of simpler times, and tells the stories of heartfelt, humorous, and special human relationships. Other than writing, among many careers both paid and unpaid, he is a former semi-professional hockey goaltender, a music fan and music reviewer, an avid sports fan, photographer, and a military radio and amateur radio operator. He now resides in Somewhere, U.S.A., but his heart always remains along Belmont Avenue in good old Paterson, and Haledon, New Jersey.

Other Work by Mr. Paul John Hausleben

The Time Bomb in The Cupboard and Other Adventures of Harry and Paul

The Night Always Comes, Another story from the Adventures of Harry and Paul

Reunion, A sequel to the Night Always Comes and Another story from the Adventures of Harry and Paul

The Miracle Tree, Another story from the Adventures of Harry and Paul

The Chronicles of Henson

Heaven's Gain
The Final Adventure of Harry and Paul

Geyer Street Gardens
Beneath the Mask of a Hockey Goaltender
Another story from the Adventures of Harry and Paul

Where the River Bends and Curls

And a few others too!

You may write to the author at ctte27@gmail.com

Published by God Bless the Keg Publishing LLC
Henrico, Virginia, U.S.A.
You may write to the publisher at
Godblessthekegpublishing@gmail.com

"Life's simple pleasures are so often the best ones!"

Follow Paul John Hausleben on Facebook and enjoy samples of his photography, receive updates on new releases, and enjoy his general meanderings

www.ingramcontent.com/pod-product-compliance
Lightning Source LLC
LaVergne TN
LVHW030910080826
845145LV00010B/2848

* 9 7 8 1 7 3 3 0 9 2 7 2 2 *